A New Chapter

Susan Coventry

Cover Design: Woodchuck Arts
Edited by: FirstEditing.com

Also by Susan Coventry

See You Then
Starring You and Me

DEDICATION

For my two beautiful daughters

CHAPTER 1

"Don't turn around," Kelly ordered from her position behind the cash register.

"Why not?" Emma asked, her head bent over a stack of books that had just arrived.

"Because someone is staring at you from self-help. A very handsome someone, I might add."

"If he's in the self-help section, I don't know that I want to turn around," Emma responded drily.

Kelly chuckled, but her laughter was quickly cut off and replaced by the sound of a man noisily clearing his throat.

"Emma, is that you?"

The voice sounded vaguely familiar, but Emma couldn't quite place it. In any case, she couldn't very well ignore it. She turned around slowly to face the man who had been accused of staring at her from the self-help section. *Oh no, not him. Why now? Why here? Why, why, why?*

"Yes, it's me. Hello, Zack," Emma replied coolly.

She hadn't seen Zack Kostas since her cousin's wedding five years ago, and she'd hoped to never see him again. They had been paired up together as groomsman and bridesmaid, and she had spent half the night fending off his advances. It wasn't because he was bad looking or uninteresting; it was the fact that both of them were taken! Last she heard, Zack had married his date from the wedding, and they lived in Ann Arbor. Why on earth was he in her bookshop in her hometown after all these years?

"Great to see you," he said, his eyes lit up with genuine pleasure.

Kelly had been glancing back and forth between the two of them, and now she spoke up. "Emma, aren't you going to introduce me to your... friend?" she asked, breaking out the smile she usually reserved for their best customers.

Realizing that she had no choice, Emma made the introductions, determined to ignore the appreciative once-over that Kelly gave Zack.

"So, you're standing behind the counter. Does that mean that you're the owner of A New Chapter? Great name, by the way."

"Yes, I am," Emma answered proudly. "I must say I'm surprised to see you here; I thought you lived in Ann Arbor." *Rats!* She didn't want him to think that she had kept tabs on him after all these years.

"Actually, I just moved here. My folks live in Clarkston, and I wanted to be closer to them, since..."

Just then, a little girl with wavy dark brown hair and a bright smile rushed up to Zack and wrapped her arms tightly around his legs.

"Daddy, Daddy, come to the kid's section. There's something I want to show you."

Daddy? Zack Kostas, playboy extraordinaire, is a daddy? Emma was shocked, although, why should she be? The man was married, after all. For some reason, she just didn't see him as the "family" type.

"Just a minute, sweetie. Daddy's talking to someone. Why don't you go back to the coloring table, and I'll be there soon?"

Zack's daughter looked up at Emma with big, expressive brown eyes and then narrowed them at her dad.

"Ok, but hurry up," she demanded before running off.

"Where was I?" Zack asked, thrown off by the appearance of his daughter.

"You were just explaining why you moved here," Kelly answered sweetly.

Ok, Emma was officially going to kill Kelly after the store closed! She had no interest in why Zack moved to Clarkston; she just wanted him to leave so she could get back to work.

"That's right," Zack said, turning his attention back to Emma. "I'm divorced, and I decided to move here so that my parents could help out with Gracie."

Ah-ha, that explained it. Emma could relate to his divorced status, having gone through her own divorce six months ago. In any case, she wasn't prepared to swap sob stories with this man.

"Well, it was nice to see you. I really should get back to work though. I have a mountain of new books to shelve and—"

"I can take care of that, Emma," Kelly offered eagerly.

Ok, since Emma couldn't actually kill her, she was at least going to cut her off from reading romance novels! Kelly was a hopeless romantic, and she was undoubtedly trying to set up Zack and Emma as the next couple in her "happily ever after" world. Kelly was in for a rude awakening!

Zack glanced between the two of them and said, "It's ok. I understand. Didn't mean to keep you. I just wanted to come over and say hi."

Emma experienced a flicker of guilt. Maybe he was just being nice. She shouldn't condemn the man for being an asshole five years ago, should she? Maybe he'd changed now that he had a daughter...

"If Gracie likes books, I conduct a story hour for kids every Saturday morning at eleven. It's free, and she's welcome to come." *Yep, my guilt got the best of me.*

"Thanks for the suggestion. I'll let her know."

Her good deed done for the day, Emma turned back to the business at hand, and Zack drifted away toward the back of the store.

"Wow," Kelly whispered as soon as he was out of sight. "He is absolutely delicious!"

"He's a man, not a pastry, Kell, and if you knew his backstory, you might feel differently."

"So, enlighten me. How did you two meet, and holy Greek God!"

Emma reluctantly let out a giggle. "I'm not going to tell you the story while he's still in the store. Oh look, Mrs. Simmons just walked in. Why don't you see if she needs any help?"

Mrs. Simmons was one of their "regulars," and she almost always bought a book from the classics section. Lately, Emma had noticed her hovering around the erotica shelf, and she might have even paged through one of the books when she thought no one was looking. That wouldn't have been such a big deal with most customers, but Mrs. Simmons was an eighty-year-old, gray-haired grandmother who dressed like a throwback from the 1950s. To say she was prim and proper was an understatement. Emma and Kelly had shared a good laugh over the idea of Mrs. Simmons reading *Fifty Shades of Grey*, but hey, who were they to judge?

Kelly stepped out from behind the counter and approached Mrs. Simmons just as Zack and Gracie walked up, each with a couple of books in their hands.

"We just need to pay for these, and we'll be on our way," Zack said apologetically.

Looking into Gracie's eyes as she placed her selections on the counter, Emma couldn't help but soften her stance. Zack couldn't be that bad if he had created such a beautiful and seemingly well-behaved little girl.

"I didn't mean to rush you," Emma said, extending her olive branch. "I just got a big shipment of books in today, so I'm anxious to get them priced and on the shelves."

"It looks like you have a thriving business. I'm glad to see that an independent bookstore can still survive; they seem so few and far between these days."

"You're right, but I'm determined to stay afloat."

"Well, the store looks great. Gracie already said that she'd like to come back, so I'm sure you'll see us again."

Oh boy. "Great," Emma said, hoping that she sounded enthusiastic.

Emma rang up their purchases and gave Gracie her own bag with a complimentary kid's bookmark. She adopted a neutral expression while she bagged Zack's books about single parenting. Gracie rewarded Emma with a beaming smile and then tugged on her dad's hand to lead him out of the store.

When Zack had one foot out the door, he turned around and gave Emma a wave. *Damn it, why had I still been looking?*

As soon as Emma changed the sign on the front door to "Closed" and turned the lock, Kelly started in with her questions.

"Ok, so what's the deal with Mr. Tall, Dark, and Handsome?"

Emma went about running the register tape for the day's sales and tidying up the front counter while she relayed the short version of the story to Kelly.

"Zack is a college buddy of my cousin Phil. You know, the one who currently lives in Charlotte. Anyway, Zack and I stood up together in Phil's wedding five years ago, and that's how we met. I haven't seen him since, so it was a bit of a shock that he showed up here today."

"And?" Kelly said, tapping her toe impatiently. "There's got to be more to the story than that."

Emma could try to trick her best friend, but it was pointless. Kelly would get all of the details out of her in the end no matter what.

"And he came on to me all night long, even though we were there with our future spouses! The tragic irony of the tale is that we both ended up divorced. Crazy, huh?"

"No, I don't think it's crazy at all. I think it's destiny," Kelly replied earnestly. "You might not believe in fate, but I do, and I think that there's a reason why Zack showed up here today."

Emma set the register tape down and let out a heavy sigh. "Kelly, you are hereby officially cut off from reading romance novels. I forbid you to so much as lay a finger on one when it comes into this store. Understood?"

"Nice try, but you're just trying to deflect. It's obvious that you find each other attractive, and hello, who wouldn't find that dude attractive? He's so…"

"Delicious? Yes, you already said that. Listen, he's the classic playboy, and I plan on staying as far away from him as possible." *Although, now that we live in the same town, that's going to be a little more difficult.*

"Maybe he's changed. Have you considered that? Think about how much your life has changed in the past five years. His obviously has too."

Kelly's words resonated with her as Emma drove the mile and a half home from the bookstore. Her friend was right. Emma's life had changed drastically in the past five years, and she hoped it was on the upswing. The divorce process had taken the wind out of her sails, and she was just beginning to feel stable again. She would never forget the day that

Mark had told her he wanted out. His words were forever etched on her brain, and whenever she recalled them, she felt hurt and confused all over again. Her husband had simply decided that he didn't want to be married anymore. He hadn't had any specific complaints, and he'd sworn up and down that there wasn't another woman, which Emma had believed. No, Mark had "come to the conclusion that marriage was not for him." He wanted to be "free" to live a life without restrictions.

If Emma had a dollar for every hour she had spent analyzing those words, she probably wouldn't have to work at all. But thank God for the bookstore; it had been her anchor throughout the divorce process and beyond. Mark had promised it would be a "congenial" divorce, and it was, relatively speaking. He'd signed off on any and all rights to the bookstore, and now Emma owned it free and clear. Sometimes she wondered if that was supposed to be her consolation prize. *Tell her what she's won… her very own bookstore!* Looking back on the time when she had first opened the shop three years ago, Mark had been so supportive of her. He had been her cheerleader through it all, insisting that she follow her passion. Had he set her up with everything he thought she wanted just so he could leave her? Was that supposed to soften the blow?

"Just stop!" Emma shouted out loud, and realized that she still sat in her parked car in the garage. She didn't even recall opening the garage door. This was exactly why she tried not to relive those awful days. The questions swirled around and around in her mind, but there weren't any satisfactory answers. Nowadays, she found solace at work and with her friends, and of course with books. Books were the one thing she could always count on, and they would never let her down.

CHAPTER 2

Zack leaned back in his brown leather Barcalounger and took a long slug of his Heineken. Now he could finally relax since Gracie was down to sleep. He had read her one of her favorite Little Critter stories, and when he'd turned the last page, she was out.

Zack was just beginning to realize how exhausting single parenting could be. Sure, he had help from his parents, but after he worked all day and picked up Gracie, she was still raring to go. He glanced around the living room of his new home, noting all of the boxes that waited to be unpacked. The remote control for his new oversized flat-screen television sat on the coffee table, but he was too tired to walk over and retrieve it. The new books he had bought about single parenting sat unopened on the table beside him, but he couldn't bring himself to crack one open. Nope, he was truly and utterly exhausted.

Glancing at the books reminded him of the one bright spot in his day—running into Emma Murphy. *Wow, what a looker!* He had thought that five years ago, but now she looked even prettier, although there was a hint of sadness behind her eyes. He didn't blame her for the cool reception she gave him because he deserved it. He had been a bit of an asshole at her cousin's wedding. Zack would have liked to blame it all on the amount of liquor he'd consumed that night, but he knew that wasn't the sole reason. He had been six months away from getting married himself, and instead of feeling like the luckiest guy on earth, he had felt strangely empty. Foreshadowing of what was to come? Maybe, if you believed in that sort of thing. In any case, when he'd met Emma at the rehearsal dinner, he'd been instantly attracted to her. She'd had that special something that was hard to define, yet undeniable. She'd exuded warmth and a sense of ease with an undertone of sexy that he had found irresistible. And the best thing of all, she'd had no idea that she was that attractive.

Zack cringed when he recalled some of his actions from that night. He remembered resting his hand on Emma's knee underneath the table and her repeatedly shoving it aside. He may have stood too close to her when they partook in the bridal party dance, and she must have been aware of his erection pressed up against her. He vaguely recalled whispering in her ear that she was the most beautiful woman at the wedding. Ugh! What a jerk! Emma had reacted to it all with cool politeness, similar to how she reacted at the bookstore. She surely wouldn't have wanted to cause a scene at her cousin's wedding, so she had put up with his antics without encouraging him, although, a couple times, he thought he'd seen a sparkle in her eye. Zack had wondered then if they had both been single, could there have been a chance...

Here they were five years later, both available, but toting a lot of emotional baggage. Emma hadn't said, but Zack already knew that she was divorced too. He had found out through Phil, whom he talked to every few months. Phil had given him minimal details, but Zack got the impression that Emma's husband had left her and not the other way around. Zack could relate to being rejected because it had happened to him too. Alicia had traded him in for a much younger model, a guy who interned at her company. He should have seen it coming, between her extra-long work days, texting on her phone at all hours, and becoming increasingly distant and withdrawn. But nope, he had been clueless. He had truly believed that Alicia wouldn't break up their family; my God, Gracie had only been three at the time.

That was a year ago, and now Gracie would be starting preschool in one week. Zack took another long pull of his beer and set the empty bottle on the side table. No use crying over spilt milk. He was done trying to figure out what went wrong. His marriage was over, and Alicia was already living with what's-his-name in their new condo. Zack's focus now was to make sure that Gracie was ok. He had messed up his marriage, but he would do everything in his power to make a good life for his daughter. That included not dating for a while. He and Gracie needed time to heal before he brought another woman into their life. For now, he would concentrate on his role as Dad and give no further thought to the pretty lady with the light green eyes, strawberry blonde curls, and that tight, petite body.

Nope, he wouldn't give her anymore thought... tonight.

CHAPTER 3

Emma and Kelly began setting up for story time twenty minutes before eleven. Today's book was *Green Eggs and Ham,* a crowd favorite for the kids and adults alike. Kelly was in charge of snacks, and she had baked oval sugar cookies with green frosting—to represent the eggs of course. They had also set out coloring sheets of some of the pages from the book and new boxes of Crayola crayons.

This was one of Emma's favorite aspects of her job. She loved to read to the children and watch their eyes light up as she took on the various characters' voices. Oftentimes, the kids enjoyed the story so much that their parents bought the book for them, but that wasn't the only goal. Emma's true fulfillment came from instilling the love of reading into the hearts and minds of young children.

She didn't expect as many kids today because it was Labor Day weekend, the last hurrah of the summer season. Whether there were five kids or twenty, the show would go on! She was arranging the chairs in a semicircle when she heard a man clear his throat behind her. It sounded suspiciously like... yep, it was Zack, with Gracie in tow.

"Good morning," he said with a gravelly morning voice.

"Good morning," Emma returned, focusing her eyes on Gracie. "I'm so glad you could come today."

Gracie gave her a shy smile and looked up to her dad for guidance.

"Gracie, I didn't introduce you the last time we were here, but this is Emma Murphy. She owns the bookstore, and she's going to be reading to you today."

Gracie nodded her head but clung to her dad's hand for dear life.

"Do the parents stay with their children during the story, or how does it work?"

Emma was touched by his concern for his daughter, even though she tried not to be. Zack was obviously uncomfortable in the situation, and she felt obliged to put him and Gracie at ease.

"It's really up to you. Some parents sit with their kids, and others roam around the store. There are even a few who wait in their car, but I'd prefer it if you'd stay nearby."

Zack crouched down to confer with Gracie. "How about if I sit with you this time, and maybe next time you can sit here on your own?"

Gracie nodded her head enthusiastically while Emma instructed them to choose a seat and then turned her attention to the other kids and parents that had begun to file in. Six kids had turned out in total, and they were all regulars, except for Gracie, which meant the other parents left their children in Emma's charge and drifted off to look at books.

Emma had done this dozens of times, but something about Zack's presence threw her off. He sat quietly and attentively with Gracie securely on his lap, but his eyes bored right into her. Those light gray eyes with the ridiculous thick eyelashes that most women would kill for, the mane of rich brown, almost black, hair that stood up in all the right places, and the light smattering of facial hair that graced his chiseled jaw—it was too much! Zack's Greek heritage gave him that dark, roguish, smoldering look that was impossible to ignore. Did he look this good five years ago? Yes, she was sure that he had, but back then, she wasn't supposed to have noticed. Hell, she shouldn't be noticing now either!

Emma brought her focus back to the story, adopting a silly voice as she read, "That Sam I am, that Sam I am..." The kids listened with rapt attention, and when she finished the beloved story, everyone clapped, including Zack. Emma was certain that her face had turned a bright shade of pink. To distract herself from his intense gaze, she stood up and offered cookies and juice while the kids turned their attention to the coloring sheets.

"You're really good at that," Zack said once the children were happily engaged.

"Thanks. I probably enjoy it just as much as they do," she replied self-consciously.

"Nothing wrong with that. Do what you're good at; that's my philosophy."

Hmm… I wonder what you're good at? "So, do you and Gracie have big plans for the holiday weekend?" Emma struggled to find a neutral topic, and this was the best she could come up with.

"Just this before I have to take Gracie down to Ann Arbor. She'll be spending the rest of the weekend with Alicia before school starts." Zack sounded matter-of-fact, but his eyes told a different story.

"It must be difficult having to share custody. Not that I know much about it, since I don't have children myself..." Emma let her sentence trail off once she realized she was rambling.

"It's a tough thing to deal with, but we're cooperating for Gracie's sake."

Emma was silent for a few beats while they watched Gracie interact with the other children. So far, Emma hadn't noticed any signs of distress. Gracie behaved much the same as the rest of the kids, contentedly coloring while she nibbled on a cookie.

"So, what about you? What are your plans for the long weekend?" Zack asked, seemingly anxious to turn the conversation back to her.

"You're looking at it. I work today and tomorrow, but we're closed on Labor Day."

"What will you do on your day off?"

Zack may have asked to be polite, but Emma began to feel uncomfortable. She didn't want to let on that her life was rather dull outside of work. In fact, she had no plans for the holiday whatsoever. She would probably end up puttering around the house until she gave in to reading. After all, she was the only one who saw the inside of her house these days!

"I don't have any specific plans," she answered, hoping that would bring an end to the discussion.

"Well, in that case, if you'd like to grab a coffee or something, maybe we could..."

Emma didn't let him finish. "I don't drink coffee," she said abruptly.

"Tea?"

"Nope."

"Anything caffeinated?"

"Diet Coke occasionally, although I know it's not good for me." *Geez, can't this guy take a hint? I do not want to go out with him. I would not, could not! Oh God, now I'm channeling Green Eggs and Ham.*

"How about lemonade?"

Zack was obviously not giving up, and the pressure was mounting. She never was very good at saying no...

"Ok, fine, I'll meet you for lemonade." *That didn't even sound right.*

A slow, satisfied smile spread across Zack's face. "Great! Lemonade it is."

Emma shot him a weak smile. "Great."

"Daddy, is it time to go yet?" Gracie asked.

"Yes, sweetie, right after you tell Miss Emma thank you."

"Thank you," Gracie said.

"You're very welcome, Gracie. I hope that you'll come back to story time again." Emma was being sincere, even though she knew that it meant having continued interaction with Zack. If his daughter weren't so darn adorable... The two of them together were hard to resist.

"I'll call you about the lemonade," Zack said and swiped one of her business cards from the front counter.

Kelly and Emma watched as he and Gracie walked out the door. "Lemonade?" Kelly said.

"Don't ask," Emma said and huffed off to the back of the store.

CHAPTER 4

Two days later, Emma and Zack sat across from each other at a table for two in Starbucks. Emma sipped on a strawberry banana smoothie (it sounded less boring than lemonade) while Zack nursed his no-frills dark roast coffee. A brownie sat on the table between them, but no one had taken a bite yet. There had been a bit of awkwardness at the counter when Zack had insisted on paying, but now they were seated, and Emma was struck by a whole new wave of discomfort.

She had debated cancelling this morning until she realized that she didn't have Zack's phone number. He had called the store the day before to confirm their coffee "date," but she hadn't written his number down from the caller ID. Emma squirmed in her chair and wished she were still at home in her pajamas, curled up on her couch with her nose in a book. She had no business being here with Zack. What did they have in common besides their connection to Phil? Oh, and the fact that they were both divorced, which was not a stellar thing to have in common. Zack had confessed that he knew she was divorced. Based on their history, he probably wanted to make it clear that he didn't intend to hit on a married woman. Even so, the words *this was a mistake* kept repeating in Emma's head until they threatened to spill out.

"So, Emma, you're probably wondering why I asked you to meet me today," Zack said.

Mr. Cool-as-a-cucumber didn't look the least bit uncomfortable. He leaned back in his chair like he owned the place, without a hint of nervousness on his handsome face. "Well, I am a little curious," she replied.

"I wanted to apologize to you for my behavior on the night of Phil's wedding. I acted boorishly, and there was no excuse for it. I hope that you can forgive me."

Boorishly? He knows the word boorishly? Impressive. "That was a long time ago, Zack. I think we've reached the statute of limitations on boorish behavior."

Zack's loud laughter filled the nearly empty shop. "Does that mean that you're not holding a grudge?"

Hmm… how to answer? "It means that we all make mistakes and I accept your apology."

"Just so we're clear, I'm sorry for the way I acted, but not for what I said to you that night."

Emma decided to play dumb. "I don't recall. What did you say to me that night?"

"I told you that you were the most beautiful woman in the room, and that was the absolute truth."

Emma's mouth dropped open, and luckily, there wasn't a bite of brownie inside, or it would have fallen out. She collected herself, leaned forward, and asked, "How can you say that with a straight face when your future wife was also in the room that night?"

"Because it's the truth."

Emma sat back in her seat and tried to process his statement. She wasn't sure how to feel about this man. Was he just feeding her a line? What was his agenda? On one hand, he sounded sincere, but was he an expert at playing women? Well, he wasn't going to play her—that was for sure!

"Why did you really ask me here today, Zack? Since we're being *truthful* about everything…"

Zack slurped his coffee, leaned forward, and looked directly into her eyes. "I was hoping that we could start over, as friends. Other than my parents, you're the only one I know in Clarkston, and I would like it if we could become friends."

"Friends?" Emma asked incredulously.

"Yes, friends," he repeated.

Emma could honestly say that she had never had a male friend. In high school, she'd tried to pass a couple guys off as friends, but she'd secretly had a crush on them. She wasn't decided on the age-old question of whether or not men and women could just be friends. Perusing Zack's face across the table confirmed her uncertainty. *If only he were a little uglier…*

"So, what's your answer?"

"I suppose we could try it," she replied skeptically, "but I think we need to define the term 'friend' first. Go ahead, what does it mean to you?"

Finally, she had put Zack on the spot. This was more like it!

"I feel like I'm on a game show and if I give the wrong answer, I'll be sent home," he teased.

Emma didn't feel the least bit sorry for him. Oh no, if he wanted to be her friend, he would have to prove that he knew the meaning of the word.

"Ok, here goes. A friend is someone you can share coffee with, or strawberry smoothies as the case may be. If the two friends have certain things in common, say they both like sports, they could go to a game together. If one friend was having a particularly rough day and wanted to vent about something, they could call the other friend and talk about it. If…"

"Ok, ok, enough," Emma said while attempting to keep a straight face. She had to give him credit for humoring her with such a thorough answer. The guy was a good sport!

"Now it's your turn," Zack said with a serious expression. "What would I have to do as your friend?"

Hmm… interesting choice of words. "Well, you summed it up nicely, but I have a minor correction to what you said about doing things together. Suppose one friend loved books and wanted to go to a book expo. The other friend may not share that interest; however, they would accompany said friend to the expo knowing that the favor may be reciprocated down the road."

"So, if the other friend liked classic cars, they could conceivably ask said friend to a classic car show even though that might not be a shared interest?"

Emma could no longer contain her laughter. Her shoulders shook, and her face was probably crinkled up and bright pink as she burst out in giggles. "I'm glad to see that you understand the rules," she managed once her laughter subsided.

"I think I can handle it. Any other rules that I should know about?"

"Just one. No hitting on each other due to drunkenness or desperation." *Oops, maybe I shouldn't have gone there.*

Zack's face fell. "I promise that won't happen again."

"Zack, I didn't mean to... Let's just put the past behind us and move forward, ok?" She held up her smoothie. "How about a toast? To a new chapter."

He raised his coffee cup and clinked it against her glass. "I think this is the beginning of a beautiful friendship," he said, quoting from *Casablanca*.

Wow, a man who knew the word boorish *and* could quote from *Casablanca*. Little did Zack know that he had earned two gold stars on his report card already!

CHAPTER 5

"So, I went out with that guy Collin, you remember, the one that likes poetry," Kelly began.

Honestly, it was hard for Emma to keep track of all of the guys that Kelly had dated that she had met at the bookstore. Her friend had a penchant for choosing men based on the type of books they read. There was Steve, who liked mysteries, which made him "secretive" in Kelly's eyes. Then there was Chris, who read erotica, and since his name was close to Christian (as in Grey) that meant he had to be good in bed, right? Wrong, according to Kelly, who suggested that he go back and reread the books.

"Collin, yes, I remember. Was he as sensitive and caring as you thought he would be?" Emma asked sarcastically.

"Scoff all you want, but we're going on a second date this weekend, so there!"

It was Wednesday evening, and Kelly had just arrived for her five-to-nine shift. Emma was grateful that she had two capable employees to cover some of the evening and weekend shifts. She had hired Brett, a college student, to work over the summer, and he had stayed on to work a couple of nights per week. Hiring him had resulted in an unexpected increase in the number of teenage and young adult women who frequented the store. Brett was good looking in that all-American way that the young girls seemed to appreciate. Hey, if it sold more books, so be it; besides, he was a really good worker.

The store phone interrupted Kelly's dating tale, and since Emma stood closest, she picked it up. "A New Chapter, how can I help you?" she answered cheerfully.

"Question. Do friends help each other unpack moving boxes in exchange for free pizza and beer?"

A smile instantly broke out on Emma's face. She couldn't help it; the man had a good sense of humor!

"I suppose that falls within the guidelines. When do you need me?" *Oops, that didn't come out right.*

Zack chuckled gruffly. "As soon as you're able to get here."

Emma turned her body slightly away from Kelly, who was watching her with great interest. "I was just getting ready to leave. Give me your address, and I'll head right over."

After she jotted down the address and hung up the phone, she turned back around to face the music. Kelly didn't disappoint.

"That was the Greek God, wasn't it?"

"Please stop calling him that. If he finds out, it'll go straight to his ego."

"Sorry, but answer the question."

"Yes, it was Zack. He asked me to help him unpack some boxes. No big deal."

"What, are you friends now?"

"That's the plan."

"Well, get ready to fail. There's no way you can be 'just friends' with a guy who looks like that!"

Emma grabbed her purse and a new book that she was dying to read and purposely ignored Kelly's comment. "Have a good night, Kell," she said on her way out the door.

It was almost laughable how close she and Zack lived to each other. His neighborhood was two miles east of hers off of the same main road. She wound her way back into his subdivision until she found the house on a quiet cul-de-sac. It looked like the ideal neighborhood for kids, equipped with sidewalks and a mini-playground. He'd probably chosen it with Gracie in mind, which made Emma wonder if Gracie would be home tonight.

Zack answered the door wearing a maize and blue University of Michigan t-shirt and a faded pair of jeans, and she had to admit he looked delicious (to borrow Kelly's word).

"Hey, come on in," he said, holding the door open as she stepped inside.

The house was a traditional two-story colonial similar to hers, the major difference being that his was in complete disarray. There were boxes everywhere, stacked up against the walls and scattered among the scant pieces of furniture. Emma also noted that everything was beige; the walls and carpet blended together with nary a contrasting color in sight.

"Sorry about the mess. I've been trying to unload a few boxes per day, but with work and Gracie and…"

"No need to apologize. I'm here to lend a hand, so put me to work."

"Great, well, I thought we could start in the den. I have some bookshelves up, but my books are still in boxes. Maybe you can unpack them while I set up my desk."

"Makes sense. Lead the way."

Emma tried not to look at his butt as she followed him down the hall, but her curiosity got the best of her. Naturally, it was a nice one, tight and toned just like the rest of him. She wondered idly how tall he was and guessed around six foot three.

The den was a cozy room at the back of the house with a bay window overlooking the heavily treed backyard. Emma noticed that a swing set had already been assembled, which prompted her to ask about Gracie. "Where's your daughter tonight?"

"With her mom. Alicia took her out for dinner and shopping, so I don't expect her back for a few hours."

Emma stopped herself from asking more questions about his ex and surveyed the scene. "Any particular order you want the books in?"

"I'd like the business books on the shelf that's level with my desk, but you can arrange the rest any way you want since you're the expert."

Emma smiled at that. "So, what do you do for a living?" They had been so busy mapping out the rules of their friendship at Starbucks that she had failed to ask him about his job.

"I'm a financial consultant. I basically help people plan for their retirement."

"Sounds... sensible. What's your number one piece of financial advice?"

"Don't get a divorce! It'll cost you a fortune!"

Emma glanced at Zack as he sat organizing his desk. He had made the comment lightly, but there was nothing light in his expression. Zack was busy putting paperclips and pens in their assigned cubbies, but she wondered if he was purposely avoiding eye contact.

"Do you want to talk about it?" she ventured. So far, they had just skimmed the surface when it came to the topic of divorce, yet it had been such a major event for both of them. She figured one way or another it would all come out.

"Not right now," Zack said, finally looking up at her. "I'd rather talk about something else if you don't mind."

Emma completely understood. "Ok, then how about if we talk about your taste in books! I see some James Patterson, John Grisham, and Michael Crichton in here. I take it you like mysteries and legal thrillers."

"Yeah, pretty boring, right?"

"No, not at all. Kelly would say that makes you a man of mystery—a puzzle to be solved." Emma giggled at her friend's analysis.

"Hmm... I think that Kelly would be sorely disappointed. Men aren't very mysterious; we're pretty simple creatures."

"How so?"

"Well, most men I know like three basic things: food, sports, and sex. Not necessarily in that order."

The James Patterson book she had been holding dropped to the floor with a thud. Emma bent down to retrieve it, happy to be out of sight for a second to catch her breath. When she stood back up, Zack's gray eyes sparkled with merriment.

"Oops, was I not supposed to share that with my female friend?"

"No, it's fine. You were just being honest, and as your *friend*, I value honesty."

Zack leaned back in his chair and crossed his hands behind his head. "I came clean about what men want, so now it's your turn to share. What's important to the ladies?"

The rascal! And yes, that was exactly what he was, a rascal! "Based on my discussions with women, I would say: companionship, loyalty, and romance."

"Romance, as in sex, right?"

Emma put her hands on her hips and cocked her eyebrows at him. "Now see, this is why men are from Mars and women are from Venus. That's not what I said at all. Romance and sex are two different things, although they make for a nice combination when paired together."

Now it was Zack's turn to raise his eyebrows. "Please, continue. Give me an example."

Emma shook her head. "I am not continuing this discussion with you, at least, not until after dinner. I'm starved."

Zack's hearty laughter filled the small space. "Now see, here's where we agree. The number one item on my list is food!"

CHAPTER 6

Zack cleared a space for them to eat at the crowded kitchen table. He got out paper plates and plasticware and set the pizza box between them. "I have bottled water, beer, and milk," he offered, leaning into the refrigerator.

"I'll take a beer," Emma said and plopped a cheesy slice of pizza on her plate.

Zack twisted off the top on a Heineken and set it in front of her. "I take it this meal wouldn't fall under a woman's definition of a romantic dinner," he teased, picking up their conversation from earlier.

"That all depends on the two people partaking of the meal," she said around the big bite she had just taken.

"So, if the two people were in a romantic relationship, pizza and beer could be considered romantic?"

Emma grinned. "Something like that." *Enough talk about romance; it's time for a subject change.* "How does Gracie like her new home?"

"She likes that her bedroom here is bigger than the one at Alicia's condo, but she's still adjusting to the move. It's a lot to handle for a four-year-old."

"You know; I can recommend some books that were written specifically for children of divorce. I'm not trying to sell you anything, but maybe they would be helpful."

"Thanks. Maybe you can show me when I bring her to story time on Saturday."

"Sure."

"Since we're on the topic of Gracie, I wanted to mention something related to us." Zack motioned between the two of them.

Us? What us? We're just friends. "Ok," Emma said hesitantly.

"I think it would be best if we kept our friendship to ourselves for now. I don't want Gracie to get confused about what you and I mean to each other. I know she misses her mom, and I don't want her to think I'm trying to replace Alicia."

Emma took a slug of beer to buy herself a few seconds before responding. "So when I see Gracie on Saturday, I'm not supposed to act like I've been here?"

Zack shrugged and looked apologetic. "If you don't mind. At least for now. It's fine for us to talk at the bookstore, but I don't think she needs to know when we see each other outside of that."

Emma had no choice but to respect his decision. He was Gracie's dad, and he knew what was best for her, but something about his request was unsettling. She didn't like the idea of sneaking around behind the little girl's back, especially since they were "just friends." Maybe that's what Zack was concerned about—that they would become more.

"Ok," Emma replied, "but maybe after she gets to know me, she won't see me as a threat."

"I certainly hope so," Zack said.

Saturday came around quickly, and a few kids had begun to trickle in for story time. Emma hadn't talked to Zack since Wednesday, but she hadn't really expected to. What she found disconcerting was how anxious she was to see him, and Gracie too of course. She looked up each time the bell over the door chimed, but they still hadn't arrived when it was time to begin.

"Today's book is titled *Guess How Much I Love You*," Emma began. She had thought of Gracie when she'd selected the story because of its gentle reminder of the love between a parent and a child. The moral might be lost on Gracie, but it was a sweet story nonetheless. *Where are they?*

Emma had just finished reading the first page when the bell chimed again, and she knew without looking that it was them. Zack seemed frazzled as he ushered Gracie into a chair and searched around for a seat for himself. There was a bench set up behind the row of kid's chairs, and one mother scooted over to allow room for Zack to sit. Emma had paused reading in order for them to get settled, and had to stop herself from rolling her eyes. The single mom who sat next to Zack was notorious for flirting with the single dads. Her name was Janice, and today, she wore a scoop neck t-shirt that flaunted her abundant cleavage, along with snug-fitting jeans and strappy sandals. Janice brought her son, David, to story time on a regular basis, but Emma had a strong suspicion that it wasn't because David loved to read. No, Janice was definitely on the make, and she was pretty obvious about it. Of course, the single dads didn't mind being the object of her attention, and were always treated to a generous view of what she had to offer. Up until now, Emma and Kelly had just laughed the whole thing off, but something about Janice's presence today was especially irksome. She noticed that Janice had slid over just enough for Zack to perch on the end of the bench, but their legs touched thigh to thigh. Emma made brief eye contact with Zack, and he mouthed, *Sorry*, before she continued the story. She assumed that his apology was for being late and not for sitting too close to Janice. Since they were "just friends," Emma had no reason to be jealous, but she still didn't like the idea of Janice using her bookstore as a meat market.

When the story was over and the kids were munching on carrots (chosen because of the bunnies in the book), Emma glanced over at Zack. He and Janice hadn't moved from the bench, but now she had turned toward him, offering him an even better view down her shirt. Zack smiled at something she had just said, and she touched his arm lightly with her perfectly manicured hand.

Seriously? He's making time with that woman in my store? Emma continued to spy on them out of the corner of her eye in between making affirmative sounds to the children as they proudly held up their bunny drawings. Janice reached into her oversized designer handbag and pulled out a pad of paper and a pen. She jotted something down and handed it to Zack, who tucked it into his jeans pocket. *Such a player, yet he doesn't want Gracie to know about our friendship. Ha!* Here he was flirting with a stranger right under his daughter's nose. *Wait until I get a chance to talk to him alone.* Friends were honest with each other, and Emma was going to tell him exactly what she thought of his boorish behavior today!

When David was done coloring, he ran over to Janice and demanded that they leave. Janice looked miffed that her son had interrupted her and Zack's tete-a-tete, but as usual, she gave in to David's whining. She and Zack shook hands before David rushed her out of the store.

While Emma had been distracted, the rest of the kids and parents had drifted away, leaving her alone with Gracie. "Did you like the story today, Gracie?" Emma asked.

"Um-hmm," Gracie answered in typical kid fashion.

"What did you like best about it?"

"I liked that the baby bunny and the daddy bunny were best friends," she said without looking up from her coloring page.

Emma felt Zack's presence behind her and finally turned around to face him. "Hey," she said.

"Hey. I'm really sorry that we disrupted your story. We were on our way out the door when Gracie changed her mind about what to wear, and that's why we were late."

"No worries," Emma said dismissively.

"Gracie, is it ok if Emma shows me some books while you're coloring?"

"Ok," she said.

They walked a few feet away before Zack placed his hand on Emma's arm and swung her around. "Is something wrong?" he asked while maintaining a firm grip on her arm.

She attempted to pull her arm away, but the man had strong hands, and he wasn't letting go. "Well, since you asked, I thought it was in poor taste that you flirted with Janice right in front of your daughter. What happened to keeping other women at a distance?"

Zack let go of her arm and rubbed his hand across his stubbled chin. "Let me get this straight. You thought that *I* was flirting with *her*?"

"That's what it looked like to me."

"Well, then maybe you need glasses, because it was the other way around. I was merely being polite."

"Whatever. I just don't want you to use my bookstore as a place to pick up women."

"Ha! Believe me, a bookstore is the *last* place I'd think of to find a woman."

Emma's face fell, and Zack instantly realized his mistake. She turned on her heel and stomped off, leaving him stranded in the middle of the self-help section. *Good place for him too*, she seethed. Emma retreated into the small office behind the front counter and closed the door firmly behind her.

Kelly stood wide-eyed behind the register as Zack approached. "Would you please ask your boss to come out and talk to me?" he asked, his neck muscles taut with tension.

"I don't think that's a very good idea," Kelly replied. "She doesn't get angry that often, but it's probably best that you leave her alone right now."

Zack sighed in defeat. "Do you have a scrap of paper and a pen back there?"

"Yeah, sure," Kelly said, and she handed him a yellow notepad and pen.

Zack scrawled his phone number and the words *Call Me* on the pad, and then he handed them back to Kelly. "Please make sure she gets that," he said before herding Gracie out the door.

CHAPTER 7

It was Monday evening, and Emma still hadn't called Zack. She had started to type in his phone number several times, but stopped before pushing the green call button. Yes, she was being stubborn, but part of her felt like it was his responsibility to call her. Emma was replaying the ugly scene at the bookstore for the umpteenth time when her doorbell rang.

She peered through the peephole, and there was Zack clutching a bag from the Clarkston bakery, his head bowed down as if in prayer. She debated about whether or not to answer the door, but her curiosity over the contents of that bag won out.

"Oh, hi," Zack said when she swung the door open. "I wasn't sure if you were home."

"C'mon in," Emma said and stepped aside to accommodate him.

"I was on my way home from work, and I wanted to stop by and give you this," he said, handing her the bag.

Emma peered inside, and her mouth instantly watered at the sight of not one, but two of her very favorite double chocolate donuts from the bakery.

"How did you know?" she asked, looking back up to meet his eyes.

"Kelly might have tipped me off," he admitted with a grin.

"Did Kelly also tell you where I lived?" Emma had him on the hot seat, but she was enjoying her mini power trip.

"Yes."

"That traitor," Emma said, but she felt her anger slipping away. The look on Zack's handsome face was impossible to resist. His expression was a cross between sheepish and hopeful, and she decided to let him off the hook.

"These are my favorite. Thank you for bringing them." She gave him a wide smile and was rewarded with his in return.

"Does this mean that I'm forgiven?"

"Well, in all fairness, it wasn't entirely your fault. I shouldn't have snapped at you like I did. Besides, it's none of my business who you flirt with anyway."

Zack's smile disappeared. "I did not flirt with that woman, Emma. She introduced herself to me and then handed me her phone number under the guise of setting up a play date for Gracie and David. For the record, I don't find her attractive in the least."

"Is it me, or did you just sound a little bit like Bill Clinton right now?"

Zack's deep laughter echoed in her foyer. "You're impossible. Do you know that?"

"But only in the best way, right?"

"I have no choice but to agree."

"Quick study."

"I'm trying."

"I know you are, and I'm sorry for giving you a hard time."

His million-dollar smile was back again. "Can I continue to make it up to you over dinner on Wednesday night?"

"Wow, donuts and dinner? I'm a lucky lady."

"You said it, not me."

"Yes, dinner sounds good, but does this mean I have to help you unpack some more boxes?"

"Nope. I'm not asking for anything in return. Just dinner."

"I take it Gracie will be with her mom again."

"Yes. She's with Alicia on Wednesday nights and part of each weekend."

"Ok. So where would you like to go?"

"My co-workers keep talking about some restaurant in town that serves phenomenal mac-n-cheese. Do you know the place?"

"Know it? I practically live there! The restaurant is called The Union, and their food is delicious. Do you want to meet there or...?"

"No, I'll pick you up. Friends are allowed to do that, right?"

Emma resisted the urge to respond with a smartass remark and simply nodded her head yes. After all, the man was trying really hard.

"Ok, so I'll pick you up at six on Wednesday."

"I'll be ready," Emma said. Once Zack had left, she leaned against the door and inhaled deeply. "Or not," she muttered.

"When you and I go out to dinner, you don't need an hour and a half to get ready," Kelly argued when Emma had explained that she needed to leave early on Wednesday. "If you and the Greek God are just friends, why should it be any different?"

Kelly had a point, but Emma chose to ignore it. "I'm not getting ready for *him*. I'm getting ready for me. I didn't have time to take a shower this morning, and I want to freshen up."

That part, at least, was the truth. Emma had slept in after tossing and turning all night long. She'd cursed herself in the middle of the night for lying in bed questioning her decision to go out with Zack when she should have been getting her beauty sleep. Why should eating dinner at a restaurant be any more significant than eating pizza at Zack's house? Sometime around four a.m., Emma decided that maintaining a platonic relationship with Zack would be no easy feat. The question she kept asking herself was, *Am I up to the challenge?*

If her ten wardrobe changes were any indication, the answer was definitely NO! Emma surveyed herself in the mirror. She had chosen a casual cobalt blue knit dress that was belted at the waist and hit just above the knee. The color complemented her fair skin and reddish-blonde hair that fell to her shoulders. Usually Emma embraced the natural wave in her hair, but today, she had decided to straighten it, hoping it made her look sleeker and more sophisticated. She had also spent a little more time on her makeup, accentuating her pale green eyes, which she considered her best feature. Emma bolstered her petite, five-foot-three-inch frame with two-inch wedges, even though she would still feel dwarfed next to Zack. She pondered why he had labelled her the "most beautiful woman" at her cousin's wedding when she would describe herself as average. Most of the time, she felt like a pale, freckled version of the "girl next door"—attractive but in an unremarkable way. She wondered what it was that Zack saw in her...

The sound of the doorbell interrupted her musings. She rushed down the stairs, ran her hands down her smooth hair, and answered the door.

Holy wow! Apparently, Emma wasn't the only one who had taken extra time with their grooming! Zack stood there in all his masculine glory, freshly shaved, his wavy black hair perfectly tousled, and his smile gleaming. He wore a navy blue polo shirt with crisp, pleated khakis and topsiders. He could have been a guy in a Ralph Lauren cologne ad, yet here he stood on her doorstep.

They sized each other up through the screen door until Zack cleared his throat and said, "Emma, are you going to come out, or are we just going to stand here?"

How embarrassing! "I'll come out. Let me grab my purse." She scurried off into the kitchen and snatched her purse from the counter. When she returned, Zack stood in the same spot. He opened the screen door and motioned with his hand for her to come out. As Emma walked past, she inhaled the scent of his woodsy cologne, which smelled vaguely familiar. Oh yeah, she remembered it from the night of her cousin's wedding, when she and Zack had danced together, when his body had been pressed so tightly against hers that she'd felt his erection through her bridesmaid dress...

Zack followed her to the passenger door of his sporty black Range Rover. "If I were your girlfriend, I wouldn't open the door for you, but since I'm a man, I can't help myself."

Oh, there's no doubt that you're a man! "That's very gentlemanly of you. Thanks," Emma said as she slid into the car, careful not to give him an accidental peep show.

When they arrived at the popular restaurant, it was crowded as usual, so they were forced to wait in a cramped vestibule. It was difficult to carry on a conversation, so they stood quietly side by side in the tight space and waited for their table. Whenever a party's name was called, Emma and Zack had to squeeze even closer together to allow people to pass. By the time they were finally seated, Emma's face was flushed. She guzzled down half a glass of water as soon as the waitress brought it.

Zack, on the other hand, was the picture of calm while he perused the menu. "Everything looks good here. I'm not sure what to order."

I'll have the mac-n-cheese with a side of Greek hunk, Emma thought. *Oh my gosh, I did not just think that!* "We could split an order of mac-n-cheese," she suggested, tramping down her impure thoughts.

"Sure. You can't go wrong with the house special."

While they waited for their food, Emma brought up the most neutral topic she could think of—Gracie.

"How does Gracie like preschool so far?" she asked.

"Seems to love it. She's made a few new friends already, although she's been complaining about some boy in the class."

"Why's that?"

"I guess he's been teasing her on the playground. Pulling her hair, pinching her, things like that."

"Hmm, sounds like a classic case of a boy with a crush."

Zack smiled broadly, which caused a crazy flip in her stomach. "That's what I told her. Boys don't always know the appropriate way to express themselves when they like a girl."

"Spoken like a true expert."

Zack stared at her for a moment with a look of uncertainty. "Although, sometimes boys express themselves and get rebuffed," he said pointedly.

Was he talking about the wedding? If so, Emma refused to go there. Luckily, the mac-n-cheese arrived just in the nick of time. As soon as the first creamy, cheesy, luscious bite hit her tongue, Emma let out a loud, happy sigh.

Zack eyed her across the table, his fork poised in mid-air.

"What?" she asked, trying to read his expression.

"Nothing. Just glad to see you're enjoying it." Zack's forkful disappeared into his mouth, and he let out a similar sigh, followed by a thorough lick of his full, cheese-coated lips.

Suddenly Emma felt like she was watching a scene from a porn movie (not that she'd ever watched one of those). Any minute, she expected Zack to stand up and start stripping, then lean her over the table and...

"Emma?" he asked, breaking into her thoughts.

"Hmm?"

"You dropped a noodle, right there." Zack pointed to a spot just above her left breast. "Here, I'll get it for you."

He poured a drop of water onto his napkin and was just about to reach over the table when Emma yelled, "NO!" She hadn't realized how loud she was until she glanced around and saw several pairs of eyes upon her.

Zack pulled his napkin back like he'd been stung while Emma extracted the errant noodle from her dress and placed it daintily on the edge of her plate. "I got it," she said, smiling sweetly.

They finished their meal and split the bill upon Emma's insistence that friends pay their own way. When Zack pulled into Emma's driveway, they both sat still for a moment in awkward silence.

"Can I walk you to the door?" Zack asked.

"That's not necessary, but thanks for sharing the mac-n-cheese with me," Emma said, adopting a light and airy tone. She opened her door before Zack could come around, and slid out, holding her dress down as she did so. She had only taken a few steps when Zack rolled down his window.

"Hey, Emma? One more thing."

"What's that?"

"You looked beautiful tonight," he replied, and he rolled his window up before she could respond.

Emma stood rooted in place, eyes wide, and watched, bewildered, as he drove away.

CHAPTER 8

It was almost five o'clock on Friday afternoon when Emma heard from Zack again. Kelly had just left the bookstore to go on another "hot date" with her poetry-reading boyfriend, and Brett would arrive soon to take over the evening shift. This time, Emma recognized the phone number on the display and answered, "Hi, Zack, what's up?"

"Question. Don't friends share their personal phone numbers so they don't have to call each other at work?"

Emma smiled even though he couldn't see her. "Yes, I believe we've graduated to sharing our personal numbers. When we hang up, I'll send you a text from my cell phone, and then you'll have it."

"Whew, I'm glad I've moved up a notch on the friendship ladder."

Emma's grin stretched even wider. "So, is that all you called for?"

Brett walked in the door at that moment, and Emma smiled and waved when he approached the front counter. A young girl in the romance section glanced up at the same time and perused Brett from head to toe. *Some women are so obvious*, Emma thought and turned her attention back to the phone.

"Actually, I called to tell you that Gracie won't be coming to story time tomorrow. Alicia's taking her to a fair in Ann Arbor instead."

"Oh, well, thanks for letting me know," Emma replied and felt a wave of disappointment at the thought of not seeing them on Saturday.

"Since Gracie will be gone all day, I wondered if you would like to hang out with me when you get off work?"

Did he just say make out with me? No, you idiot, he said hang out! "What did you have in mind?"

Brett sat on a stool nearby and peered at Emma over the top of his stylish black-rimmed glasses. While he watched Emma, the girl in the romance section watched him, probably hoping to catch his eye.

"Well, I saw a banner in town advertising an arts and crafts show this weekend. Would that be of any interest to you?"

"Sure, I'd be interested, but I can't believe that you would be."

"Why not?"

"You just don't seem like an artsy type of guy."

Zack chuckled. "Ok, you caught me, but it was either that or a monster truck show, and I figured…"

"You figured right. I would have passed on the monster trucks."

"See, I really am learning."

"But does this mean I eventually have to go with you to one of *those* things?"

"Maybe. Isn't that written on page eight of the friendship handbook?"

Emma's loud laughter must have startled the girl in the romance section because the rather tall pile of books she had been holding toppled to the floor, and Brett gallantly rushed to her aid. The poor girl's face turned bright red when Brett bent down to help her reassemble the books into a neat pile.

"Zack, I have to go. I'm working until two o'clock tomorrow, so what time do you want to pick me up?" Emma asked.

"Oh, more progress! You didn't even ask if we should meet there."

"What time Zack?" Emma repeated with feigned impatience.

"How about two-thirty?"

"Ok. See you then," Emma replied and hung up. Brett carried the romance reader's books up to the counter, and she trailed sheepishly behind him. The girl was probably eighteen years old, and she had the fresh look of youth on her side. Emma decided to make a hasty retreat in order for Brett to work his magic. Plus, he might be able to sell her a few more books while he was at it!

"Have a good evening, Brett. Call me if you need anything," Emma said, and she gave *romance girl* an encouraging smile as she headed out the door.

The arts and crafts show was in full swing by the time Emma and Zack arrived in downtown Clarkston. Zack drove around the block a few times before they got lucky and found a decent parking spot. It was a comfortable seventy-degree day with clear skies, perfect for an outdoor festival. When Zack had picked her up, Emma thought he had looked particularly *yummy* (another one of Kelly's descriptions) in his navy blue cargo shorts, gray t-shirt, and aviators. He sported a few days' worth of scruff on his face that gave him that extra edge of true male hotness, and Emma had to remind herself not to stare.

She was dressed in her usual weekend attire: white skinny jeans, striped t-shirt, and Keds. She had let her hair dry naturally so that it fell in soft waves to her shoulders. After wearing a dress on their previous outing, Emma didn't want Zack to think that she was trying to impress him. Today, she dressed like she would if she were going to the craft show with Kelly.

They strolled slowly up and down the rows of craft tables, stopping occasionally if something caught their attention. Zack had just paused at a custom woodworker's booth to look at a child-size desk and chair for Gracie when Emma saw *him*.

There was her ex-husband, not six feet away and headed straight toward them. That would have been shocking enough, but to add insult to injury, he had his arm around the waist of a tall, leggy woman with long, glossy black hair and a dazzling white smile. The woman reminded Emma of Cher circa 1970!

"So, Emma, what do you think of this one? Do you think Gracie would like it?" Zack was still busy perusing the desk and chair and hadn't noticed Emma's expression until he glanced up at her stricken face.

"Emma, what's wrong?" he asked, but it was a little too late.

"Hello, Emma," Mark said and dropped his arm from around the Cher-wannabe's waist.

"Hello, Mark," Emma replied while Zack moved to stand alongside her.

"This is my friend, Charlene," Mark said as he gave Zack the evil eye.

"Nice to meet you," Emma said and then turned toward Zack. "And this is my *friend*, Zack," she added pointedly.

Zack removed his sunglasses and held out his hand to Mark. "You look familiar," Mark said, eyebrows knit with concentration.

"We've met," Zack replied with forced politeness. "At Phil's wedding five years ago. Emma and I stood up together."

"Ah, yes, now I remember."

Emma thought she saw a flicker of disdain pass over Mark's face, but she couldn't be sure. He had always been hard to read, unlike Zack, whose every thought registered on his face. For instance, at that moment, he looked like he wouldn't mind punching Mark right in his smug face.

"Of course, I didn't see much of Emma that night. Seems like you were monopolizing her time," Mark continued, unaware that he was waving a red cape at a fight-ready bull.

Emma laid her hand on Zack's arm and gave it a little squeeze. "Zack, I think it's time for us to go. We don't want to miss our dinner reservation."

Zack didn't even flinch; he just went along for the ride. "Right, and we wanted to take a shower first."

Ok, he didn't need to go that far! "Goodbye, Mark, Charlene," Emma said and slipped her hand into Zack's while they walked away.

When they arrived at Zack's car, Emma realized that their fingers were still entwined. Neither one let go until Zack opened the passenger door for her.

"Was that an Oscar-worthy performance or what?" Zack asked when they pulled out of the parking spot. "I felt like Liam Neeson for a second there. Man, I wanted to clock the guy, and then he made that snide comment about the wedding…"

Emma's silence must have tipped him off. She had been trying to hide her tears as Zack carried on, but her face was already damp by the time he noticed.

"Oh God, Emma, I'm so sorry," Zack said.

"It's ok," she said, swatting angrily at her tears. "He just caught me off guard, that's all. I figured I might run into him someday, but not today and especially not at a craft show. He never would have gone with me to a craft show, yet there he was with, with… Charlene."

Zack gently picked up her hand in his as a fresh stream of tears ran down her face. "I understand, Em, believe me. I went through this with Alicia. The first time I saw her with pretty boy, it made me crazy. It took every ounce of control I had not to beat the guy to a pulp."

"What stopped you?"

"Gracie. I didn't want to do anything to jeopardize my relationship with her—still don't."

"You're a good dad, Zack," Emma said softly.

"And you're a good woman. Don't let Mark or any other man make you feel otherwise."

Emma looked down at their hands. That was the second time today that they had held hands, and it struck her that it had felt like the most natural thing in the world.

CHAPTER 9

Zack put his blinker on just before they reached Emma's street, but she stopped him from turning there.

"Zack, I really don't want to be alone right now. Do you have some more boxes I could help you unpack? I'd like to do something to distract myself from thoughts of you-know-who."

"Wow, a friend who offers to help instead of waiting to be asked... impressive."

His teasing brought a smile back to Emma's tear-stained face. "What can I say, I'm a *really* good friend."

"Ok, but I have to be honest with you. The only room I have left to unpack is my bedroom."

Emma's eyes widened with surprise. "Are you serious? Everything else is done?"

"Yep. I kicked butt this week, and Gracie helped too. I saved my room for last since it's the least seen, and used, in the house."

His meaning wasn't lost on her. Emma's bedroom hadn't seen much action in quite some time either. Aside from the six months she'd been divorced, she and Mark hadn't been intimate with each other for several months preceding that. In retrospect, it was easy to see that he had been pulling away from her little by little.

"I don't mind helping. I just need to keep my hands busy…" Emma's voice trailed off when she saw the grin on Zack's scruffy face. "Oh geez, seriously?"

"Sorry. It's a guy thing. I'll be on my best behavior. I promise."

Emma wasn't so sure that she believed him, and in a private corner of her mind, she wanted him to misbehave. *The hazards of having a gorgeous male friend, I guess.*

Ten minutes later, they were in Zack's bedroom, each armed with cleaning supplies and a cold beer. His bed was unmade, and a new bedding ensemble sat on the floor, still in the package. Boxes of clothes and books lined the walls, and the only furniture, besides the king-sized bed, was a chest of drawers. There was a large walk-in closet next to the master bathroom, and Emma assumed that was where most of his clothes would go. The beige walls were void of decoration, and the oversized window was bare of curtains. The window looked out on the treed backyard, so lack of privacy wasn't an issue, but Emma couldn't imagine not having any window covering.

"This room needs a woman's touch," Emma said, and then she immediately recognized her error.

Zack laughed gruffly and ran his hands through his thick, wavy hair. "You said it, not me."

"I better just shut up and get to work," Emma said and marched over to the window with the Windex and paper towels. She vigorously wiped the handprints off of the window while Zack began to put his clothes into the dresser drawers. They were silent for several minutes before he brought up the dreaded topic.

"So, are you still in love with him?"

Nothing like cutting right to the chase. "No," Emma replied adamantly.

"We don't have to talk about it, but based on your reaction today, I thought you might want to."

Emma kept her back to him and concentrated extra hard on a stubborn spot on the window. "You want to hear something really sad? I don't know that I was ever truly in love with Mark."

"Really?"

"We dated throughout college, and the next logical step seemed to be marriage. I never stopped to question whether or not I really loved him. I just went through the motions. Sad, huh?"

Zack was silent for a moment, and Emma turned around to find him perched on the edge of the bed. "It was similar for me. Alicia and I looked really good on paper, but the reality of our relationship was a different story. I don't think either one of us was ever truly happy."

The window was more than clean at this point, so Emma set down the cleaning products and walked toward him. There were no chairs in the room, so she sat on the opposite end of the bed from Zack.

"Even though I might not have loved Mark the way I should have, I never planned on divorcing him. I made a commitment, and I fully intended to honor it. I was shocked when he decided not to."

"I hear you. When Gracie was born, I figured that she would be the glue that kept Alicia and I together. We were a family; you know…"

Emma heard the unmistakable hitch in Zack's voice, and her heart went out to him. She inched a little closer and laid her hand on his arm. "I'm sure that it was even harder for you to get divorced because of Gracie. I can't imagine what that would have been like—for all of you."

"Divorce sucks." Zack said firmly, and Emma's lips twitched at his childlike expression.

"I agree. All we can do now is move forward and try never to make the same mistakes again."

"I don't know about you, but marriage is the last thing on my radar right now. Hell, it's hard to imagine having any relationship with a woman at this point."

Emma flinched and pulled her hand away. "Hey, I'm a woman."

"I know, but that's different. You're my friend, so there's no pressure."

"What about the other stuff? You know, what you said the other day about guys wanting…"

"Sex?"

"Yeah, that." Emma found herself inching a little further away, which caused Zack to chuckle.

"Oh, I still want that," he admitted, and he gave her the most devilish grin she had ever seen.

"So having sex doesn't count as having a relationship with a woman?" Emma was constantly amazed at the inner workings of a man's brain. She obviously had a lot to learn, and who better to teach her than this man—the king of panty melters.

"Not necessarily. Remember when you said that sex and romance make a perfect combination? Well, sex and relationships don't have to go together. Sometimes we like sex just for the sake of sex."

"Hmm, and you believe that this is unique to the male species?" Emma set her hands on her hips and quirked her eyebrows at him.

Zack was obviously enjoying the turn that their conversation had taken. He adjusted his position to face her full on, their knees almost touching on the sheets. "I guess it's possible for a woman to want that too, although I've never known one."

"Well, I'll have you know that women enjoy sex just as much as men. Some just might be too shy to admit it."

"Which one are you?"

Oh God, what have I done? Emma was stuck. She couldn't move back another inch, or she'd fall on the floor. Zack looked at her like he was about to pounce, and her heart started beating double-time. To top it all off, she felt her cheeks heat up, which meant she was probably a lovely shade of beet-red!

"Um, this is not an appropriate conversation for friends to have."

Zack leaned a little closer, to where she could feel his breath on her skin. He rested his weight on his hands, which caused the muscles in his biceps to bulge. *Great, now I'm looking at his muscles!*

"Emma, let me just say that if you *ever* feel the urge to have sex just for the sake of it, I'm your man.

No need to pick up a stranger at a bar or anything like that. It's not safe, and I can promise you I would never hurt you."

Emma almost melted under his intense gray-eyed gaze, but suddenly her conscience kicked in, and she stood up from the bed, putting a safe distance between them.

"I'll keep that in mind," she said flippantly. "Now, let's get back to work."

CHAPTER 10

Emma didn't hear from Zack for the next few days, and she decided that it was for the best. Their last interaction had been a little too close for comfort, and a break was just what she needed. Besides, she had a particularly busy schedule at A New Chapter that week. On Tuesday, there was a local author coming in to do a book signing, and on Thursday, Emma was hosting the store's first ever book club meeting.

Emma was constantly generating ideas on how to keep her store alive, and reaching out to the community was one of them. She had advertised in all of the local papers and participated in a live interview on Clarkston's independent television channel to encourage people to join the new book club. Anyone who joined would receive a discount on that month's book selection. This month's book was *The Nightingale* by Kristin Hannah, which was one of Emma's favorite reads of the year.

Emma and Kelly were setting up chairs at the back of the store when Emma's cell phone buzzed in her pants pocket. She was annoyed at herself for carrying the darn thing around instead of leaving it in her purse. Before Zack, her phone hadn't been blowing up with personal calls so she had let it be, but now…

"Hey, Em. What are you up to?"

"I'm in the process of setting up for a book club meeting at the store, so I only have a few minutes." Emma held up her index finger to Kelly, who was attempting to move a large table by herself.

"I won't keep you, but I have a favor to ask. Now, I'm not sure where this appears in the friendship handbook, but… "

"Just get to the point, Zack," Emma said, suppressing a smile while she rolled her eyes.

"Ok. A coworker of mine invited me to his wedding reception on Saturday. I know it's short notice, but I wondered if you would go with me. I hate going solo to weddings, and we wouldn't have to stay long, unless we're having a good time… "

Emma turned her back on Kelly, who was making obnoxious *hurry up* faces at her. "I don't think so, Zack. Sorry."

"Why not?"

She should have known that he wouldn't give up that easily. The bell chimed at the front of the store, and a couple of women walked in toting their book club books. Emma motioned to Kelly to greet them.

"Zack, I really don't have time to talk about this right now. I just don't think it's a good idea, that's all."

"Even if I promise to be on my best behavior? No repeats of the last time we were at a wedding together. I swear."

Say no, Emma, just say no! "Oh, alright, but I'm holding you to your word."

"Cool, thanks. You're the best!"

"Yes, I know. Call me tomorrow with the details."

Emma put all thoughts of Zack and weddings aside when she began the book club meeting. She gave a brief synopsis of the novel and then initiated some discussion questions, and the group took over from there. Emma felt right at home among the lively group of women and one brave guy, who shared her love of reading. During the meeting, Kelly went around with a tray of punch, cheese, and fruit. At the end of the hour, Emma announced the book selection for the following month and passed out a store coupon for twenty percent off.

After the last person left the store, Emma and Kelly turned and gave each other a double high five. *If only I felt this elated about going to the wedding with Zack,* Emma thought while she drove home.

Emma had just crawled under her covers and was about to switch her phone off when it rang. She glanced at her bedroom clock—nine thirty—and then back down at Zack's name on the display. *Why is he calling me now?* She debated about whether or not to answer for all of five seconds before she tapped the green button.

"Hello?"

"So, I was lying in bed thinking about you and decided I had to call."

Oh boy. "Why were you thinking about me in bed?" Emma asked as she pulled the covers up to her chin. She pictured him lying under his new brown and blue plaid comforter that they had made his bed with on Saturday. *Would he be wearing boxers, briefs, or nothing at all?*

"Well, knowing how women are, I thought you might want a little more information about the wedding on Saturday. In case you need time to buy a new dress or get your hair done or whatever."

Wow, he really did know women! "Ok, why don't you start with the reason you were invited to this wedding on such short notice."

"The invitations went out long before I started working at the company, but Justin—he's the groom—didn't want me to feel left out. Most of my coworkers will be there, so I feel like I should at least make an appearance."

"And you didn't want to go alone."

"Exactly."

Emma heard him rustle around and tried not to picture him bare-chested with his defined biceps, wavy black hair, and devilish grin. "I usually work until five on Saturdays, so what time do I need to be ready?"

"Is seven o'clock ok?"

"Sure."

"Oh, and Alicia is going to pick Gracie up after story time and have her overnight, so I don't have to worry about a curfew. You know, in case you want to keep me out late… "

Flirty man! "Zack," Emma warned.

"Sorry. Even though we're friends, I am still a man after all."

Don't I know it. "I'm well aware, but best behavior, remember?"

"Define best behavior."

"Goodnight, Zack."

"What are you wearing right now? Just curious."

"Goodnight, Zack," Emma repeated, even though a giggle erupted unbidden.

"Hmm, a nightie or sweats? Or maybe, none of the above..."

"I'm hanging up the phone now."

"I'm thinking tank top and skimpy underwear."

Emma erupted into full-out laughter. "You're incorrigible."

"But only in the best way, right?"

"If I agree, will you let me go this time?"

"Absolutely."

"Well, then, I agree."

She heard the rustle of covers again and then, "Goodnight, Emma."

"Goodnight, Zack."

CHAPTER 11

The next day, during a lull at the bookstore, Emma lamented to Kelly, "I don't have anything to wear."

"You're welcome to borrow something of mine, but I still can't believe you said yes."

"I know, I caved. He caught me at a busy moment, and I was just trying to get him off the phone."

Kelly shook her head. "Yeah, right. I think that subconsciously you really wanted to go with him, and that's why you said yes. I've been reading about the power of the subconscious mind, and..."

"Not helping, Kell. I don't need you to psychoanalyze me; all I need is for you to find me something to wear!"

"Fine. When Brett comes in to relieve us, we can go to my apartment, and you can dig through my closet."

"Thank you."

"But I still say you're in for big trouble tomorrow night."

"Why is that?"

"Because weddings are romantic, and when two good-looking single people attend a wedding together, well, you know what can happen."

"Yes, but when the two people are *friends*..."

"Friends, schmends. Call it whatever you want, but don't say I didn't warn you."

Kelly's closet was like a gold mine. She was a self-proclaimed "serial dater," and she had clothes for every occasion. Emma was a couple of inches shorter than her, but they still wore roughly the same size. Emma rifled through the dresses, which Kelly had aligned neatly in one section of her closet, and held them up one by one.

"Too flashy," Kelly said about a short silver-sequined number.

"Too boring," she said about a black shift dress.

Emma pulled out a deep purple dress and was just about to put it back without asking for Kelly's opinion when...

"Wait, that one's perfect," Kelly blurted out.

The dress was sleeveless with a deep vee in the front and the back. The skirt portion was simple and draped nicely to the knee, but there would be a lot of skin showing up top, and that made Emma nervous.

"I don't think so, Kell. The top portion is a little too breezy for my liking."

Kelly giggled. "It won't show as much as you think, Em. Try it on, and you'll see. The color is perfect for you."

Some friends were good for the ego, and Kelly was definitely one of them. They had met during their senior year in college and had been inseparable ever since. Kelly had been there for Emma's wedding, through her divorce, and at the opening of A New Chapter. She had been working for a marketing firm prior to the opening of the bookstore, but she hadn't been happy there. When Emma had offered her a job, she had jumped at the chance. Emma had put her in charge of marketing and promoting the store, and she attributed much of its success to Kelly's sales skills. Emma was the true book lover, who excelled at interacting with the customers, giving book recommendations, and choosing the inventory, while Kelly promoted the shop from behind the scenes. They complimented each other perfectly, and Emma couldn't imagine her life without Kelly in it.

Having seen each other in all manner of dress and undress, Emma discarded her khakis and plaid button-down shirt and slipped into the purple dress. She turned in a complete circle in front of the mirror on the back of Kelly's bedroom door and waited for her friend's reaction.

Kelly's golden brown eyes sparkled, and her smile lit up the room. "You look beautiful, Em."

Emma had to agree. The color complimented her light skin and reddish-blonde hair, and the vee in the front didn't show nearly as much skin as she thought it would. Of course, her breasts weren't as ample as Kelly's, so there wasn't as much to show, but she still felt sexy nonetheless.

"All you need is your black patent pumps, and you're good to go," Kelly said.

"I love it, Kell."

"You're going to knock Zack's socks off tomorrow. And maybe the rest of his clothes too!"

On Saturday morning, Emma felt surprisingly calm about attending the wedding with Zack. She was even looking forward to it. She'd convinced herself that it would be a fun night out with a friend and that was all there was to it! She had just finished setting up for story time when she heard Zack's voice. She went toward the front of the store to greet him and Gracie, and stopped dead in her tracks.

Emma's eyes swung from Zack to Gracie to Alicia and back to Zack again. She recalled him telling her that Alicia was going to take Gracie home after story time, but she didn't expect her to come in the store. It was probably the norm for divorced parents to present a united front for their child's benefit; however, it caught Emma off guard to see them all together. Gracie looked like the picture of happiness as she clasped both of her parents' hands.

"See, Mommy. This is Miss Emma, the lady who reads me stories," Gracie said sweetly.

Alicia gave Emma the once-over and granted her a cool partial smile. "Nice to see you again, Emma."

"You too," Emma managed, and she looked to Zack to fill in the blanks.

"Gracie wanted her mom to see where she comes for story time," he explained with an unreadable expression on his face.

Emma got the impression that he wasn't thrilled with his ex-wife's presence, but he was forced to tolerate it for the sake of their daughter.

"Will you be staying?" Emma asked, adopting a neutral tone.

"Yes, I think so," Alicia replied.

"Well, then, all of you can take a seat, and I'll begin in a few minutes."

The three of them walked away, and Emma slipped behind the counter where Kelly had stood and watched the entire interaction.

"Well, that was awkward," Kelly said.

Emma took a few sips from her water bottle and shrugged her shoulders. "That's an understatement. I wish Zack would have given me a heads-up that she would be here."

"Maybe he didn't know until the last minute."

Emma glanced at her watch. "I've got to get back there. Wish me luck."

As she walked to the back of the store, she squared her shoulders and took a couple of deep breaths. *Why should I be nervous about her being here? Zack and I aren't together, so it's no big deal.* She was determined to ignore Alicia's presence and concentrate on the kids, which turned out to be easier said than done. Whenever Emma glanced up from reading *The Very Hungry Caterpillar*, she noticed that Alicia was studying her intently. While the kids looked at each other or at the illustrations in the story and the other parents looked discreetly down at their phones, Alicia's eyes stayed focused directly on the storyteller.

Emma felt a surge of relief when the story was finally over and she could move away from Alicia's penetrating gaze. Emma was bent over the craft table when she overhead Alicia tell Gracie that they had to leave.

"But, Mom, I want to do the craft," Gracie complained.

"Why don't we ask Miss Emma if you can take the craft with you?" Zack suggested in an attempt to keep the peace.

"That's a good idea," Alicia said.

Alicia and Gracie drifted off to look at books while Zack approached Emma. "Can Gracie take the craft to go?" Zack asked and rolled his eyes.

Emma's discomfort slipped away when she saw that Zack was obviously more distressed than she was. "Sure," she said and handed him the craft items.

"I'm going to walk them out. Be right back," he called over his shoulder.

Alicia and Gracie had wandered to the front of the store, but Gracie turned and ran back to Emma. She skidded to a stop and said, "Bye, Miss Emma. Thanks for the story."

"You're very welcome," Emma replied and smiled as Gracie raced back to her parents. Alicia gave Emma a brief wave and then they all filed out.

Zack returned five minutes later and looked apologetic.

"Well, that was interesting," Emma said quietly. The store was still busy, and she didn't want customers to overhear their conversation.

"Tell me about it. When Gracie and I pulled up, Alicia was waiting in the parking lot. I had no idea that she would show up early."

"I'm sure that Gracie wanted her here. It's really no big deal," Emma said, although she still felt a little shaken from the encounter.

"There might have been more to it than that. Gracie's been talking about you quite a bit, and I think Alicia wanted to check you out."

"Why? She already met me at Phil's wedding."

"I know, but that was a long time ago. Listen, I don't know what her motivations were, but I'm sorry if she made you uncomfortable."

"I'm fine, Zack. She was perfectly... polite."

"Yeah, about as polite as a mother bear protecting her cub."

Emma smiled up at him. "She'll ease off as soon as she realizes that I'm not a threat."

"You're probably right," Zack said, but he didn't look convinced.

CHAPTER 12

Zack knotted his tie and took one last look in the bathroom mirror. He brushed an imaginary speck of lint off of his suit jacket and turned away in disgust, not at his appearance, but at the sudden case of nerves that he felt in his gut. Part of him wished that he hadn't asked Emma to accompany him tonight, and part of him was thrilled that she had said yes.

The reason for his nervousness was simple; he liked the way things were going with Emma, and he didn't want to mess it up. So far, he had kept to his word about only wanting her friendship, even though inside he knew it was a lie. There was no doubt that he was attracted to her, and at times, he thought the feeling might be mutual, although they were both reluctant to act on it.

Zack kept telling himself that it was the right decision for Gracie, but he was starting to question his reasoning. Gracie seemed to enjoy Emma's company just as much as he did. Well, maybe that was a slight exaggeration, but still, Gracie was always excited to see her on Saturdays. What would be the harm of bringing Emma around while Gracie was there too? He could explain to Gracie that while he liked Emma, that didn't mean he was going to marry her or that she would ever replace Alicia. *Why does just the thought of that discussion make me break out in a sweat?*

Aside from Gracie's feelings on the subject, he wasn't sure where Emma stood. She seemed to be content with their current "friends" status, and he hadn't seen any real indication that she wanted to change it. Other than that day in his bedroom, when they had been talking about sex...

Oh yeah. That was a scene that kept replaying in his mind, especially at night, when he was lying in bed having trouble sleeping. When he had offered to be Emma's sex buddy (well, not in those exact words), he thought he had seen a glimmer of interest. She had been quick to squelch it, but her eyes had given her away, not to mention the hitch of her breath when he had leaned in close to her on the bed.

She could have slapped him or at least berated him for the suggestion, but she hadn't. She had simply moved to the other side of the room, as if putting distance between them would prevent him from wanting her. Or prevent her from wanting him...

In any case, he had enough experience with women to know when someone was interested. Emma could deny it all she wanted to, and he could use Gracie as his reason not to get involved, but in the end, it wouldn't matter. They shared a mutual attraction, and if he played his cards right and took

good care of Emma, she would come around. He
was almost sure of it.

CHAPTER 13

When Emma swung open the door on Saturday evening, Zack's mouth gaped, and his eyes grew wide.

"Wow, Emma, you look amazing! Friends can say that, right?"

Emma chuckled. "Yes, of course. You're looking pretty fine yourself."

Zack puffed out his chest. "Why thank you, ma'am."

As they walked out to the Range Rover, Zack put a hand on her elbow, presumably to keep her from tripping in her heels. Emma decided not to fight it and let him play the role of the gallant gentleman. When he opened the car door and she slid in, the hem of her dress rose, and she caught him peeking at her legs. *So much for the perfect gentleman!*

"How long of a drive do we have?" Emma asked as she tugged the hem of her dress back down.

"About thirty minutes," Zack replied with a smirk.

"What?"

"You can't wear a dress like that and expect me not to look at your legs," Zack said unapologetically.

Emma rolled her eyes but didn't try to hide her smile. "So it's a guy thing, I take it."

"Pretty much. I'm sure I won't be the only guy who checks you out tonight."

"Really? Even if I show up on your arm?"

"Doesn't matter. You're going to have to face it, Em. You're a looker. In fact, I should probably warn you about a couple of my coworkers."

"Ok... "

"Dan, my boss, is single and horny as hell. I swear his goal in life is to have more women than he has Facebook friends! Then there's Rick and his wife who are confirmed swingers... "

"Hold up," Emma said, turning in her seat to face him. "Are you serious? You actually know people who do that?"

"You'd be surprised what people do behind closed doors. Not everyone is as squeaky clean as you are."

Emma's eyes bulged. "Excuse me? Who says I'm squeaky clean?"

"You married Mark right after college, correct?" After she nodded, he continued. "So I'm going to guess that you might have slept with one or two guys before him and, since your divorce was fairly recent, no one since him. Am I right?"

Emma turned away from him in a huff. *So I don't sleep around. What's wrong with that?*

"Not that there's anything wrong with that," Zack said, borrowing a line from *Seinfeld*.

"I happen to believe that sex is a meaningful act that should be between *two* people who actually care about each other. If that makes me squeaky clean, then so be it!"

"I agree with you."

Wait, what? "You do?"

"Sure. Just because I'm a flirt doesn't mean I sleep around, Em."

She was saved from further discussion when he pulled up to the reception hall, and they were immediately approached by a valet. Emma had never been to Buhl Estate before, but she knew it was a popular wedding venue. Zack placed his hand on the small of her back and guided her into the exquisite ballroom. Some of Zack's coworkers spotted them right away and waved him over to a group of tables toward the back wall. Emma felt several pairs of eyes upon them while they made their way across the empty dance floor.

"We can leave whenever you're ready," Zack whispered in her ear.

"We just got here!" Emma exclaimed. It felt good to get dressed up and go out with a handsome man. She didn't want to think about the evening ending before it had even really begun.

When they reached his coworkers, Zack shook hands with some of the men, smiled and nodded at some of the women, and then introduced them all to his "friend" Emma. A few people looked skeptical about the label, but Emma just smiled and said hello. They were barely seated when Zack's boss asked them what they would like to drink.

When Dan went off to the bar, Zack leaned over and whispered, "Didn't know you liked hard liquor. Thought you were a beer girl."

"I hardly think of rum and Coke as hard liquor," Emma said. "Besides, you've never offered me anything but a beer at your house, so how would you know?"

Zack was about to retort when an attractive middle-aged woman wearing a tight black dress and a seductive smile approached their table.

"Hi, Zack," she said, completely ignoring Emma's presence.

"Hey, Brandy. How's it going?"

"Better now that you're here."

Zack let out a strangled laugh and glanced over at Emma, who was trying to suppress a giggle. "Brandy, this is my… "

"Yes, I heard. Hello Zack's *friend*, Emma," Brandy purred.

"Brandy works at the front desk at Bradford Financial," Zack explained while tugging at the white collar of his dress shirt.

"It's nice to meet you, Brandy," Emma said. She could have said something totally inappropriate, and Brandy wouldn't have noticed. The woman's eyes were glued to Zack, and he squirmed uncomfortably under her intense scrutiny.

"Save me a dance later, Zacky," Brandy said, and she sashayed away without waiting for his response.

The minute she was out of sight, Emma turned to Zack and teased, "Zacky?"

"Yes, I know. It's obnoxious. The woman adds a 'y' to the end of everyone's name, not just mine."

"Whatever you say, Zacky," Emma said with a grin. "When you told me about your coworkers, you failed to mention Brandy."

Zack was about to reply when Dan returned with their drinks. "Drink up, buddy. The night is young!" Dan proclaimed and winked at Emma.

Zack took a long pull on his beer and scooted his chair closer to hers. It was an obvious show of possession, but Dan seemed oblivious. He sat down across from them and attempted to engage Emma in conversation.

"So, Emma, what do you do?"

"I own A New Chapter." Since Dan looked confused, Emma added, "The bookstore about a mile north of downtown Clarkston."

"Ah, yes. I've heard of it, but I haven't been there. Now that I know you own it, I'll have to stop in."

"Why, Dan? I thought you told me that you didn't like to read," Zack said with unmistakable sarcasm.

"Well, I like to read some things," he said. "Do you sell *Playboy* there?"

Zack didn't give Emma time to answer. He stood up abruptly and pulled her with him, almost spilling her drink in the process. "Hey, there's the bride and groom. We should go say hello," he said and quickly steered Emma away.

"Thanks for the save; otherwise, I was going to have to smack your boss," Emma hissed through her plastered-on smile. The bride and groom had spotted them, and she didn't want to look like an unhappy guest.

Zack introduced Emma to Justin and his lovely bride, Trisha, who looked just like a bride should look on her wedding day. Emma observed the happy couple wistfully while they chatted with Zack about their wedding ceremony and shared a laugh over their eight-year-old ring bearer, who had dropped their rings on his way up the aisle.

The longer they stood there with the beautiful couple, the sadder Emma became. This is what it should have been like on her wedding day. She should have been buoyant and effervescent like Trisha instead of plagued with doubts and worries. Emma wondered what the guests at her wedding had seen when they had looked at the bride. Had some of them been able to tell that she seemed less than ecstatic as she was pronounced Mrs. Emma Babcock? (She had reclaimed her maiden name, Murphy, after the divorce.) The overriding feeling Emma remembered having on her wedding day was that she was giving something up rather than gaining something. It wasn't about her independence or her dreams of success. She had achieved all of that when she had opened the bookstore. No, what she had given up that day was her chance to have a true and satisfying love, the kind of love that would last a lifetime. Now that Mark was out of her life, she still wondered if she would ever find that kind of love.

It took her a moment to realize that Zack was leading her back to their table. "Are you ok? You look a little pale."

"I'm fine," she replied. When they sat back down, Emma noticed that a fresh drink had been placed at her seat—Dan's handiwork, no doubt, although he was nowhere to be seen. When Zack became engaged in a lengthy discussion about financial matters with his coworkers, Emma quietly sipped on her rum and Coke. Zack glanced over at her occasionally, and she kept giving him a reassuring smile. An hour later, there were three empty glasses on the table in front of her, and the crazy thing was she didn't remember how they'd all gotten there.

Sometime later, the lights were dimmed, and the guests filled the dance floor for the first slow dance. Sure enough, Brandy appeared out of nowhere and asked *Zacky* to dance.

"Sorry, Brandy. I promised the first dance to Emma." Zack held out his hand to Emma, and she gladly took it. She wasn't entirely sure that she would have been able to stand up without it.

As Brandy slinked away, Zack led Emma to the crowded dance floor. Her surroundings were fuzzy, like she was looking at everything through the bottom of a Coke bottle. Shapes were distorted, lights flickered, and colors blended together. The sea of people looked like one big blur to her, so Emma trained her focus on Zack.

He held her stiffly at first, keeping a respectable space between them, but Emma needed more of his support to stay upright. She closed the distance between them and entwined her arms around his neck. *There, much better.*

Emma noticed the look of surprise on Zack's face, but he didn't pull back. In fact, he might have pulled her a little closer, because she heard the rustle of her dress against his suit pants. She leaned her head against his broad, hard chest and concentrated on the strong rhythmic thuds of his heartbeat in her ear. Emma couldn't be one hundred percent certain, but she thought she felt something else that was hard a bit further down. She lifted her face up to find Zack smiling down at her with a look of amusement dancing in his eyes.

"Sorry," he said and shrugged. "Some things are beyond my control."

Emma erupted into a fit of giggles and ignored the curious stares around her. Once she gathered herself back together, she took a step back, but Zack's hands remained firmly locked on her hips.

"It's my fault this time," she said, slurring her words a little. "I'm the one who got too close."

Zack leaned forward and brushed her hair back. "There's no such thing as too close, Emma."

Luckily, the disc jockey announced a line dance, so Zack and Emma broke apart. When they made their way back to their table, Emma stumbled and Zack put his arm around her waist and tucked her close to his side.

"I think it's time to take you home," he said.

"But why? I'm having such a good time," Emma implored, slurring her words once again.

"I believe you, but if we stay much longer, I'm afraid your good time is going to come to an abrupt and potentially embarrassing end."

Emma didn't have the strength to argue. While Zack said his round of goodbyes, she took one last sip of her drink. "Goodbye, everyone," she called merrily, and Zack quickly led her out of the room.

CHAPTER 14

On the drive home, Emma leaned her head back and closed her eyes. Her body was completely relaxed, but her head was spinning, and she was afraid to move. Now she understood why Zack had hurried her out of the reception hall. One more drink would have probably sent her right over the edge, and she wasn't keen on throwing up with an audience. Hopefully, she would be able to keep the contents of her stomach down until Zack got her home.

"What made you drink so much tonight?" Zack asked softly.

"I'm not sure," she lied. "Someone kept bringing me drinks, and I lost count."

"Hmm," Zack replied thoughtfully.

Emma peeked through her eyelashes at him. "That's the only reason, Zack," she insisted.

"Ok, I believe you. I just wondered if being at a wedding made you feel sad. To be honest, that's how I felt when I saw Justin and Trish together."

Emma shut her eyes again. "Is this confession time?"

"Just forget I said anything," he said dismissively.

Zack hit an unexpected bump in the road, and Emma grabbed her stomach with both hands.

"Sorry. Do you need me to stop?"

"No, I've got this," she said as the sloshing in her stomach ceased.

"Zack?"

"Yes?"

"I did feel sad tonight. It just brought everything back, ya know?"

Zack reached over and squeezed her hand. "For me too," he said.

"Well, aren't we a couple of sad sacks?" Emma said.

"Yeah, let's talk about something else."

"Like what?"

"Like how I enjoyed dancing with you tonight."

Uh-oh. "It was kind of nice," Emma admitted while keeping her eyes tightly shut. *Maybe if I don't look at him it will be easier.*

"Emma?"

"Yes?"

"Since we're confessing, will you answer a question for me?"

And this is why I don't drink that often! People tend to do and say things that they wouldn't normally do or say. "I don't know, Zack. It depends on the question."

Never one to back down from a challenge, Zack forged ahead. "Were you attracted to me at Phil's wedding? Even the tiniest little bit?"

Thank God that it was too dark for Zack to see that her cheeks were flushed. "Um…"

"Whatever your answer is, we never have to speak of it again. I promise. It's just something that I've wanted to know."

Emma blinked her eyes a couple of times and realized that they were now sitting in her driveway. "Um, Zack… "

"Sorry. I shouldn't have asked."

"ZACK!" Emma shouted. "I need you to get me in the house right NOW!"

He finally clued in on the urgency of the situation and rushed around to open the passenger door. Instead of waiting for Emma to step out, he reached in and lifted her into his arms with ease. "Key," he demanded.

Luckily she had fished it out of her purse while he had been driving, and she quickly thrust it into his hand. Cradling her in one arm, he unlocked the front door in a flash and asked, "Where to?"

Emma didn't open her mouth for fear of what might escape. Instead, she pointed frantically to the nearest bathroom, which Zack reached with a few long strides. He flicked on the light and gently set her feet on the floor, and she motioned for him to get out. *Friends don't need to share everything!*

Once she had eliminated the majority of her rum and Cokes, Emma stood up, thoroughly rinsed out her mouth, and sheepishly cracked open the bathroom door. Zack must have turned on the light in her living room, and she carefully moved toward it with one hand against the wall for support.

Zack had discarded his suit jacket and loosened his tie, and he stood in the middle of her living room looking nothing short of… delicious. *Oh God, and now I threw up in front of him.*

The room started to spin, and Emma felt the blood rush out of her head. Zack flew across the room in no time and scooped her up in his arms before she hit the floor. "Let me get you up to bed," he said firmly.

Even through the haze, Emma liked the way that sounded. Of course, in this situation, it didn't hold quite the same meaning.

"Thanks," she whispered and directed him to the master bedroom.

Zack flicked on the lights as he went, but he never loosened his hold on her. Emma leaned her head against his chest and marveled at his strength for the second time that night. The man was made of pure muscle!

He gently set her on the bed and propped her up against the mountain of throw pillows that she had collected. "You need water and aspirin," he said.

"In the bathroom." Emma pointed toward the doorway that led to the master bath.

Zack returned shortly and set the glass and pills on her bedside table. "Do you think you can handle some water?"

Emma's hands covered her face, and she had kicked off her heels onto the floor. "Light. Too bright."

"On it," Zack replied, and he jumped up to switch off the light. "Better?"

"Yes, thank you."

The bed creaked as Zack perched on the edge. "Sit up for a sec and drink some water."

He held the glass for her, and Emma sipped the cool, clear liquid.

"I'm going to hate myself tomorrow," she moaned and leaned back against the pillows.

"Yeah, probably," he affirmed and brushed her bangs back from her damp forehead.

They were silent for a few minutes, and Emma realized that she must have fallen asleep, because the sound of the bed creaking awakened her.

"Where are you going?"

"You fell asleep. I was just going to let myself out."

Suddenly Emma didn't want to be left alone. Being drunk was bad enough, but being drunk and alone was much worse. "Can you stay a little longer? Please." In other circumstances, her plea might have sounded suggestive, but she was pretty sure she could get away with it in her inebriated state.

"Ok," Zack said. "Scoot over a little."

Oh boy, maybe this wasn't such a good idea after all.

"Don't panic, Em. If I'm going to stay for a while, I just want to be comfortable."

Emma moved over so that Zack could prop himself up next to her. She had exchanged the king-sized bed she had shared with Mark for a queen-size, because she wanted as few reminders of *them* as possible. The new bed gave her plenty of room to spread out, but with Zack's large body lying next to her, the bed suddenly felt very small. She was afraid to move over too much lest she fall onto the floor.

"Emma?"

"Yes?"

"I can practically hear your brain working. You can relax. I'm not going to try and seduce you."

"I didn't think…" she stammered.

"Rest assured, if you and I ever have sex, I want you to be fully aware of it!"

CHAPTER 15

The next morning, Emma finally roused around nine o'clock. Her first thoughts were that her head hurt, she had a horrible taste in her mouth, and she was still wearing Kelly's purple dress. Then images from the prior evening flashed through her mind and made her wince with each recollection. What a disaster! Zack must have covered her with blankets and left a full glass of water on her bedside table before he'd left last night. She would definitely have to call him later and thank him for taking such good care of her.

Emma extracted herself from the covers, drank the water, and slowly rose from the bed. She felt a little shaky, but at least her stomach wasn't roiling. In fact, she actually felt hungry. Since today was Sunday and Brett was working at the bookstore, she could take her time getting ready. She decided to change out of the dress and go downstairs in search of food.

She slipped into her gray sleepshirt with the phrase "I Woke Up Like This" stamped across the front and had just opened her bedroom door when she heard a noise and stopped in her tracks. The kitchen was out of her sight, but she swore the sound had come from there. Emma stayed perfectly still and cupped her ear with her hand. Yes, the humming sound was definitely coming from the kitchen, and it could only belong to one person... Zack!

Emma saw no choice in the matter. He'd already seen her at her worst, so there was nothing left to hide. She carefully made her way down the stairs and around the corner into the kitchen.

Holy wow! Zack stood at the stove with his back to her while he cracked eggs into a pan... shirtless! He was clad in a pair of Superman boxer shorts and nothing else! The vision was enough to make Emma feel dizzy all over again, and as she leaned against the wall for support, she bumped against a kitchen chair, causing a loud clatter.

Zack whipped his head around and broke out in a huge grin. "Well, well, look who's finally up."

Emma didn't know where to look. Now that he faced her full-on, the view was even more spectacular. She had seen the exercise room in his house and knew that he liked to lift weights. That explained the defined biceps, shoulders, and pecs tapering down to a narrow waist, and that sexy indention where his boxers hung low on his hips. Even the man's feet were sexy! Add in the olive-toned skin, just-woke-up wavy black hair, and that confident-as-all-hell smile, and...

"How are you feeling this morning?" Zack asked, seemingly oblivious to her perusal. "Nice shirt, by the way."

Emma glanced down at her sleepshirt and crossed her arms over her chest, realizing that without a bra, he could probably see the outlines of her nipples.

"Don't worry about it, Em. We're all friends here," he said, chuckling before he turned his attention back to the stove. "Breakfast will be ready in a few minutes if you want to grab a robe."

Emma battled with herself for a few seconds and then decided that if Zack could stand around in just his boxers, she could wear her sleepshirt. *How did I know he was still going to be here?*

Emma slumped into the nearest chair. "I feel ok, but I'm a little surprised to see you this morning. Where did you sleep?" The last thing she remembered was Zack crawling in to bed with her. *Oh God.*

"After you fell asleep, I came downstairs and crashed on the couch. I didn't want to leave in case you needed me."

Zack plated their eggs and toast and delivered them to the table. He brought her a bottle of water from the fridge and poured himself a glass of orange juice. Emma watched him move around her kitchen with ease and had to smile. This was the first time he'd officially been over, and he was the one making her a meal!

"You really didn't have to do all of this, although I appreciate it," Emma said when he joined her at the table.

"Wouldn't a friend do this for you? Kelly, let's say." Zack plunked a large helping of scrambled egg in his mouth and chewed thoughtfully.

"Yes, but Kelly wouldn't be sitting here in just her underwear."

Zack leaned back in his chair and laughed. "I didn't want to sleep in my suit. Besides, I thought I'd have time to get dressed before you came down. I had planned on serving you breakfast in bed."

Emma arched her eyebrows at him. "That would have been going above and beyond friend duty." *In fact, that was perilously close to boyfriend/girlfriend territory.*

Zack shrugged. "I wasn't sure how you'd be feeling this morning, so I thought I'd stick around to find out. Now that I know you're fine, I should take off."

When Zack stood up to gather their empty plates, Emma found herself at eye level with his Superman boxers, and she couldn't help but wonder what was underneath. Of course, she knew what was there, but she didn't really *know, know.*

"Are you a fan?"

"Huh?" she asked, guiltily.

"Of Superman? Or do you like Batman better?"

"I like Superman," she admitted, suddenly feeling overly warm.

"Me too," Zack said and smiled softly.

Emma felt trapped. If she stood up, Zack would certainly see her tightened nipples straining against her sleepshirt, but if she remained seated, she would continue to have her face in his...

"I'll just put these in the dishwasher, and then I'll be on my way."

"Ok," Emma said, and she watched his fine backside as he moved away. *Who knew having a sleepover with a friend could feel so dangerous?*

Zack went to get dressed while Emma stayed at the kitchen table sipping her water. Physically she felt much better, but she couldn't say the same for her emotional state. Having Zack in her house, taking care of her, made her wish for things that she might never have. She worried that she was getting too attached to him for her own good. They talked and laughed together like friends would; however, there was no mistaking the electric charge between them. If Zack had been a different kind of guy, he might have taken advantage of her last night, yet he hadn't. Other than a few flirty comments and some long glances—oh, and their sultry slow dance—he had been a perfect gentleman. Everything was fine and well as long as everybody kept their clothes on, but the Greek version of Superman moseying around in his boxers almost tipped her over the edge!

When Zack rejoined her in the kitchen, he was dressed except for his jacket and tie, which were draped casually over his arm. It looked like he had finger-combed his hair, and he still wore that sexy grin.

"I'll walk you to the door," Emma said, and she stood, immediately crossing her arms over her chest again.

Zack had his hand on the door knob when he turned to look her directly in the eyes. "Emma, I've been thinking…"

Uh-oh, this could be bad… very bad.

"And I wondered if you would like to have dinner with me and Gracie one night this week?"

Or it could be good... very good. "Yes, I would love that," Emma replied, sincerely touched by his change of heart.

"Great. I'll give you a call during the week, and we'll set something up."

Emma nodded, afraid that her voice would catch if she spoke. She knew how much Zack loved his little girl and wanted to protect her. It felt like a pretty big deal for him to invite Emma over.

Zack was just about out of sight when Emma called out to him, "Oh, and Zack?"

"Yes?" He turned around.

"About that question you asked me last night—the answer is yes." Emma shut and locked her front door before he could respond. Her heart pounded rapidly in her chest as she stepped away from the door. She had just admitted that she had been attracted to Zack on the night of Phil's wedding. *What will he do with that nugget of information?* she wondered.

Emma couldn't stop herself from peeking out her living room window and watching him drive away. Zack glanced up at the house, and although he couldn't see her, she saw him perfectly clearly. He was still grinning—the rascal!

CHAPTER 16

"So nothing happened?" Kelly asked incredulously.

"Nothing," Emma repeated.

"Wow, Em. You might be the only woman I know who could resist a naked man who makes your breakfast. Impressive."

"He wasn't naked. He had boxers on. Besides, I was a mess. I don't know why he stayed with me as long as he did."

"I think it's pretty obvious," Kelly said.

"What is?"

"The guy is just biding his time until he can get in your..."

Emma's eyes grew wide, and she made a frantic motion to cut Kelly off.

"Hello, ladies," Zack said as he sauntered up to the counter.

Kelly swiveled around in her chair and smiled sweetly. "Good afternoon," she said.

"Hey," Emma said, praying that he hadn't overheard their conversation. Emma couldn't recall hearing the door chime, and Zack had slipped in undetected, which is kind of difficult for a man of his stature to do.

Kelly hopped down from her chair and mumbled some excuse about having paperwork to do in the office.

"So, what brings you in?" Emma asked. This was the first time that Zack had popped into the store unannounced. *Shouldn't he be at work?*

"I had to go meet with a client in White Lake, so I thought I'd stop by and say hi on my way back to the office."

Did I imagine it, or do his gray eyes hold an extra sparkle today? "Oh. Well, hi then."

Zack chuckled. "Emma, you're not embarrassed about the other night are you?"

She shifted uncomfortably, glad that he couldn't see her wringing her hands behind the counter. "Which part? The part where I threw up or the part where I begged you to stay over?"

The corners of his mouth curled slightly. "You didn't beg me. I wanted to stay."

They were interrupted by a frazzled-looking mother of two toddlers who approached the counter. Emma held her index finger up to Zack and answered the woman's question about a popular book on child-rearing.

After the woman walked away with her kids in tow, Emma turned back toward Zack, who gave her a full-on smile. "What?"

"I like to watch you work," he admitted. "You're in your element here, and it's cool that you get to do what you love. In fact, I should let you get back to work."

"So that's it? You just stopped to say hi?"

"Yep. Oh, and I wanted to ask you what night is good to come over and have dinner with Gracie and me?"

Emma relaxed her shoulders, glad to steer the conversation away from the wedding fiasco. "I'm free on Thursday or Friday night this week."

"Let's do Friday. I already mentioned the idea to Gracie, and she seemed excited. She asked me if you liked macaroni and cheese, and I told her yes, since that's what we ate at The Union. I hope you don't mind the boxed kind, though, because that's Gracie's favorite."

Emma smiled. "No problem. Do you need me to bring anything?"

"Just yourself."

The way he looked at her when he said that... "What time?"

"Six o'clock?"

"Ok."

Zack had one foot out the door when he turned around and called, "I stocked up on the rum and Coke."

She put her hands on her hips and stuck her tongue out at him as he went away laughing.

When Wednesday rolled around, Emma expected to hear from Zack, since Gracie was most likely with Alicia. When she climbed into bed that night, he still hadn't called, and it struck her that maybe he had a date. Since they were just friends, it would be perfectly acceptable for him to go out with someone else—her too, for that matter. But why did the very thought of him dating disturb her? The idea of Zack focusing those gray eyes on some other

Susan Coventry

woman and touching someone else with those amazing hands while smiling that devilish smile...

Ok, this was bad. Very bad. Emma had been skeptical about Zack keeping up his end of the friend bargain, and here she was thinking about his eyes and his hands and his mouth. Not good at all! She would have to ask him never to wear the Superman boxers in her presence again. Wait a minute, she couldn't do that, because then he would know that she was still attracted to him. Thank goodness Gracie would be there on Friday night. Zack wouldn't be able to strut around half-naked then.

Emma soothed herself to sleep with visions of creamy macaroni and cheese and the sound of Gracie's laughter dancing in her head—until the damn boxers showed up again. "Ugh!" she shouted and buried her face in a pillow.

The next day, just before closing time, Emma decided to call Zack. Up until now, he had been the one to call her, and since she was a modern woman, there was no reason why she couldn't call him. Besides, it wasn't like she just wanted to hear his voice. She actually had an important question to ask.

"Hello?" Zack answered, sounding pleasantly surprised.

"Question," she said. "What are Gracie's favorite types of books?"

Zack lowered his voice and replied, "Just a minute."

He must have covered the phone with his hand, because his voice was muffled when he said, "Go up to bed, and I'll be there in a few minutes."

"Oops. I didn't think that Gracie would still be up. Sorry about that."

"No worries," Zack said. "So, her favorite books right now are the Little Critter series."

"Good taste. I want to bring her a book tomorrow night, but I wasn't sure what she liked."

"I can name some of the ones she already has." He rattled off a few titles, and Emma jotted them down.

"Ok, that helps. Thanks."

Emma wasn't sure what else to say, so she was just about to end the conversation when Zack said, "I missed you last night."

Huh?

"I wanted to call, but since you were coming over for dinner this week, I didn't want to seem like a pest. I don't want to be the kind of friend that calls *too much*, if you know what I mean."

Emma giggled and was oddly touched by the sentiment. "You're not a pest, Zack. I would have liked to hear from you. In fact, since we're confessing, I missed you too." *Why was it always easier to say such things over the phone?*

"Yeah?"

She heard the smile in his voice and knew she wore a matching one. "Yeah," she replied softly.

"Good to know."

Emma suddenly heard a very loud voice yell, "DAAAAAD!"

"Time's up," Zack said apologetically.

"Ok. Well, I'll see you tomorrow, then."

"We can't wait."

Neither can I, Emma thought when she hung up the phone.

CHAPTER 17

Emma arrived at Zack's house at exactly six o'clock. Clutching a bag from A New Chapter in one hand, she rang the doorbell with the other.

She heard Gracie's voice yell, "I'll get it!" followed by the sound of her feet pounding across the floor. When Gracie flung the door open, Emma melted. She hadn't expected such an enthusiastic greeting. Plus, Zack was standing in the background looking all kinds of wonderful.

"Come on in," Zack said, beaming.

"What's in the bag?" Gracie asked.

Zack shot Gracie a disapproving look, but her curiosity kept her from noticing.

"This is for you," Emma said and handed Gracie the bag.

Gracie eagerly tore into it and pulled out the Little Critter book *When I Grow Up.* Her face lit with excitement, and she exclaimed, "These are my favorite!"

"What do you say to Miss Emma?"

"Thank you, Miss Emma. I love it!"

"You're very welcome. I love Little Critter books too."

Gracie raced off to the living room with her new book, and Zack motioned to Emma to follow him into the kitchen. The table was already set for three, and a pot of noodles bubbled on the stove. Zack had also prepared a salad, and there was a fresh loaf of bread on the counter that had come from the local bakery.

"Wow, first breakfast and now this. I'm going to get spoiled." Emma said.

"Don't count on it. This is about the extent of my culinary expertise. Most nights, we eat cereal or something microwavable."

Zack's back was to her while he stirred the noodles, and Emma felt a pang of empathy for him. She didn't have any other friends who were single parents, and she suddenly realized how difficult it must be. He worked full time and took care of a house and a four-year-old, yet he never complained. He had such a positive attitude, and Emma admired that about him.

"I could cook for you sometime," she ventured.

Zack turned toward her. "I didn't mean for you to feel sorry for me, Em."

"No. It's not that at all. I just thought that since you've cooked for me, I could return the favor sometime."

Zack stared at her for a few beats and then said, "Sure. That would be great."

Just then, Gracie ran into the kitchen and asked if dinner was ready.

"Almost," Zack said. "Why don't you ask Miss Emma what she would like to drink?"

"I made lemonade," Gracie suggested.

How can I refuse? This little girl is absolutely adorable. "Lemonade sounds perfect," Emma replied.

Once they were seated and Zack had dished out the macaroni and cheese, Gracie said, "I get to say the prayer."

Zack nodded and held out his hands to Gracie and Emma around the small table. Emma swallowed hard as she slipped one hand into Zack's warm, masculine grip and reached out her other hand to Gracie. Gracie's small, soft hand rested gently in Emma's while she said the prayer.

"Dear God, please watch over me and Daddy and Mommy and Papa and Nana and Miss Emma. And please tell Robby to stop pinching me on the playground. Amen."

Emma couldn't contain her laughter, and thankfully, Zack and Gracie followed suit.

"Does Robby pinch you every day?" Emma asked.

"Yes," Gracie replied vehemently before stuffing her mouth with a heaping spoonful of macaroni.

"When I was in kindergarten, there was a boy in my class who used to pull my hair all the time. Sometimes, boys do things like that."

Zack raised his eyebrows but didn't add anything to the conversation.

"Did you ever do that, Daddy?" Gracie asked innocently.

Zack looked between the two of them and set his fork down. "Yes, I did. However, I only picked on the girls that I liked."

"Well, I don't like Robby! Can I be done now?"

Zack eyed her plate and said, "Two more bites."

Gracie complied and then ran away from the table, shouting something about playing with her dolls.

Zack stood up to clear the table, and Emma jumped up to help. "She's a lot like you," Emma commented while they loaded plates into the dishwasher.

"How so?"

"Her exuberance for one and her sense of humor for two."

"You forgot to mention her good looks."

"Well, that's a given." She had said it off-handedly, but Zack stopped what he was doing and gazed at her intently.

"What? Friends can find each other attractive."

"Yet they're not supposed to act on it?" Zack smiled, but his eyes were dead serious.

His intensity did something funny to her insides. "Not if they want to remain friends," Emma answered, refusing to back down.

"Why can't they be both friends and lovers?"

Ok, the word "lovers" just made my spine tingle. "Because that complicates things." *Why do I feel like I am about to lose this argument?*

"You mean sex?"

"Shh," Emma hissed, worried that Gracie might overhear.

Zack chuckled. "You can't even say the word, can you?"

"What word?" Emma felt the heat creeping up her neck, and she quickly averted her eyes.

Zack laughed louder this time. "Sex. You can't say the word sex."

Once again, Emma was reminded of why it was so difficult to be friends with this man. "That is ridiculous," she said, becoming more flustered by the second.

Zack reached out and clasped her wrist in his steel grip. "Say the word, and I'll let you go."

"Real mature," Emma said, but damn if a little giggle didn't escape.

"Let's hear it." Zack tightened his grip on her wrist, which gave her spine another jolt.

Emma felt like she was burning up. She would have liked to blame it on the heat from the stove, but she knew better. Zack seemed to sense that victory was near, because his smile grew even wider. Emma scanned the area to make sure that they were alone, and then she looked him directly in the eyes.

"Sex," she breathed.

Usually, she'd describe Zack's eyes as light gray, but at that moment, they took on a different hue. *A different shade of gray*, she mused with a secretive smile. He hadn't let go of her wrist, and now he yanked her closer until there was a mere sliver of space between them. Zack cupped her chin with his free hand and gently rubbed his thumb back and forth across her flushed cheek. Emma didn't move an inch—couldn't have even if she'd wanted to. Time was suspended. Her vision filled with only him. He tilted his head, eyes trained on her lips, and then...

"DAAAAAD!"

They broke apart abruptly just as Gracie rushed into the kitchen. Emma turned her back to them and resumed cleaning the kitchen.

"Can we watch a movie now?" Gracie asked.

"Sure, sweetie," Zack replied, but his voice sounded a little strained. "Go ahead and pick one, and then we'll be there in a minute."

When Gracie bounded out of the room, Emma's and Zack's eyes met again. He made an exaggerated motion of wiping the sweat off his brow to acknowledge their close call. Emma broke out in a huge grin and let his sense of humor wash away the tension.

"Like I said, it complicates things," she reiterated and flounced out of the room.

Gracie selected the movie *Tangled* for them to watch, and while Emma had heard of it, she had never seen it. Aside from her interaction with kids at the bookstore, Emma wasn't around children that often. She was an only child, so she didn't have nieces or nephews, and her friends that had kids were so busy that she rarely saw them. While watching a kid flick on a Friday night might not be everyone's idea of a good time, Emma was perfectly content. She enjoyed the innocence and enthusiasm that most kids displayed, and Gracie was no exception. The fact that she was Zack's child made her even more fun to be around.

Zack slipped the disc into the machine while Gracie and Emma took up positions on the couch. Emma didn't mind at all when Gracie nestled right beside her, but Zack's face showed a flicker of surprise as he came over to join them. Emma watched him wrestle with the question of where to sit, since there was room on either side of Gracie or her, but when Gracie patted the spot next to her, the decision was made. Secretly, Emma was glad. It would be easier for her to concentrate on the movie without Zack's nearness to distract her.

Wrong-o! Partway through the film, Zack placed his long arm along the back of the couch and started fiddling with Emma's hair. At first, she thought it was just a coincidence, but when he didn't stop, she realized what he was up to. Gracie was so enthralled with the movie that she hadn't noticed, but Emma shot Zack a knock-it-off glare over the top of Gracie's head.

He got the message, because he pulled his hand away and turned his attention back to the television. But a few minutes later, his hand was back, and this time, his fingers caressed the sensitive skin on the back of her neck! Emma was torn between wanting to throttle him and wanting to give herself over to his magic hands. But then she looked down at Gracie staring wide-eyed at the television screen while Eugene professed his love for Rapunzel. Emma certainly didn't want to draw attention to herself, so she decided to allow Zack to continue his... teasing.

Oh yes, he knew exactly what he was doing. He alternated between drawing lazy circles on her skin, massaging her neck muscles, and running his hand down the back of her hair. And it was driving her absolutely crazy with need. Every so often, she glanced over at him, and he appeared to be deeply engrossed in the movie. Occasionally, their eyes would meet, and she saw a cross between desire and amusement written on his face.

Emma shifted around in her seat, which caused him to give up his ministrations for a moment, but as soon as she got settled, he started up again. This time, he slid his entire hand just under the collar of her shirt, and she almost jumped. Her whole body responded when he brushed his hand back and forth between her shoulder blades. By the time the credits rolled, Emma was completely aroused.

Gracie let out a big yawn, which brought Emma quickly back to reality. Zack smoothly extracted his roaming hand, stood up, and briskly informed Gracie that it was time for bed.

"Say goodnight to Miss Emma," Zack said.

"Actually, I need to get to bed too," Emma said, struggling to sound casual. "I'll just let myself out."

Zack gave her a knowing look. "No need to rush. I can put Gracie to bed and come back down."

There is no way in hell... If Emma stayed, she was afraid of what might happen, and she wasn't ready for that—yet. She firmly shook her head but smiled down at Gracie. "I'll see both of you tomorrow for story time, right?"

Gracie nodded her head enthusiastically, and Zack said a resigned, "Yes."

"Ok. Well, thanks for dinner and the movie. I had fun."

Gracie wrapped her arms around Emma's waist and gave her a tight squeeze. "Me too," she said.

Emma was somewhat taken aback by the display of affection, but then again, Gracie was Zack's child. He obviously didn't have trouble showing affection either.

When Gracie pulled away, she said, "Daddy, you have to hug Miss Emma goodbye too."

Oh boy! The devilish grin was back as Zack immediately opened his arms to invite her in. It was impossible to say no with Gracie staring up at her, and Zack waited expectantly. Emma stepped into his arms and was wrapped up in a warm, tight hug. In that brief moment, she felt a swirling combination of emotions: desire and lust mixed with comfort and friendship. It was an intoxicating cocktail that buzzed through her veins. Better than rum and Coke any day!

Emma was still reeling when they walked her to the door. They stood and waved goodbye while she drove away, and when they were out of sight, Emma was left with only one emotion—loneliness.

CHAPTER 18

Emma was accepting a delivery from the UPS driver the next morning when Zack and Gracie entered the store. Gracie waved to Emma and then sprinted to the kid's section while Zack stood nearby and waited for Emma to finish up.

Mike, the UPS guy, chatted her up like usual, only this time they had a rapt audience. Kelly had insisted that Mike had a crush on Emma, but she'd been married for most of the time that he'd been making deliveries to the store. Now that he knew she was single (thanks to Kelly), he found ways to linger just a little bit longer each time he delivered a package. Mike was good looking in that all-American, clean-cut, athletic kind of way. Emma and Kelly had often commented to each other about how lean and hard his body was from lifting boxes all day long. He wore the typical brown uniform with the shorts, and they'd often admired his muscular calves and tight buns.

Today, however, Emma was acutely aware of Zack's inquisitive gaze upon her, so she listened politely to Mike but didn't offer any encouragement.

"So, I was wondering if you would like to..."

Mike's voice trailed off when Zack sauntered over to Emma, placed his arm around her waist, and gave her a peck on the cheek.

"Hey, Em," Zack said, and he gave her waist a squeeze.

Emma couldn't hide the look of surprise on her face, but she quickly collected herself. "Um, Zack, this is Mike. Mike, Zack."

Zack and Mike shook hands firmly and sized each other up. While they both cut impressive figures, Zack was a few inches taller than Mike and broader through the chest. Next to Zack's exotic good looks, Mike looked pale in comparison. *Oh God, why am I comparing them?*

"Nice to meet you, Zack. I'll see you later, Emma."

"Wait. What did you want to ask me?" Emma called as he hurried toward the door.

"Never mind. It's not important," Mike replied before he hopped into the delivery truck and drove off.

Emma glanced around to make sure that no one was nearby, and then she swatted Zack on the arm. "What was all that about?"

Zack shrugged. "I didn't like the way he looked at you, and as your friend..."

"Don't pull that friend crap on me," Emma hissed.

Zack leaned in until they were mere inches apart. "It's no different than the way you reacted about Janice, or were you just giving me a *friendly* warning about her?"

Before Emma could reply, Janice walked in with her bratty son in tow. "We'll have to finish this discussion later," Emma huffed, and she made her way to the back of the store. Emma felt Zack's presence two steps behind her, but she didn't look back. She was so furious with him that if she had turned around, she might have punched his too-handsome-for-his-own-good face!

She scored a minor victory when Zack chose the seat farthest away from Janice, but then she was irritated with herself for caring. *Zack and I aren't dating, so why should I care who he sits by? And why should he care if the UPS man flirted with me?*

Emma managed to get through story time by avoiding eye contact with Zack. Once the majority of the children and parents had left, he approached her near the craft table.

"What is it?" she asked without looking up.

"I know we need to talk, but I have Gracie tonight. Can I call you after she goes to bed?"

Emma softened at the sound of regret in his voice. The man had her tied up in knots. She had been so wound up from his antics the night before that she had had trouble sleeping. Now, he had riled her in a completely different way.

"That will be fine," she muttered.

Gracie gave Emma a hug before they left, and Zack simply lifted his hand in a brief wave. Once they were gone, Emma let out a long breath just as Kelly emerged from the office.

"What now?" Kelly asked.

"Zack went all *caveman* on me when I was talking to Mike. I don't get it. We're supposed to be friends, but the past few days…"

"It's felt like something more," Kelly finished.

"The thing is, he's the one who suggested that we should be friends in the first place. He didn't even want Gracie to know that we were seeing each other, and all of a sudden, I'm eating macaroni and cheese with them. I don't get it."

"It's crystal clear to me. You two have a mutual attraction that you've both admitted to, and now Zack wants to move the relationship to the next level, if you know what I mean." Kelly wiggled her eyebrows.

That may be true for Zack, but what about me? What do I want? Emma would have to think long and hard about her answer before Zack called.

"What are you going to do?" Kelly asked.

"Honestly, I have no idea."

When Emma's phone rang later that night, she felt a flutter of nerves in her belly. She had struggled all day long over what she was going to say to Zack, but now that the time had arrived, she had no idea what would come out of her mouth.

"First question. Are you still mad at me?"

Ugh, of course, he has to melt me right at the beginning! "I'm not so much mad as I am confused," Emma admitted.

"What are you confused about?"

Zack's voice was calm and patient, and Emma responded in kind. "I'm confused about us. I thought we were doing just fine as friends, but lately…"

"I've been crossing the line," Zack finished with a heavy sigh.

Emma remained silent, expecting him to add more. Zack was one of the most expressive men she'd ever met, so she'd be surprised if he clammed up on her now.

"I'm sorry, Em. I have the best intentions, but then I get around you, and I can't help myself. You're so beautiful and funny and smart, and I just want to…"

Emma's heart thumped overtime, and her throat had closed up. His words were so sweet, so sincere, so…

"Well, you know. But I'll try harder to rein myself in. I promise. I don't want to do anything to ruin our friendship. If that means keeping my hands off of you, then that's what I'll do."

Uh-oh. Now I'm even more confused. Here he was trying to appease her, but is that what she really wanted? For him to keep his hands off of her? Those magic hands! Maybe they could try dating, and she opened her mouth to suggest it, but he was still talking…

"So, no more sleepovers, neck massages, or discussions about sex. No holding you back from dating the UPS guy, as long as he's solid, and no more strutting around in my Superman boxers. Forget the innuendos and the rum and Cokes. From here on out, everything's rated G. How's that sound?"

Um, extremely boring! "Ok," she croaked, glad that he couldn't see the grimace on her face.

"Great. Now that we've settled that, I have another question."

"What is it?"

"Would you like to go shopping with me tomorrow? One of my very good friends mentioned that my house could use a facelift, and I'd like your help."

Emma smacked herself on the forehead and rolled her eyes. So now he was going to act the perfect gentleman *and* take her shopping. *How could things possibly get any worse?!*

Resigned, she replied, "Sure, I'll go shopping with you."

"Pick you up at ten?"

"That will work."

"I'm so glad we sorted things out, Em. I feel a lot better now. Do you?"

Not exactly. "Yes. I'll see you tomorrow, Zack."

As soon as they disconnected, Emma balled her hands into fists and pounded them against the couch cushions. One way or another, this man was going to be the death of her!

CHAPTER 19

Emma trailed behind Zack while he pushed the cart up and down the aisles of HomeGoods. When he had picked her up that morning, neither of them had made mention of their conversation the night before. They were just two buddies out shopping on a beautiful fall day, except why did he have to smell exceptionally yummy? Was it his body wash, or did he wear cologne? Had he always smelled this good, or was she just more aware of it today? These were the questions that Emma pondered as they perused row after row of furniture, knick-knacks, and wall hangings.

"So, what do you think of this one for my bedroom?" Zack asked innocently as he pointed to a painting of a beach scene in a distressed wood frame.

The painting evoked images of sun-drenched days on a white powder sand beach somewhere deep in the Caribbean. The water was a brilliant shade of blue, and Emma could see herself kicked back in a beach chair, sipping a fruity drink and reading a dirty novel. Funny thing was, she could see Zack in the image too, lounging next to her in a form-fitting pair of board shorts, bare-chest bronzed from the sun, and grinning at her from behind his aviators. And then he turned to her and said...

"Whatcha thinking, Em?"

Emma snapped out of her reverie when she realized he was talking about the painting and not her lusty musings. "I love it."

"I like it too. Can't you just imagine lying on this beach? Soaking up the hot sun, sand between your toes, and a cold drink in your hand?"

While you rub coconut-scented sunscreen on my back... Crap, I'm doing it again! "Yes, I can totally imagine it," she said while he hefted the painting into the cart.

"Sold!" he said enthusiastically. "Now, what else do I need?"

"How about a mirror? If you mount it on the opposing wall, you'll be able to see the reflection of the painting."

"Wow, you're good at this. Thanks for helping me out, Em."

"No problem. That's what friends are for." She gave him a half-smile and continued walking up the aisle.

An hour later, they hauled Zack's purchases to the Range Rover. In addition to the painting, he'd bought a large wall mirror, a kitchen clock, a set of cherry wood picture frames, and a cut crystal vase.

"Do you want to grab some lunch before I take you home?" Zack asked, pointing to the Panera restaurant in the shopping plaza.

"Sounds good."

Zack was definitely making good on his promise to rein his behavior in, but she missed their flirty banter. *Figures, you always want what you can't have,* Emma thought when they sat down to lunch.

While they ate soup and salad, they chatted about Gracie, the bookstore, and Zack's job. They kept to topics that were light and easy, and Emma found herself relaxing again. It was probably best that they stick to being friends so nobody's feelings would get hurt, Gracie's included. By the time they were back in the car, Emma felt much better.

"Hey, do you want to come over and supervise while I put up my new decorations?" Zack asked.

Emma hesitated for a moment. She could pretend to have other plans, but why? What would be the harm in pounding a few nails into the wall? "Sure, why not? Will Gracie be home soon?"

"I'm not sure. Alicia took her to a movie and lunch. She said she'd text me when they were on their way back."

Emma felt a pang of jealousy, which she logged right up there with her other ridiculous emotions as of late. Alicia was Gracie's mother, so of course they had a close bond. Someday, Emma hoped to share a bond like that with her own child, although she wondered when and if that would ever happen. She was thirty years old, and although she didn't completely buy into the theory about her biological clock ticking, maybe it was… She had assumed that she and Mark would have had children one day, and now here she sat with her hunky male friend, husbandless and childless.

"Em? Is everything ok?"

"Yep, everything's good," she replied and hoped that he would believe her.

"A little more to the right."

"That good?"

"No, go back to the left."

"How about now?"

"Hmm... a touch higher."

"I can't hold this much longer, Em."

"You want it to be right, don't you?"

"Yes, but hurry up. My arms are killing me."

"Come down about an inch."

"Ok, that's it. The picture is going right here. Grab the pencil and put a mark on the wall."

Zack and Emma stood on his bed in their bare feet. Zack's arm muscles strained as he held the beach painting in place above his headboard while Emma awkwardly reached over him to place some pencil marks on the wall. Standing this close to him had her senses on high alert. Their arms brushed a few times while Zack struggled to keep the painting in place and maintain his balance at the same time.

"Aah," he said, when he leaned the picture against the headboard. Zack shook out his arms before he bent over to retrieve the hammer and nails from his bedside table. Emma tried not to glance at his backside but failed miserably.

What is it about a man holding a tool? What makes it even hotter is when he knows how to use said tool...

Emma looked up to find Zack staring at her intently. "You seem to be drifting off a lot today. Are you sure you're ok?"

"I'm positive," she snapped, irritated that she couldn't get anything past him. "Let's just finish this."

Emma watched Zack pound the nails into the wall, his t-shirt rising up with each stroke of the hammer. He had dressed simply in a gray shirt and blue jeans, but it was impossible to ignore the way he filled out his clothes.

"Ta-da. What do you think?"

Zack stepped back to examine his handiwork and crash... fell right into Emma, and they tumbled onto the bed in a heap. He hadn't noticed that she had been standing right behind him, and she had been so distracted by her daydreams that now they lay tangled together in the middle of his bed.

They both froze—their heavy breathing the only sound. Zack looked like he was about to speak, but Emma stopped him with a finger pressed to his lips. She shook her head and then fisted her hand in his shirt. Their eyes locked and shone with acknowledgement at what was about to happen.

Zack leaned in closer, but he hesitated until Emma gave him a nod. And then his lips were on hers, warm and soft, with just the right amount of pressure. Emma sank into the sensation and opened her mouth to greet his tongue as their kiss intensified. Zack's hands cradled her head, and she arched into him even though it wasn't easy, pinned down as she was under his large, hard body.

Emma's hands had somehow found their way up the back of his shirt, and she ran them over his taut muscles. Zack's right leg wedged between hers, creating a fabulous friction just where she needed it. She became vaguely aware that his right hand had begun to untuck her shirt from her jeans. The anticipation of where that hand would travel next had her squirming beneath him.

Zack pulled his lips away and gazed down at her as if to ask for further permission. Before Emma could respond, the sound of a car door slamming jolted them to an upright position.

Zack scrambled off of the bed while Emma hurriedly tucked her shirt back in and ran her hands over her hair. "Shit. It's Gracie and Alicia," Zack said.

Emma was already poised at his bedroom door, ready for flight. "What should I do?" she asked, hating the panicky sound of her voice.

"Let's just go downstairs and act normal. You were just helping me put up a picture."

Emma took a deep breath and followed him down the stairs. They made it to the bottom just as Alicia and Gracie stepped in.

"Hi, Daddy and Miss Emma," Gracie said, seemingly unsurprised to find Emma there.

Alicia looked at Zack and Emma with an air of disdain, and perhaps a flicker of jealousy too. "Hello, Zack. Emma."

Emma wondered if her face looked as flushed as she felt. "Nice to see you," she said, hoping the lie would cover up her discomfort.

"Bye, sweetie," Alicia said, and she bent down to hug Gracie. "Zack, can I talk to you outside for a moment?"

Emma flinched at Alicia's condescending tone, but she knew that Zack would agree for Gracie's sake. "Go ahead. I'll keep Gracie company," Emma said.

The door clicked shut behind them, and Emma led Gracie into the living room, where she spotted the Little Critter book that she had given her lying on the couch. "How about if I read to you until Daddy comes back?"

"Ok," Gracie replied enthusiastically.

Emma sat down, and Gracie sidled right up next to her, just like she had the other night. As Emma opened the book and began to read, she pushed all of her worries aside. She could analyze what had happened between her and Zack later, but right now, Gracie deserved her undivided attention. Emma read slowly and varied her intonation to match the characters' expressions. Gracie listened closely and giggled at Emma's silly voices, blissfully unaware of any discordance between the adults.

Zack entered the room just as Emma finished the story. He wore a neutral expression, but Emma noticed the strain around his eyes. He opened his arms wide, and Gracie jumped into them. "Did you have fun today?"

"Yes, but I missed you," Gracie said.

"I missed you too, sweet pea." The minute he set her down, Gracie raced up the stairs.

"I'm going to play with my dolls," she called, and the next minute, her bedroom door slammed shut.

"So much for missing me," Zack said and smiled.

Emma was still trying to get her bearings. Between the kiss, the interruption, and the emotional reunion she had just witnessed, her head was spinning.

"I could use a drink. How about you?" Zack held out his hand to her.

Emma let him pull her up from the couch and lead her into the kitchen, where she plopped down on the counter stool. Zack extracted two bottles of water from the fridge and sat down beside her.

"So," he began.

"So, what happened with Alicia?"

"You want to talk about Alicia?"

"Well, yeah."

"I thought you might want to talk about the kiss."

"Shh," Emma hissed. "We can't talk about that now."

"Em, four-year-olds don't have a super power that allows them to hear through walls. We're safe."

Safe? I don't think so. Safe is sitting at home reading a book and munching on potato chips. Safe is NOT getting caught messing around by his ex-wife and child!

Just then, Gracie came bounding down the stairs, and Emma shot Zack an I-told-you-so look.

"Dad, I'm hungry."

"Didn't you eat with Mommy?"

"Yes, but I didn't finish it all."

Perfect excuse for me to leave. "Zack, why don't you drive me home and then you and Gracie can have dinner together."

"You can eat with us too," Gracie suggested sweetly.

"Thanks for inviting me, but I'm not really hungry right now," Emma replied, noting the disappointment in Gracie's eyes. "Maybe some other time."

Zack looked disappointed too, but he stood up and said, "C'mon, Gracie. Let's take Miss Emma home."

On the drive, Gracie chattered on about the movie that she had seen while Emma listened with one ear. Every so often, she caught Zack studying her, but she tried to ignore it. When he pulled up in front of her house, Emma hastily said goodbye and hurried up the sidewalk. She glanced back to see Gracie waving wildly from the back seat, and Emma waved back until they were out of sight.

When Emma entered her quiet house, relief washed over her. So why was it that five minutes later she was back to feeling lonely?

CHAPTER 20

That night, after tucking Gracie into bed, Zack debated calling Emma. In fact, he lay in bed with the phone in his hand and stared at her number on the screen until the light faded to black.

"Damn it," he muttered and set the phone down on his stack of books. He had promised not to cross the line with her, and yet, just a few hours ago, in this very spot, he had kissed her. And of course, it hadn't been an average kiss, a so-so kiss that could be easily forgotten. No, it had to be *that* kind of kiss, the kind that left him wanting another and another and... well, more.

What had stumped him was Emma's reaction. The way she had looked at him with desire burning bright in her eyes. The way she had fisted his shirt and pulled him closer. Those weren't the actions of a woman who just wanted to be his friend. He let his mind wander to what might have happened had Gracie not come home when she had. And then he felt like a total dirt bag!

Now was not the time to be selfish. After all, he was the one who'd told Emma that Gracie came first, and the last thing he wanted to do was hurt her. His little girl had been through so much already— more than a four-year-old should have to go through. First the divorce, then the move, and now… Emma.

The more time he spent with her, the more he wanted her. He liked everything about her: her laugh, the way she blushed when he got too close, her petite frame, curly hair, and crooked smile. Somehow she had become the first person he wanted to share things with, from the tiniest minutiae of his day to the big topics like divorce and parenting. He felt comfortable in her presence, yet energized at the same time. Of course, some of that was sexual energy, but still!

And now he had returned to the image of them kissing, which wasn't going to help him get to sleep anytime soon. "Damn it," he said again and crawled out of bed. "If I'm not going to sleep and I'm not going to call her, then I might as well work out."

Zack quietly slipped down the hall and into the spare bedroom where he had arranged his exercise equipment. Pumping iron almost always made him feel better, so he attacked the weights with vigor.

He started with bicep curls and remembered how light Emma had felt when he had carried her up the stairs the night of his coworker's wedding. He moved on to overhead presses and thought about hanging the beach painting over his bed while Emma had supervised. He did some squats and recalled Emma's slim legs trapped beneath his. During his last set of flies, he remembered how soft Emma's hands had felt when she had caressed his back and…

Ok, this is definitely not helping matters! Zack glanced at his watch—ten o'clock. It would be too late to call her now. She was probably already asleep, and besides, she hadn't called him either. There was nothing to do but wait. Emma probably needed some time to process what had happened, and she might not have welcomed his phone call anyway.

Zack returned to his bedroom and picked up his phone on the off chance he had missed her call. Nope, nothing. He stripped and stepped into the shower, letting the warm water soothe his aching muscles. Maybe he would call her tomorrow. If not tomorrow, then definitely the next day. If it was time she needed, he would give it to her.

By the time he got back into bed, he was thoroughly exhausted. It had been a hell of a day. He wouldn't give the kiss any more thought tonight, but he couldn't promise himself not to think about it tomorrow…

CHAPTER 21

"So, after all that, he didn't call you last night?" Kelly asked with her hands on her hips.

"No, can you believe it?" Emma replied, still miffed about it herself.

It was a slow Monday afternoon at A New Chapter, and they leaned against the counter relaying their latest man troubles. Kelly had just finished complaining about Collin, the aspiring poet who had turned out to be insensitive, and now it was Emma's turn to vent.

"I suppose I could have called him, but..."

Emma let her words trail off when she heard the door chime, and Mike entered with a large box hoisted on one shoulder. He smiled warmly at her as he set the box down on the counter and handed her the device for her electronic signature. When Emma looked up, Kelly had disappeared, presumably so that Emma and Mike could be alone.

Mike glanced around warily and then said, "I didn't realize that you had a boyfriend."

Emma's eyes widened. "Oh, you mean Zack? He's not my boyfriend. He's... we're..."

"It's ok, Emma. You don't have to explain."

"No, I'm serious, Mike. Zack is not my boyfriend," she repeated a little too emphatically.

"Oh. Well, then, maybe I should finish asking you what I started to ask the other day."

"Please do," Emma said, wondering for a moment why she was encouraging him. Mike was nice enough, but she didn't feel that extra oomph around him. Not like she did with Zack. Still, it might be nice to go out with someone who didn't come with an ex-wife and child.

"So, I wondered..."

Oh no, not again. This could not be happening.

The door chime announced his presence, although Emma had already spotted Zack over Mike's shoulder. He approached her while excitedly waving two tickets in the air.

"Hey, Em. Mike."

Mike's head whipped around, and his face fell. "Hey. I was just leaving."

"You don't have to leave on my account. I'll wait," Zack said politely, but Emma recognized the edge in his voice.

"I'll talk to you later, Emma. Have a good day," Mike added, and he walked away, his head hung in defeat.

Kelly had resurfaced and stood nearby giving Zack the evil eye.

"What?" he asked, glancing between Kelly and Emma.

"Kell, we'll be in the office for a few minutes," Emma growled, and she motioned for Zack to follow her. Once they were behind closed doors, she turned on him.

"What the hell, Zack?"

"What did I do?"

Emma raised her eyebrows at him. "You really have no idea?"

"No. Please enlighten me."

"Ok, I will. First off, you didn't call me last night to tell me what Alicia said after she caught us… well, you know. Second, you come waltzing in here like you own the place and scare Mike off again after you promised that you wouldn't interfere. What gives?"

Zack ran his hands through his hair, obviously frustrated too. "Just when I think I understand women, I realize that I don't have a clue. The reason I didn't call you last night is because I figured you were freaked out about the kiss and needed some time to decompress. I wasn't ignoring you or the significance of the *event*, I was just giving you time. Regarding the UPS guy—if my coming in here is enough to scare him off, then he's not worth your time. You deserve better."

Emma's jaw dropped. In a heartbeat, she had gone from being furious at him to wanting to wrap her arms around him. She took a couple of deep breaths instead.

"So, what do you have in your hand?"

Zack smiled and held up the tickets. "I happen to have two tickets to a country music concert at DTE Music Theater for this Friday night. Since you like country music, I figured you might want to go with me."

Emma eyed him suspiciously. "How do you know that I like country music?"

"I might have snooped around in your entertainment cabinet when we had the sleepover," Zack replied unapologetically.

Emma frowned, but she couldn't stay mad, not when she saw the amusement in those twinkling gray orbs. "And what else did you discover besides my CD collection?"

"I found a lot of dirty movies. Now I know how you spend your free time," he said with a grin.

Emma broke out into laughter, which erased the remaining tension between them. "I do not have a dirty movie collection. Well, maybe just one or two."

"Anyway, what about the concert? Will you go with me?"

"I wish I could; however, I won't be here. I'm going to Chicago for a bookseller's trade show."

Zack visibly deflated. "Oh. Did that just come up?"

"No. It's an annual event that I've gone to since I opened the shop. I made the arrangements months ago."

"Hmm."

"Is there someone else you could take to the concert?" *Say no, say no!*

"I don't know anyone else who likes country music except you."

"Sorry, Zack." He looked so forlorn that she wanted to hug him, but she resisted. "I hope that you didn't pay a lot for the tickets."

"Actually, I got them for free. Dan passed them out to a few of the guys and Brandy."

Oh no, not the bimbo. "You could go with them," she suggested weakly.

"Nah, I'll just skip it. So, tell me more about your trip to Chicago."

"There's not a whole lot to tell. It'll just be a bunch of book nerds like me walking around the convention center checking out what's new in the world of books."

"How long will you be gone?"

"I fly out on Thursday morning and fly back Sunday morning."

"Chicago's a great city. What else will you do there besides go to the book show?"

Emma was touched by his interest. "I'll be at the show for most of the day. By the time it's over, I'll probably get some dinner and then go to bed. Nothing too exciting."

"Who will you go to dinner with?"

Hmm... now it sounds like he's fishing. "I know a few people who will be at the show, but I'll probably end up eating on my own. Why?"

"Just curious. No hidden agenda, Em. Just asking as your friend."

Back to that again. Maybe the kiss didn't mean anything after all. "Well, I'll be fine on my own. I'm getting used to it." *Liar!*

"Well, if you get lonely or anything, you can always give me a call."

She searched his eyes and saw nothing but sincerity there. Emma stepped forward and put her arms around him. "Thanks, Zack," she whispered.

He was obviously caught off guard by her show of affection, but he quickly recovered and wrapped her tightly in his embrace. Emma reveled in the feeling of warmth and security while she leaned into his hard chest, her head tucked under his chin. She was no nurse, but she could have sworn his heartbeat was a little faster than normal. Of course, hers probably was too.

Zack ran his hands up and down her back as he held her close, and for once, he didn't seem inclined to speak. A tap on the office door caused them to pull apart.

Kelly poked her head in. "Sorry to interrupt, Em, but there's a local author here who would like to talk to you."

"Be right there," Emma said.

"So…" Zack began.

"So…" Emma repeated.

"Can I call you tonight?"

"Of course."

"Good." Zack gave her his full-out devilish grin, and then turned and sauntered out the door.

After he left, Emma tried to give her undivided attention to the local author, who was there to pitch her latest children's book, but her mind kept drifting, first to the kiss, then to the hug, then back to the kiss again. As the author showed her the illustrations in the book, Emma decided that being in Zack's arms ranked right up there with reading and chocolate. It had been a long time since a man had made it on her top three list, and it was then that Emma realized that she was in big, big, trouble!

CHAPTER 22

Emma leaned her head against the window of the airplane and watched the Detroit skyline disappear. It seemed fitting that now her body was in the clouds along with her head. She had been thinking about Zack and Gracie all morning long.

Zack had called her as promised on Monday evening and filled her in on his conversation with Alicia. Apparently, Alicia had tried to read him the riot act about it being too soon to introduce another woman into Gracie's life. Zack had retaliated with, "Well, what about the intern? Why does he get to be a part of Gracie's life?" He had also gone on to defend Emma and had pointed out how much Gracie liked her. Evidently, that had shut Alicia up, at least for now.

Zack had asked Emma to have dinner with him and Gracie on Wednesday, but she worked until closing that night. In lieu of dinner, she had received a sweet phone call at the store, where first Gracie and then Zack had said their goodbyes. Emma warmed at the thought that someone—make that two someones—would actually miss her that weekend.

The plane touched down smoothly at O'Hare Airport a short time later. Emma pushed all thoughts of Zack aside while she deplaned, retrieved her luggage, and caught a taxicab to the McCormick Place Convention Center. It was still early enough that she would have time to drop off her bag and get to the trade show right when it opened. It helped that she was staying at the hotel that was connected to the convention hall.

Before long, Emma was completely immersed in a sea of books. She meandered up and down row after row of booths showcasing books of every kind. Halfway through, her tote bag bulged with literature and freebies from the various tables that she had stopped at. As always, Emma gravitated to the children's books, and as she paged through them, she was reminded of Gracie—and the other kids who came to story time, of course.

By four o'clock that afternoon, Emma was exhausted. Between the early flight and all of the walking she had done, she wanted nothing more than to take a nap and order room service, which is exactly what she did. After dinner, she curled up in the chair in front of the window and enjoyed the expansive view of Lake Michigan while she cracked open the latest James Patterson novel. The book was engaging, but her attention kept drifting out to the lake, where boats sailed by, full of smiling passengers. Chicago's nightlife was already in full swing, and here she was tucked away in her hotel room, alone. She was considering venturing outside for a walk when her cell phone buzzed. Just like that, her melancholy mood slipped away.

"Hello, Zack," she answered.

"Hey, pretty lady. How's the windy city?"

Pretty lady? That's a new one. "Bustling as always. I'm looking out at Lake Michigan from my hotel room right now."

"Sounds nice, but why aren't you out on the town?"

"It's not as fun when you're alone. Besides, I'm kind of tired. It's been a long day."

"I wish I were there," Zack said.

Does he mean in Chicago or with me? "What would you do if you were here right now?"

"Well, for starters, I would take you out for a nice dinner."

"Then what?" Emma wrapped her arms around her legs and gazed out at the lake, letting Zack's voice warm her from the inside out.

"Then we would go bar-hopping or, wait, even better, shopping on the Magnificent Mile."

Emma giggled. "You are the only man I know who doesn't mind shopping."

"It's not that I love to shop, Em. It's that I like to see you smile."

Oh boy. Was that a line? If it was, his delivery was great, because she was tingling all over. "And what would happen after we went shopping?" It was easy to flirt when he was hundreds of miles away.

"Well, that would depend." His voice dropped a couple of octaves lower.

"On what?"

"On what you were in the mood for."

Ok, I've done it now. Might as well keep going. "So, it would be my choice?"

"Yep, because I would be up for *anything.*"

Emma cleared her throat noisily, and Zack chuckled gruffly. She was trying to formulate a witty response when she heard Gracie's voice in the background. Emma wasn't sure whether she felt relieved or disappointed at the interruption, although she leaned toward disappointed.

"I should go," Zack said, sounding disappointed too. "Call you tomorrow."

"Ok."

Emma still felt tingly when she slipped under the covers. She let herself imagine what it would be like if Zack really were there with her, and she finally drifted off with a soft smile on her face.

The next day, Emma wandered around the show and collected all the information she could about how to be a successful bookseller. She loved this part of her trip, but she wasn't looking forward to another lonely night in the hotel room. She had decided that tonight, she would at least go out to dinner and maybe walk along Michigan Avenue for a little while before settling in.

Emma left the convention center around four thirty and was heading back toward the hotel when she felt the vibration of her cell phone in her purse. She stepped out of the flow of foot traffic and hurriedly extracted her phone. She hadn't expected to hear from Zack until later, so she was surprised to see his name on the display.

"Hi," she answered and slipped back into the stream of people leaving the convention.

"Hey. Are you still book shopping?"

"No. I'm on my way back to the hotel."

"How did it go today?"

Wherever Zack was calling from, there was a lot of background noise, and it dawned on Emma that he might have gone to the country concert after all.

"Good. Where are you? It sounds noisy."

"Huh? I can't hear you. It's really loud here."

Emma giggled. She had just entered the lobby of the hotel, and she stopped to catch her breath. She set down her heavy tote bags and fanned her face to cool off.

"Where are you?" she repeated, louder this time to make sure that he heard her.

"I like your dress."

Wait, what? She must have misunderstood him, or maybe he had said it to someone else. "What did you just say?"

"I said I like your dress."

Emma looked around wildly but didn't see any sign of Zack. How ridiculous of her to think that he might be there! "How do you know that I'm wearing a dress?"

"Look over your right shoulder."

Emma's heart leapt to her throat as she did what he had asked. She swung around and almost dropped the phone onto the gleaming white tile floor. There in front of her, not ten steps away, stood Zack, phone to his ear, with a smug smile plastered across his gorgeous face.

"Surprise," he said unnecessarily.

Emma wished that she had something to hold on to, because she suddenly felt light-headed.

Luckily, Zack reached her in a few long strides and wrapped her in a tight hug. She gripped his forearms, looked into his eyes, and sputtered, "But how, when, why...?"

Zack tipped his head back and laughed. "Slow down, Em. I'll explain everything, but first tell me that you're happy to see me."

Like he has to ask! "Yes, of course I'm happy to see you! I'm just shocked."

"Well, why don't we drop those bags off in your room, and then I'll explain over dinner."

Emma was about to open her mouth to ask more questions but decided it was probably better not to. She had already made quite a spectacle of herself in the middle of a crowded hotel lobby. She could at least wait to quiz him when they had more privacy.

Zack effortlessly hefted the tote bags over his shoulder and led her to the bank of elevators. "Which floor?" he asked while they waited among a throng of people.

"Fifteen," she croaked. On the ride up to her floor, Emma kept sneaking glances at Zack. She still couldn't believe that he was there, and she was almost afraid to take her eyes off of him in case it was all an illusion. He caught her looking a few times and just gave her that devilish grin that she had come to know and... love?

"Which way?" Zack asked when they stepped off the elevator.

Emma pointed down the hall and stopped in front of her door. "Right here," she said and extracted the room key from her purse. Zack followed her inside, set the tote bags on the king-sized bed, and sauntered over to the window to take in the view of Lake Michigan.

"Wow. Gorgeous," he commented with his back to her.

"I agree," she said, although she was referring to him rather than the view.

He slowly turned around, and she felt dizzy all over again. "Are you ready for dinner?"

"Not until you answer my questions. Tell me why you're here, Zack."

He took a step forward, and she inhaled sharply.

"Because I hated the thought of you eating alone?" He quirked his eyebrows at her.

"Try again."

He took another step toward her. "Because I missed you."

Oh my God. I'm going to pass out. "How did you get here?"

"I drove." He took another step.

"You drove for *five* hours to take me out to dinner?" Emma's voice had raised, and her heart pounded rapidly. He was only an arm's length away now.

"That about sums it up. Yes." Zack stopped right in front of her and let his gaze roam freely over her. "That ok with you?"

Emma swallowed hard and hoped that she wasn't blushing. She looked into his eyes and nodded.

"Good." Zack reached out and brushed her cheek with the back of his hand.

The gesture was so simple yet so intoxicating that Emma had to suppress a moan. "Where are you taking me for dinner?"

Zack chuckled and took a step back. "I was thinking about Timothy O'Toole's. It's an Irish pub that serves excellent fish and chips."

Emma let out a breath. The spell had been broken, and they were back on *friendly* ground again. "Sounds great. Should I change?" She glanced down at her kelly green dress and nude-toned wedges and looked back up to meet Zack's appraising eyes. *Uh-oh. He looks hungry, but not for food!*

"No. We should probably get going. Besides, I like the dress."

"Ok. I need to freshen up, and then we'll go." Emma hurried off to the bathroom and closed the door firmly behind her. She leaned her back against it and took a few deep breaths. She then used the facilities, gargled with mouthwash, and reapplied her lipstick. When she came back out, Zack was standing by the window once again, with his hands tucked in the front pockets of his khaki pants, seemingly deep in thought. She still couldn't get over the fact that he was there, standing in her hotel room, looking drool-worthy as ever with his wavy, dark hair curling slightly at the edge of his collar and...

He turned around to catch her staring. "Ready?"

For dinner, yes. For whatever comes after, I'm not sure. "Yes." Emma grabbed her jean jacket and purse and followed him out the door.

CHAPTER 23

Emma and Zack hopped in the back of a cab and relaxed while the taxi driver wound his way in and out of the busy traffic. The quiet interior of the cab was like a haven compared to the hustle and bustle of the city. The contrast was similar to what was going on inside Emma's head. Zack's presence had both comforted and energized her at the same time.

"Is Gracie with Alicia this weekend?" Emma ventured.

"No. My parents have her. I'm not sure who was more thrilled, them or Gracie."

"It's great that you have their help."

"I don't know what I'd do without it."

"So what did you tell them about this weekend?" Her real question: *Do they know about me?*

"I told them the truth, that I was going to see a friend in Chicago." Zack reached over and squeezed her knee before turning his attention out the window.

Emma wondered if it was just her or if he felt the presence of a third passenger in the cab—Sexual Tension!

"I'm glad you're here," she said.

"Me too."

Zack gave her a hand out of the cab, but he didn't let go when they entered the pub. It was early enough that they were shown to a table for two, but before long, the place would be packed. Zack pulled out her chair and then took the seat across from her. His legs were so long that he stretched them out alongside hers under the table. Emma tried to concentrate on the menu, but the feel of his pant leg brushing up against her bare skin distracted her.

An attractive young waitress approached to take their drink orders. She was fitted in a tight black t-shirt with the restaurant name imprinted on the front. Emma noticed the way she perused Zack like he was the daily special, but Zack appeared unfazed.

"What are you drinking?" the waitress asked.

"Rum and Coke, Em?" Zack chuckled at their private joke.

"No. I'll have a Bud Light," Emma said, shooting him a glare.

He just smirked and ordered a Heineken.

"I'm not getting drunk tonight," Emma said vehemently after the waitress had gone.

"I wouldn't think so, because then I'd have to sleep over again, and you never know what might happen."

He might have been teasing, but they both knew there was a hint of truth behind it. "Speaking of sleep, where did you plan on staying tonight?"

"One of my college buddies lives in the city. I figured I would give him a call, unless…"

The waitress came over with their drinks and took their food orders, which gave Emma a few minutes to collect herself. She took a long slug of beer while Zack studied her across the table.

"No pressure, Em. Let's just have a good time tonight, ok?"

"Ok." They clinked beer bottles, and Emma relaxed again. After that, they talked about various topics and enjoyed the ambiance of the busy pub. They had both ordered fish and chips, and Emma tucked into hers with gusto. Who knew flirting would work up such an appetite?!

"One more beer before we go?" Zack asked.

"Sure, but that's it for the night," Emma warned.

When the waitress set Zack's beer down, she bent over so far that her boobs threatened to spill out of her shirt. She had been fawning over Zack all night, and Emma wanted to shout, "HELLO, he's with me!"

"Some set of boobs, huh?" Emma asked, straight-faced.

Zack coughed and sputtered as if his beer had gone down the wrong pipe. He wiped his mouth with a napkin and shook his head at her.

"What? Like you didn't notice."

"How could I not notice?" He chuckled and shook his head some more.

"I knew it. Why do men like boobs so much anyway? They're just globs of fat."

"I don't know, Em. Maybe because we don't have them?"

"Well, women like that make it tough for women like me."

"How so?" He looked genuinely curious.

"Hello, Miss Average-sized over here." She pointed down at her chest. *Oops, that may have been a mistake,* she thought, because now Zack stared right at them.

"News flash, Em. All boobs are good."

"Oh, so size doesn't matter?"

Zack let out a hearty laugh that caught the attention of the people at the next table. "Do I really need to answer that?"

Emma laughed too. "I walked right into that one, didn't I?"

"Maybe I should be asking you the size question." Zack wiggled his eyebrows at her.

"It's not the size of the tool, but how you use it that counts... or something like that," she said and slugged down the last of her beer.

"Hmm, we'll see," Zack said, and he rubbed his hand over his day-old stubble.

What was that supposed to mean? Emma felt herself flush and averted her eyes. Luckily—or not, depending on how she looked at it—the booby waitress reappeared with their bill. Zack instantly reached for his wallet and handed her his credit card.

"Ooh. Zack Kostas. Are you Greek?" Booby asked.

Emma wanted to scream, *"Yoo-hoo! I'm still here!"*

"Yes, I am," Zack answered smoothly. "Yet here I am in an Irish pub."

Booby giggled. "There are a lot of good Greek restaurants in the city too. How long are you here for?"

Ok, that does it! Emma cleared her throat and was just about to speak when Zack reached across the table and grabbed her hand.

"I don't think we'll be leaving the room much for the next couple of days."

Holy wow! Emma smiled sweetly at the waitress until she turned and scurried away.

Emma and Zack were still laughing when they left the pub and had joined the stream of people on the busy sidewalk.

"Where are we going?" Emma asked when he took her hand and tucked her close to his side. Emma wrote off the gesture as practical—it would prevent them from getting separated in the crowd.

"Shopping," Zack replied, as if she should have known the answer.

He'll get no argument from me! Emma took in the array of sights and sounds while they made their way up Michigan Avenue. She couldn't be sure what made her feel more alive, the city or the sensation of Zack's fingers entwined with hers. They were jostled by passersby several times, and Emma reveled in the jolt she felt every time their bodies came into contact. Conversation was kept to a minimum because it was difficult to hear over the noise, but Emma didn't mind. It was rare to feel comfortable with someone in silence, but Zack seemed fine with it too.

When the American Girl doll store came into sight, Zack pointed, and Emma nodded. Once they stepped inside, Zack let go of her hand.

"Gracie loves this stuff. Will you help me find something?" Zack asked.

"Sure. I used to love to play with dolls when I was a little girl," Emma said, and she picked up one of the dolls on display. "Since I didn't have siblings, I would talk to my dolls as if they were real."

"Gracie does that too. I would have liked for her to have a sister or brother, but now, who knows…"

Zack's head was bent over a box of doll accessories, but Emma heard the regret in his voice.

"Do you have siblings?"

"I have a younger brother, Damian, who lives in California. He's a bit of a free spirit and the complete opposite of me. We were close as kids, but I don't see much of him anymore."

"Because he lives so far away?"

"That and the fact that we have such different lifestyles. He's a confirmed bachelor who has no intention of ever being 'tied down' with a wife and kids. Some might say that he has a fear of commitment."

Emma gave Zack a curious sideways glance.

"What?"

Why does he always have to catch me looking? "Nothing," Emma said dismissively.

"That look was not nothing. Spill it." Zack set down the doll clothes he had been looking at and gave her his full attention.

Emma sighed. "I was just thinking that maybe you and your brother aren't so different anymore. Didn't you tell me recently that you couldn't imagine having another relationship?"

"I guess I did say that, didn't I?"

"Yes, or something along those lines." Emma did her best to act like she didn't care one way or another what Zack's thoughts on relationships were. In fact, they shouldn't even be having this conversation.

"What about this outfit for Gracie's dolls?" Emma asked, trying desperately to change the subject.

For once, Zack went along with her. "I think that she would love that," he said.

A few minutes later, they were back on the sidewalk, with Zack clutching an American Girl doll bag instead of Emma's hand. The lightness that she had experienced at the pub had been replaced by a different feeling that Emma couldn't quite identify. Whatever *it* was, Emma was determined to ignore *it*. The night was still young, and she didn't want the fun to be over yet.

"Let's go to Crate and Barrel," Emma suggested enthusiastically. "You could still use a few more things for your house."

"Like what?" Zack asked, but he followed her as she led them down the street.

"I'll know it when I see it," Emma answered.

Zack rolled his eyes, but his mood seemed to have lifted, and that spurred Emma on.

He trailed her throughout the store while she browsed a variety of home goods and kitchen gadgets.

"Here it is!" Emma stopped and pointed.

"A heart-shaped waffle maker? And why do I need this in life?"

"Does Gracie like waffles?"

"Yes."

"Well, think about how excited she'll be when she sees heart-shaped waffles on her plate!"

"Emma, is this really about Gracie?"

Emma pretended to be offended. "Of course it's about Gracie. Don't be ridiculous."

Zack stared at her for a few beats. "You know what? You're right. I think I need to have the waffle maker."

Emma gave him a toothy smile and picked up the box. "Stick with me," she called over her shoulder.

"Oh, I plan on it," Zack said.

When they left the store, Zack suggested they go somewhere for dessert, and Emma readily agreed. They ended up at the Ghirardelli store, where they bought one hot fudge sundae to share.

The minute she tasted the delicious combination of cold vanilla ice cream and rich hot fudge, Emma let out a long, happy sigh.

Zack smirked at her across the table before sampling it himself. Emma watched the spoon disappear between his full, moist lips and envied it. With her focus on his mouth, it was easy to recall their steamy kiss on his bed, and Emma had the sudden urge to repeat it. With each bite they took, the room seemed to grow warmer and warmer until Emma hastily discarded her jean jacket.

After the last bite, when Zack lazily licked his lips, Emma thought she would throw herself across the table at him. He might have felt the same way because he suddenly asked, "Are you ready to get out of here?"

"So ready," Emma replied, and they rushed out the door to hail a cab.

CHAPTER 24

On the cab ride back to her hotel, Emma's thoughts ran wild, and at the center of them all was Zack. They sat several inches apart, but Zack had clasped her hand and held it tightly. Emma glanced down at her small hand engulfed by his and felt a rush of desire surge through her veins. *If I'm this turned on by such a simple touch, how would it feel to be naked beneath him?*

Her logical brain kicked in every so often, trying to warn her that this was a bad idea. Zack had been very clear about not wanting a relationship, and Emma had agreed that the timing was bad. But didn't they already have a relationship of sorts? Sure they had labelled it a friendship, but it had been shrouded with chemistry from the start. Emma wasn't concerned about getting hurt, but she didn't want anything to ruin whatever it was that she and Zack had.

Why does it have to take so damn long to get back to the hotel? Emma was afraid that if they had to wait much longer, she would talk herself out of it. Zack's silence wasn't helping matters. Every so often, he would look over at her with a serious expression, but then he would run his thumb across the back of her hand and send a delicious shiver up her spine. It was maddening!

When the cab driver finally pulled up in front of her hotel, Emma breathed a sigh of relief. She stepped out into the cool night air and waited for Zack to pay the fare. He then joined her on the sidewalk, but he clamped a hand on her arm to stop her from entering the hotel.

"Are you sure about this, Emma? Because if you're not, I'll walk away right now, and there will be no hard feelings. I'm sure that my buddy would take me in tonight."

Emma looked into those intense gray eyes and melted. "You're a good man, Zack."

"I mean it, Em. This could change things." He motioned back and forth between them.

"I know that."

He loosened his shoulders when he saw her lips turn up in a smile. "It might even make us *better* friends."

"*Closer* friends," she whispered. Emma was vaguely aware of the people having to step around them as she made up her mind. "Come upstairs with me."

Emma held her breath while she waited for his response.

"After you," Zack said and followed her through the door.

On the elevator ride up to the fifteenth floor, Emma and Zack were separated by a family of four each hauling a piece of luggage. They grinned at each other across the elevator car while the kids bickered and the parents attempted to control them. The family got out on the same floor as they did but turned the opposite way down the hall. Emma's heartrate sped up as she fished her room key out of her purse while Zack stood one step behind her.

The hairs on the back of her neck stood up as he leaned over her and took the key from her trembling hand. "Allow me," he said and swiftly opened the door.

The room was dark except for the sliver of light that poked through the partially opened curtains. Zack set his shopping bags down on the floor, and Emma placed her purse and jacket on the desk by the door. They turned to face each other at the same time, and in a flash, Zack pulled her roughly into his arms.

Emma instantly twined her arms around his neck, and she tilted her head up just as his lips crashed down on hers. Together, they were like a pot of water that had just reached the boiling point. Zack's hands were at the small of her back, and he lifted her off the ground so that she could wrap her legs around his waist. He backed her up to the bed as he continued to plunder her mouth, and she clung to him, fully immersed in his kiss.

They tumbled onto the bed together, and Zack released her to sit back on his haunches. Their breathing was heavy while he untucked his shirt and pulled it over his head. Since it was dark, Emma could only see the outline of his bare muscular chest, but she knew that it was spectacular. She reached up and ran her hands over his pecs, and he stared down at her through hooded eyes. He stilled as she let her hands roam down to the waistband of his pants and ran her index finger just underneath it.

Emma's dress had ridden up when they had fallen to the bed and just barely covered her panties. While she continued to caress his chest and abs, Zack placed his hands on her exposed thighs and slowly inched them upward. Emma stopped him just before he reached her underwear.

"You first," she demanded, tugging on his belt buckle.

Zack chuckled gruffly and immediately moved his hands to his belt. Emma scooted herself up a little higher against the headboard to afford a better view. She was tempted to reach over and flick on the lamp, but she didn't want to miss a single minute of the show. His belt had already been discarded, and now Zack put his hands on his zipper. Emma sucked in a breath as he pulled it down to reveal the bright red and blue Superman boxers that she had seen before.

She shifted her gaze upward, and it was met with Zack's self-satisfied grin. "You wore those on purpose," she accused, but this time, her voice was laced with desire.

"Just in case," he said, his deep voice like a caress. Zack removed his pants and tossed them off to the side. "Now, where was I?"

He crawled back over to her and put his warm hands back on her thighs, pushing her dress up to reveal her panties.

Maybe he won't be able to see, Emma thought, but Zack stilled, and she knew that she was busted.

"Days of the week underpants! Wow, Em, I didn't know they made those in women's sizes!"

Luckily, her face was shadowed so that he couldn't see her blush. "I didn't expect anyone else to see them except for me," she said defensively, but he was already travelling up her body and taking her dress with him.

"It's a good thing you're wearing the correct day; otherwise, I'd be concerned."

Emma could no longer concentrate on Zack's words because he had flung off her dress and had his hands poised on her bra hook. His head was bent over her, and she looked up to meet his questioning gaze. It was almost as if he was giving her one more chance to back out, but Emma wasn't interested.

"Go ahead," she urged, and seconds later, her bra had been slipped off and discarded with the rest of their clothes.

Zack's big hands instantly covered her breasts, and his gentle yet tantalizing movements caused her to gasp.

"God, you're so beautiful, Em. Everything about you is beautiful."

They lay side by side, and Emma ran a hand down the middle of his chest while he continued to fondle her breasts.

"You're beautiful too," she breathed.

Zack inhaled roughly when her hand dipped further down to cup him right over the Superman symbol. His own movements halted when she began running her index finger up and down his hard length. Their faces were just an inch apart, but their eyes studied each other's bodies and the way they responded to each touch, each caress.

"I want you so much," Zack said, and he flipped Emma onto her back. He bent his head to her breasts and took first one and then the other into his mouth, sucking and tugging until her nipples were taut peaks. Emma arched her hips, trying desperately to gain contact with his, but Zack held himself just out of reach.

"Zack. Please. Now." Her voice came out in ragged gasps.

Zack ignored her pleas as he kissed his way down her body and over her panties while Emma writhed beneath him.

Where is his will power coming from? "Zack, I mean it. I need you inside of me... now!"

Her words finally got through, because Zack heaved himself off of the bed and stumbled around in search of his pants.

Emma knew what he was looking for and was glad that he was prepared. While he sheathed himself, she wriggled out of her *Friday* undies and tossed them off the side of the bed. Zack stood transfixed by the vision of her naked body until he jolted back into action, but not before Emma caught a glimpse of his... oh my God, assets!

"Problem?" Zack asked gruffly as he straddled her.

"What if it doesn't fit?" she asked with a mix of awe and fear.

The devilish grin was back and practically lit up the room! "I'll go slow," he promised before leaning down to kiss her lush swollen lips.

And they were back in business. Emma sank into the bed and reveled in the sensations while Zack carefully and exquisitely filled her until they couldn't possibly get any closer.

"Told ya," he teased, and then he began to move.

Emma wrapped her arms tightly around him and unabashedly gave in to the pleasure. Hands and lips and tongues, strong arms and hard chest, friction and heat, whispers and sighs, she embraced it all right up until the final moment when they reached the sweet spot and then collapsed in a satisfied heap.

CHAPTER 25

Shortly after, Emma watched Zack's muscled back disappear into the bathroom, and she let out a relaxed sigh. She closed her eyes for a moment and may have drifted off, but the sensation of the bed dipping under Zack's weight brought her back to life. He sidled up next to her so that their sides touched, and he picked up her right hand in his.

"Hi," he said softly.

"Hi," she replied, giggling. Emma watched Zack play with her hand in the air, twisting it this way and that and studying it from various angles.

"So, confession time. Did you come to Chicago with the intention of seducing me, or did you really just come to take me out to dinner?"

Zack turned his head toward her on the pillow. "Probably a little bit of both," he admitted. "However, I would have settled for the dinner if that's all you wanted."

Even though they had just had mind-blowing sex, Emma believed him. Zack had given her multiple opportunities to turn him away, but she hadn't, and lying here naked beside him, she had no regrets. Not a one.

"Yet you wore the Superman boxers just in case."

He chuckled. "I figured it wouldn't hurt my chances," he said.

"You figured right."

He let go of her hand and turned sideways. He reached over and brushed her hair back from where it had stuck to her cheek. "So, how are you feeling?"

"About what we did?"

"No. I meant, are you sore from my..."

Emma cut him off by pressing her lips against his. She scooted over to get closer to him and felt his erection brush against her bare skin. "I'm not sore," she replied, and then clasped him with both hands. "But now I know what you were referring to in the pub when we talked about size!"

Zack let out a happy groan. "God, Em, if you keep doing that..."

"Yes?" She enjoyed watching him squirm beneath her hands.

Zack didn't finish his sentence. Instead, he moved his right hand from where it had been resting on her hip to between her legs where she was damp and ready for him again. Emma moaned as he explored her with his fingers while keeping his eyes locked on hers. She relished the intimacy of their motions in the dark quiet room, and they came together for the second time in a succession of rapid explosions.

Emma flopped on her back to catch her breath while Zack cleaned himself off with tissues from the bedside table. When he was finished, he gathered her into his arms with his front to her back and cradled her with his big, warm body. Emma had always been petite, but she felt even more so in Zack's presence. She felt a rush of feminine power when he nuzzled into her neck.

"I don't know if I can keep this up all night, Em."

"You're doing a pretty good job so far!" she teased, wiggling her butt against him.

"What time do you have to be at the show tomorrow?"

The show! Emma had almost forgotten about it. That was the reason for her trip to Chicago after all. "I have a wake-up call scheduled for six o'clock, but the show doesn't start until eight."

"You need two hours to get ready?"

"No, but that gives me extra time to respond to emails and take care of some business things."

"Hmm…"

"Hmm, what?"

"Now that I'm here, maybe we can use the extra time in a different way." He reached his hands up to cup her breasts and gave them a playful squeeze.

Emma twisted back around to face him. "Who says we have to wait until tomorrow?"

Six o'clock came way too soon, and Emma flung one arm out from under the covers to answer the wake-up call before it woke Zack. When she sat the phone back in its cradle, she snuck a peek at his sleeping form. He was sprawled out on top of the bedspread with nothing on but his Superman boxers.

Emma smiled at her knowledge of what was underneath and of how many times they had been together the night before. Neither of them had wanted to go to sleep, but they had finally collapsed sometime around two a.m. Before that, they had discussed the plan for Saturday, which included a myriad of tourist activities once Emma returned from the show. Zack had said something about eating breakfast together before she left, but she hated to wake him. The morning light afforded a much better view of his magnificent body, and she took a few more minutes to admire it before she hauled herself out of bed.

Emma padded across the room in her "I woke up like this" sleepshirt and slipped into the bathroom undetected. She felt groggy from lack of sleep, and a little sore if she were being honest, but she wouldn't worry Zack with that. If she told him, he might suggest that they abstain, and that was the last thing she wanted!

Emma slumped against the shower wall and let the spray of warm water beat down on her. She rolled her neck and shoulders around to work out the kinks, and she might have let out a moan, which reminded her of all of the sexy sounds that she and Zack had made the night before.

Zack, Zack, Zack. One night with him and now he is all I can think about! Emma decided that it was probably a good thing that she was going to the show for a few hours. She needed to get her head on straight before…

"Hey, how come you didn't wake me up?" Zack asked as he slipped into the shower behind her.

Emma turned around to face him and bumped right into his rock-hard chest. *Move your eyes up, move your eyes up,* she chanted in her head, but her eyes moved down of their own accord. It turned out his chest wasn't the only thing that was hard that morning. Once she raised her eyes, she came face to face with the devilish scoundrel himself, looking like the cat who had swallowed the canary.

"Haven't you had enough yet?" he teased, and he splashed her with a handful of water.

Emma sputtered and wiped the water droplets off of her face before she returned the gesture.

Zack grabbed her around the waist and pulled her against him. "Good morning," he said with a gravelly voice.

"Good morning," she replied and then was silenced by a no-holds-barred morning kiss. *I could get used to waking up like this.*

She put a hand against the shower wall to steady herself while Zack reached around her for the bar of soap.

"How'd you sleep?" he asked while he lathered up.

Emma watched with fascination as the soap bubbles travelled down his chest and over his abs and further down until they pooled at his feet.

"I slept fine, but it wasn't nearly long enough," she managed.

Zack vigorously rubbed the soap between his hands again and then ran them down each muscular leg all the way to his sexy toes.

Men's feet aren't supposed to look that good, Emma thought, distracted once again.

"Can you pass the shampoo?"

Emma passed him the mini hotel-sized bottle and watched him pour some shampoo into the center of his large masculine hand. She enjoyed the intimacy of showering with him, and found herself entranced by his every move. *Get a grip, Em. It's nothing you haven't seen before!*

"Did you already wash your hair?"

"Not yet. I was just about to when you waltzed in."

Zack smirked and motioned for her to spin around. "Lean your head back."

Emma did as she was told because, well, why shouldn't she? She was amply rewarded the second Zack's fingers came into contact with her scalp. He rubbed the shampoo in with firm circular motions that caused her to emit an "aah" and then an "ooh."

"Seems like I've heard those sounds before," he teased.

"And you'll probably never let me forget it," she replied without malice. She was enjoying the scalp massage way too much to be irritated or embarrassed.

After Zack rinsed her hair, he quickly went to work on his own. When he had finished, he reached around Emma and shut off the water. They stared at each other for a few beats until Zack said gruffly, "You should probably get ready to go."

"You're right," she said and accepted the towel he handed her. Part of her wished that he would scoop her up in his arms and take her back to bed, but Emma knew that she'd never make it to the show if he did that. She would have skipped the show altogether if she hadn't signed up to hear a talk from a successful independent bookstore owner.

They dried off in silence, and when they hung their towels back on the rack, it struck Emma that she didn't feel the least bit uncomfortable being naked with Zack. Apparently, he felt the same, because he trotted out of the bathroom wearing nothing but a smile. Emma finished getting ready and emerged from the bathroom to find Zack seated at the round table in front of the window, sipping coffee and reading the hotel's complimentary newspaper. Once again, she was struck by the casual intimacy of the scene.

Zack stood up and met her at the door, where she had slipped into her shoes and had slung her purse over her shoulder.

"I'll walk you out since I need to grab my overnight bag from the car," he said.

Emma glanced over at the bed and saw his Superman boxers lying there. Her face flushed when she turned back to look at him.

"What? I didn't want to put on dirty underwear after I just showered!"

Emma didn't even want to think about him going commando in his khakis, or she would never leave. "Let's go," she said, shaking her head as they walked out the door.

Surprisingly enough, when the elevator reached her floor, it was empty. Zack motioned her inside and stepped in behind her. The minute the door closed, he backed her into the corner.

"What, what... are you doing?" she sputtered.

"I've always wanted to make out in an elevator. They make it look so sexy in the movies."

And with that, Zack dipped his head into the crook of her neck and nibbled on it, causing Emma to moan. From there, he moved around to her front and bent his head to her breasts, where he sucked on her nipples right through her top.

Emma squeezed her legs together and watched the floor numbers light up as they descended, praying that the elevator wouldn't stop until they reached the lobby.

Zack pressed his hips against hers while he kissed his way up from her breasts to her lips. He had just sucked her bottom lip between his when the elevator pinged. When the door slid open, they were simply two innocent passengers standing on opposite sides of the car—albeit two very aroused passengers.

Emma gave Zack a shaky wave goodbye before she got swallowed up in the foot traffic that was headed toward the convention center. She glanced back once and swore that she saw him laughing as he faded from sight.

CHAPTER 26

When Emma returned to her room a few hours later, she was surprised to find it empty. The only evidence that Zack had been there was his overnight bag resting at the foot of the bed. Idly, she wondered where he might have gone while she set her purse down and went into the bathroom. There, in a note propped up against the mirror, was her answer.

Went to brunch with my buddy. Meet me at Navy Pier at noon. Z.

Emma felt giddy while she changed from her skirt and blouse into jeans and a hooded sweatshirt. She and Zack had the whole day and night ahead of them with no other commitments. Reality would kick in tomorrow morning when they had to return to Clarkston, but for now, they were as free as the seagulls swirling out over Lake Michigan.

A short while later, Emma emerged from the taxicab at the entrance to the pier and anxiously looked around for Zack. She spotted him leaning against a cement pole, looking casually sexy in his faded jeans and Chicago Bears sweatshirt. He had on dark-tinted sunglasses, which, combined with his olive-toned skin, stubbled jaw, and wavy black hair, made him look deliciously roguish. *The man is a walking, talking advertisement for the Greek isles,* Emma thought as she approached him.

Zack greeted her with a dazzling smile and a brief hug. "For a minute there, I thought that you might have forgotten about me," he said.

Ha! That will never happen. "I'm only five minutes late," she replied indignantly.

"I'm teasing, Em. Come on. Let's walk."

It was a cool, fall day with the usual wind whipping off of the lake, but the skies were clear, and the sun was warm as they strolled along the pier. Their hands naturally intertwined, and Emma felt the comfort and the sizzle between them. Zack's touch, along with the sights, smells, and sounds of the famous Chicago boardwalk, made for a heady combination. They meandered in and out of shops and then sat for a while on a bench overlooking the lake. Sailboats tossed about on the waves, and gulls squawked noisily overhead.

Gazing out over the water, Zack reminisced about the times he had visited Chicago as a child, which led into some amusing anecdotes about his family. His parents sounded a lot like the characters from *My Big Fat Greek Wedding:* loud, opinionated, and loving. Emma envied the picture of family life that Zack portrayed and encouraged him to keep talking.

Eventually Zack said, "Enough about me. What was your childhood like?"

Emma squirmed uncomfortably on the wooden bench and feigned interest in a passing tour boat. "There's not much to tell. I don't have the kind of stories that you do."

Zack crossed a leg over his knee and turned sideways to face her. "What do you mean?"

"My parents weren't the touchy-feely type. It's not that they didn't love me, but I grew up knowing that I was an 'accident.' They never meant to have children, and they didn't quite know what to do with me. As soon as I graduated from college and married Mark, they sold our house, bought a motor home, and now spend the majority of their time travelling across the country. I only see them a few times a year."

Zack was silent for a few minutes while he digested her explanation. "That must be tough, not to see them that often."

"Not really. I'm used to it." *Liar!* "Maybe if I'd have had children, they would have stuck around, but since that's not going to happen anytime soon..."

Emma glanced up at Zack and saw a mixture of emotions on his face: concern, sadness, and maybe even pity, which was the last thing she wanted from him.

"Do you still want to have kids... someday?" he asked.

"Absolutely," she replied without hesitation. "Being an only child and growing up in a quiet household has made me want the exact opposite. I want the noise, the mess, and the chaos that comes with having children. I long to sit around a dinner table that is full of people and lively discussion. Hell, I might even want a dog or a cat underfoot. Sounds cliché, right?"

Zack studied her intently and reached out to tuck her hair behind her ear. "No. I think that it sounds perfect," he said solemnly.

Emma got lost in the depth of his light gray eyes and basked in the connection that she felt with him in that moment. It was becoming easier and easier to open up with Zack, and she marveled at the fact that he was one of the very few people who made her feel that way. With Zack, the guard around her heart was slipping, and if she wasn't careful, she would end up laying herself completely bare to him.

"Let's stop with the serious stuff. Time's getting away from us, and we still have a lot to see!" Emma stood up and grabbed his hand, giving it a little tug.

"Ok, ok. Where to next?"

"Next" included a ride to the top of Willis Tower, the tallest building in Chicago, followed by a quick lunch consisting of Chicago-style hotdogs and beer, and then on to The Bean. Emma and Zack lingered there for a long time, snapping goofy pictures of each other and laughing hysterically. A friendly female tourist who had been watching them with interest offered to take some shots of them together. Fully aware that the woman had her eye on Zack, Emma hammed it up big time by plastering him with hugs and kisses. Afterwards, they sat in Millennium Park, scanning the photos and laughing all over again.

After a while, Emma noticed that the air had become cooler and ominous clouds had gathered overhead. Emma wasn't ready for the day to end, but her feet and legs were tired from walking, and she didn't relish the idea of getting caught in a downpour.

"Back to the hotel?" Zack asked.

"You read my mind," she replied. Once they were tucked securely into a cab, she let her mind wander to what they might do when they got back to the hotel room. When she shot him a sideways glance, he smirked at her and squeezed her hand, which may have been an indication that he knew exactly what she was thinking and was all for it. She could only hope!

"I need to call Gracie when we get to the room," Zack said as soon as they stepped off the elevator.

"Of course," Emma said. "Do you want me to stay out until you're done?"

"I'm not sharing state secrets, Em. I'm just calling my daughter!"

Emma giggled nervously, unsure of the protocol in this situation. She highly doubted that Zack had told Gracie that he was with Emma in Chicago, and she didn't want to make him uncomfortable by hovering nearby. She stepped into the bathroom while he was dialing just to give him a few minutes alone. While she was in there, she attempted to arrange her wind-blown hair into some semblance of order but was mostly unsuccessful. A few minutes later, she rejoined Zack where he stood by the window. Emma heard Gracie's cheerful voice tell him all about the great time that she was having with Nana and Papa, and Emma smiled at the little girl's vivaciousness. It came as a surprise when, just a few minutes later, Gracie's tone sounded almost tearful as she asked her daddy when he was coming home.

It was then that Emma realized the significance of Zack's role in his young daughter's life. Gracie was still very impressionable and needed the love and reassurance that only a parent could provide. Emma understood that Zack's first priority had to be Gracie and that any other relationship had to come second, at least for now. Just because they'd had sex didn't mean that they had entered into a committed relationship. She didn't want that anyway, and neither did Zack. It was way too soon, yet why did everything feel different? What did this mean for them going forward? Emma shook her head to fend off the worries while Zack said goodbye to Gracie.

"I'll see you tomorrow afternoon, sweetie. I love you up to the sky."

When Zack turned around to face her, Emma's expression must have been telling. He gently took her hand and led her to sit with him on the edge of the bed.

"What is it, Em? What's wrong?"

She employed her go-to tactic of denial. "Nothing's wrong. Why would you think anything is wrong?"

"Maybe because your face is puckered up like you just sucked on a lemon."

His description coaxed a slight smile out of her, but she kept mum.

"From what we've discussed about friendship, you should be able to tell me anything: the good, the bad, and the ugly."

"Isn't that the name of a movie?" she asked, trying out the next stall tactic—deflection.

Zack chuckled. "Come on, Em. Be serious. What's on your mind?"

She moved to a cross-legged position and breathed a heavy sigh. "Has anyone ever told you that you can be very persistent?"

"Is that a code word for pain in the ass?"

A loud laugh escaped that time, and she finally gave in. "Ok, here goes. Listening to you on the phone with Gracie and knowing how much she needs you—it just really touched me."

"And?"

"And it also made me wonder where that leaves us. I mean, Chicago has been wonderful, but what happens when we get home? Are we still supposed to pretend to be *friends* in front of Gracie? Are we still relegated to seeing each other when she's not around? I just don't understand how this is going to work."

Zack leaned back on his forearms and blew out a breath. "First of all, we *are* friends, Emma. There's no *pretending* to be friends. Just because we had sex doesn't mean we're no longer friends."

She was about to protest, but he held up his index finger for her to wait.

"As for your other questions, I don't have all the answers. I didn't plan on getting divorced. I didn't plan on meeting you again, and I certainly didn't expect to have these... feelings so soon. So, if you're feeling a bit overwhelmed, then that makes two of us. I was kind of hoping that we could figure it out as we go along."

"Wait a minute. Can you rewind a little?"

He looked at her with raised eyebrows. "To which part?"

"To the part where you said that you didn't expect to have *these feelings*. What kind of feelings are you referring to?" *You had to go there, didn't you, Emma?*

Zack leaned forward, and his lips curled up in a slow, sultry smile. "I'm referring to the feeling of not wanting to be apart from you. The feelings that make me do crazy things like drive for five hours just to see you. The feelings that cause me to think about you all day long and dream about you at night. The feeling of wanting you so bad that I ache. The feeling..."

Emma put a finger to his lips to stop him. "I got the picture," she whispered, and then she leaned in to replace her finger with her lips.

Emma and Zack spent the remainder of the evening wrapped in each other's arms. Their lovemaking alternated between hot and heavy, and soft and slow. There was no more talk about what happens next, because there was simply not enough time. They were too busy kissing, sucking, nibbling, and exploring each other to talk. Instead, they found a rhythm all their own and practiced it repeatedly until it became a perfect song.

The following morning, they had their first mini-argument.

"Why won't you let me drive you to the airport?" Zack huffed while he packed up his belongings.

"I already told you. I'm taking the airport shuttle."

"But you set that up before I got here. Why wouldn't you want to ride with me instead?"

"Because it will be a hassle for you to get in and out of the airport when you could just get started on your drive home." Emma had stopped packing, and they glared at each other across the room.

"I told you that I don't mind. Besides, it will give us some more time to spend together before..."

Before reality comes crashing down. "Ok, look, Mr. Persistent. I don't like airport goodbyes. Ok? That's the real reason."

Zack moved across the room in a blur, and then she was pressed tightly against him. Emma blinked her tears away and cursed herself for being a big baby while she clung to him. When they parted, her eyes were still watery, and Zack held on to her forearms to steady her.

"I'm sorry for pushing, Em," he said.

She flapped her hands around dismissively. "It's not your fault. I think it stems from my parents leaving all of the time. I just don't like goodbyes."

He pulled her in again and ran his hand down the back of her hair in a soothing motion. "I'm not going anywhere," he said. "I promise."

Emma breathed him in and let herself relax in his strong comforting embrace. This time, when they pulled apart, she offered him a shaky smile.

"I think we just had our first argument, and I'm glad to see that you did the right thing by letting me win!" With that, she flounced to the door, calling over her shoulder, "Come on, it's time to go."

Zack rolled his eyes, grabbed both of their bags, and followed her out the door. There was no make-out session in the elevator this time because it was full of passengers. They did get to stand smashed together, however, and Emma soaked up his closeness before they were deposited on the lobby floor. The airport shuttle waited in the pick-up area outside of the lobby doors, but Zack stopped her with a hand on her arm.

He kissed her firmly and said, "That was not a goodbye kiss. That was an I'll-see-you-later kiss."

Emma gave him a full-on smile and started to board the bus, but she turned around at the last second. "See you at home," she said before the door closed behind her.

CHAPTER 27

Five hours is a long time when you're in a car by yourself, Zack thought as he made his way home. He had thought about Emma during most of the drive, which was in keeping with what he had confessed to her the day before.

Ugh. So much for playing it cool. He had tipped his hand after spending one weekend in her arms. One weekend!

It's not my fault. She looked up at me with those doe eyes and asked about my feelings. Yeah, dork, but you didn't have to tell her everything.

When he had finished chastising himself, he switched to thinking more positive thoughts. Images were more like it. Images of her under him, over him, and beside him—her petite body heated and responsive to his every touch. She hadn't been shy, that was for sure. And he loved it. Loved every minute of it. It wasn't just the unbelievably awesome sex either. It was everything: her laugh, her smile, her bright eyes and flushed cheeks. The way that she sparred with him and didn't back down when he was being *Mr. Persistent.* Zack laughed out loud at the nickname.

When his steamy thoughts caused a reaction in his pants, he toned it down and pulled up some G-rated images, such as them walking along Navy Pier and taking candid photos of each other at The Bean.

Inevitably, his thoughts wandered to their discussion about what would happen next. Here was where he floundered, because, honestly, he had no idea. He wasn't convinced that Gracie was ready to include Emma in their lives, at least not on a permanent basis. Gracie saw Emma as "the one who told her stories," not as "the one who was stealing her daddy's heart." Zack chafed when he recalled the discussion he had had with Alicia about Emma. Alicia had tried to warn him that it was too soon for Zack to introduce a woman into Gracie's life, yet she was already living with her intern. When he had called her out on it, Alicia had made the excuse that she kept her activities with Gracie separate from what's-his-name. *What was his name anyway?* Zack had been referring to Alicia's live-in as everything but his real name, and now he'd forgotten what it was! Oh well, the point was, it had pissed him off. He had a right to live his own life without interference from Alicia, or did he? Certainly, as the mother of his child, she had the right to voice her concerns, but still, it irked him.

If he were being completely honest, some of what Alicia had said rang true. They hadn't been divorced for that long, and Gracie was still adjusting to their separate living arrangements. It seemed like a lot to ask for her to accept Emma into their lives too. His thoughts swirled around and around in this vein, so when he saw the exit sign for Clarkston, he was pleasantly surprised. Zack shook his head and chuckled. "Emma Murphy, what on earth have you done to me?"

CHAPTER 28

Instead of driving straight home from the airport, Emma went directly to the bookstore. After spending the weekend with Zack, she dreaded going home to an empty house, plus she wanted to check in with Kelly and see how business had fared in her absence.

Kelly looked up in surprise when Emma entered the store, and she said, "Hey, Em. Welcome back. How was the windy city?"

"It was... interesting." Emma felt her face flush while Kelly gave her the once-over.

"What does that mean? Did you pick up a mysterious stranger at a bar and have sex with him?"

"That's your fantasy, not mine," Emma replied drily.

"So? Don't make me beg. What happened?"

Emma swung her head around to see if there were any customers within hearing distance. There were only two young women in the store, but their heads were buried conspiratorially in the romance section.

"Zack showed up," she said and waited for Kelly's reaction.

Kelly's caramel brown eyes bulged, and she leaned forward intently. "He showed up in Chicago?"

"Yes. He was waiting for me in the hotel lobby after the show on Friday."

"Holy..."

"I know. I was as shocked as you are."

"So what happened next?"

"We hung out. We toured the city together, had dinner, that sort of thing..." Emma's voice trailed off as the two young customers approached the counter, each with an armload of Harlequin romances.

"Have you read any of these?" the taller of the two girls asked Kelly and Emma.

"Only like every one of them," Kelly answered enthusiastically. "This one with the cowboy on the cover is particularly juicy."

The girls giggled and left the store, happily swinging the bags that contained their treasures.

"So, get to the good stuff. Did you and Zack do it?"

"Really, Kell?" Emma turned away and examined a stack of new books that had arrived while she had been in Chicago.

"Sorry. Let me rephrase the question. Did you and Zack *make love*?"

Emma still couldn't bring herself to look Kelly in the eye, but if Zack was Mr. Persistent, then Kelly was Ms. Persistent, so she decided to give in. "Yes," she said quietly.

"Wow, Em. That's huge."

In more ways than one, she thought giddily, deciding to keep that part of the story to herself. "It's not that big a deal. You do it all the time."

"I know, but that's me, not you. You're the relationship type of girl."

Emma turned to face her. "What are you trying to say?"

"I'm saying that you don't do casual sex, which means that you and Zack must be in a relationship now. No more of that friendship crap you tried to pull off."

Emma suddenly wished that she had gone straight home. She wasn't ready to voice her fears to Kelly or anyone else. She had thought about Zack the whole way home, and after replaying the events of the weekend over and over, she was still unsure about where they stood. She purposely hadn't called him yet because she wanted more time to process it all.

"I don't know what to call it, Kell. It's all so new."

Kelly had to have heard the waver in Emma's voice because she backed off. "Well, I'm here if you need someone to talk to."

"I know. Thanks. So, tell me what happened at the store while I was gone."

Emma half-listened as Kelly related stories about some of their regular customers, including Mrs. Simmons, who had finally broken down and bought the *Fifty Shades* series. Kelly said that it had been hard for her to keep a straight face when she rang up the purchase. She went on to say that Brett had done an excellent job of leading story time on Saturday, and the kids (especially the girls) seemed to love him.

"Oh, and Mike asked about you yesterday," she added as an afterthought.

"Really?" Emma was surprised given their last interaction.

"I felt kind of sorry for the guy. He really has a thing for you."

"What did you tell him?"

"I told him that you were in Chicago at a book convention and that you'd be back on Monday. He asked about Zack, and I said that you two were just friends. If I would have known that you two hooked up, I would have discouraged Mike."

Great, now I have to let Mike down again. "Being single is a lot harder than it looks," Emma said, exasperated.

"Welcome to my world," Kelly said, shaking her head.

"Sorry, Kell. I was so busy talking about myself that I forgot to ask you about...."

"Collin."

"Yes, the poet. How's that going?"

"We're through. It turned out that he wasn't so sensitive after all."

"Why am I not surprised?" Emma rested her chin in her palm and gave Kelly her full attention.

"The good news is that I met Luke, and we have a date next weekend."

"I can't keep up with you, Kelly. Did you meet him here?"

"Yep, in the history section. He's a history teacher at Clarkston Junior High School, and he wanted to read up on World War II."

"So that makes him..."

"Worldly. I like a man with a global world view. Someone who thinks beyond himself."

Emma had to laugh, but then, to soften the blow, she gave her friend a hug.

"What was that for?" Kelly asked even though she had hugged Emma back just as tight.

"Just because I love you. Your eternal optimism never ceases to amaze me."

Emma let Kelly's romantic outlook infuse her while she drove home. She unpacked, put on her favorite country music CD, and made herself a bacon, lettuce, and tomato sandwich. She puttered around the house for a while and congratulated herself for not checking her phone every other minute. It made perfect sense that Zack would want to spend some time with Gracie since he had been gone all weekend. Emma immersed herself in her James Patterson novel until she decided that it was a reasonable time to call.

Zack answered on the first ring, but he sounded a little frazzled. "Hey, Em."

"Hey, am I interrupting something?"

"No. I just saved Gracie from having a meltdown when she couldn't find her favorite doll. I used my superpower for finding lost toys and just finished tucking her in."

"You really are Superman, then," Emma said and giggled at her reference to his boxers.

"Something like that," he replied, chuckling.

Emma thought she heard the rustling of covers, like he was getting into bed. "Whatcha doing right now?"

"Climbing into bed."

Bingo! "Wish I was there," she purred flirtatiously.

"That makes two of us," Zack replied, lowering his voice.

"I don't know if I thanked you properly for taking me out to dinner this weekend." Emma snuggled a little deeper under the covers, smiling at her boldness.

"Oh yeah? How would you like to thank me?"

"Well, first, I would give you a long, deep kiss with lots of tongue."

More rustling of covers. "And then?"

"Then I would undress you all the way down to nothing."

"Keep talking."

Now it was her that squirmed. "Next, I would run my hands down your bare chest and over your abs until I reached your…"

"DAAADDD!"

"Damn, I have to go." Zack must have covered the phone, but she heard him yell, "Hold on, Gracie."

Emma's good mood evaporated just like that. "No problem. I'll talk to you tomorrow," she said, and then he hung up without even saying goodbye.

CHAPTER 29

Zack called Emma the very next day, just after she had opened the store at ten o'clock.

"I'm sorry for hanging up on you," he began. "Gracie had a really tough time settling down last night."

That makes two of us, Emma thought. "I understand. Do you think she was upset because you were gone all weekend?"

"No. I think she was worried about going to school this morning. I might have to make an appointment with her teacher to discuss that boy who's been teasing her on the playground."

"Ah, man troubles. Been there, done that," Emma said lightly.

"What man troubles are you having?" he asked suspiciously.

"None really, except that I haven't seen a certain man in twenty-four excruciatingly long hours."

Zack erupted in warm laughter. "I'd like to remedy that. In fact, that's why I called. How about meeting me for lunch today?"

"I would love to. However, I'm the only one here. I gave Kelly the next couple of days off since she worked all weekend."

"Ok. What if I brought lunch to you?"

"That sounds wonderful as long as you don't mind if we're interrupted."

"How could I mind when I'm the king of interruptions?"

Emma's smile stretched so wide that her cheeks hurt. "It's a date then... or something like that," she amended, feeling a little flustered.

"Are you blushing right now?" he teased.

"No," she replied emphatically.

Zack seemed barely able to contain his laughter as he said, "See you at noon."

Emma busied herself by paying bills, checking on inventory, and assisting the few customers who ventured in. Before she knew it, the bell chimed, and Zack walked in holding a McDonald's bag and a drink tray.

"How did you know?" Emma asked, placing a hand over her heart adoringly.

Zack set the food and drinks down, took a quick glance around the store, and leaned over the counter to kiss her. It was a brief meeting of lips, but it sent a tingle down her spine all the same. Emma breathed in the spicy scent of his cologne and suppressed the urge to climb over the counter to get closer. He looked and smelled delicious, almost overriding the tantalizing aroma of the McDonald's french fries!

"I'm an observant guy. When I spent the night, I saw an empty Mickey-D's bag in your garbage can."

"I should chastise you for snooping around, but I'm too hungry. Let's eat!" Emma motioned for him to come behind the counter and into the tiny office. She shoved a pile of papers aside and wheeled her chair around to sit beside him. "We'll have to keep the door open in case any customers come in," she explained while Zack pulled hamburgers and french fries out of the bag.

They dug into the food for a few minutes and simply enjoyed the pleasure of each other's company. When they had finished eating, Zack reached over and twirled a lock of Emma's hair around his index finger. It was a simple gesture, but it felt meltingly intimate.

"Are you free on Wednesday night?" Zack asked as he continued to play with her hair.

"Um-hmm. What do you have in mind?"

"Well, let's see." He leaned in and gazed into her eyes, which she was sure were glazed over with desire.

"We should probably eat something to boost our energy, and then…"

Just then, the door dinged, announcing a visitor. "Hold that thought," Emma said and stood up to greet… Mike.

This isn't his usual time to make a delivery, and he's not carrying any packages. I'm screwed. Emma forced a smile and said, "Hi, Mike. What can I do for you?" The minute she said Mike's name, she heard Zack's chair scrape across the floor. She knew without turning around that he stood just a few steps behind her. She could practically see him puff out his chest and swore she felt waves of jealousy roll off of him.

Mike stopped in his tracks. His frustration was obvious as he replied, "I don't have any deliveries for you today, but I thought I'd stop by and see if you had any outgoing packages for me to pick up."

He had never done this in the three years that Emma had owned the shop, so she knew it had just been an excuse to see her. Zack cleared his throat as if to speak, but Emma jumped in to prevent a scene.

"No, I don't, but thanks for stopping by," she said calmly.

Mike nodded and quickly exited the store. Emma turned around and bumped right into Zack's hard chest. She gave him a push to indicate that they should go back into the office. This time, she closed the door firmly behind them. Zack leaned back against the desk while she stepped in between his legs.

"You might as well have pounded your chest with your fists out there, Tarzan," she scolded.

He wrapped his arms around her waist and pulled her closer. "He interrupted us," Zack said by way of explanation.

"That's no reason to act all alpha male on me." Her words trailed off because now he was kissing the sensitive hollow between her neck and shoulder.

"I'm tired of that guy sniffing around you," Zack said, but his words were muffled as he dragged his lips across her throat to the opposite side of her neck.

Emma tilted her head back and enjoyed the sensations that had assaulted her body. Zack's hands slipped down to cup her backside, closing the one-inch gap between their hips. If she had any doubt that he was as turned on as she was, it was instantly erased. He was stiff and unyielding against her.

"I don't care about Mike." Emma's words came out in a breathy pant because now Zack's hands were on her breasts. Her nipples immediately rose to full attention, and Zack pulled back to stare at her while his hands continued to play.

"I want to be the only man that you think about, Em. Not the UPS guy or any other guy. I want to be the only one you desire."

Emma opened her mouth to speak, but the words were stolen from her by Zack's kiss. His lips covered hers, hard and demanding. Her arms automatically entwined around his neck, and she pressed herself flush against him. When their tongues met, Emma's desire spiked even higher until the sound of Zack's phone buzzing in his pocket broke the spell. They reluctantly parted, but Zack kept one arm wrapped around her while he retrieved his phone. He looked down at the display and swore, and then he shoved the phone back in his pocket.

"Is there a problem?" Emma asked, her breathing still unsteady.

"Just work stuff. I need to get back." Zack cupped her face with his large hands and gazed at her intently.

"We're going to finish this on Wednesday," he stated firmly.

Emma gave him a mock salute and then leaned in and gently kissed his full lips. "Plan on it," she said, and then she stepped back and opened the door. Zack gave her butt a playful squeeze as he brushed past.

He was almost to the front door before Emma spoke again. "Thanks for lunch."

"Welcome," he called over his shoulder.

"Oh, and Zack?"

He turned around. "Yes?"

"There is no other guy."

His mega-watt smile lit up the whole store, and Emma giggled as he walked backward across the parking lot to his car, grinning broadly at her the entire way.

CHAPTER 30

Emma couldn't wait to leave the bookstore on Wednesday afternoon. Zack was coming over to her house after work, and she had a lot to do. Kelly arrived a half an hour earlier than usual to relieve Emma, encouraging her to go home and "primp for the Greek God." Emma didn't even bother with a retort; she simply grabbed her purse and hurried out the door.

When she and Zack had talked on the phone the night before, Emma had suggested that they meet at her house for a change. Her motivation was two-fold: one, she wanted to cook for him and, two, she didn't want to risk being interrupted by Alicia and Gracie. Zack did his part by telling Alicia in no uncertain terms that he wouldn't be home until eight o'clock, so Emma looked forward to three uninterrupted hours with him!

Emma had planned a simple meal, since she doubted that eating would be the primary focus of the evening. She set to work coating chicken to bake, and once it was in the oven, she prepared a tossed salad. She had stopped by the Clarkston bakery on her way home and picked up an assortment of cookies for dessert.

Kitchen duties complete, Emma hustled up the stairs to prepare herself for the evening. First, she ran a warm bath and sprinkled in her favorite vanilla-scented bath salts. She lounged back in the tub and thoroughly shaved her legs and various other areas until her skin was silky smooth. She didn't bother re-washing her hair because it would take too long to dry. Instead, she spritzed in a curling product and fluffed it up with her hands. Emma had worn dress slacks and a blouse to the bookstore that day, but she wanted to ramp it up a notch for Zack. She rummaged through her closet until she found a denim skirt that she hadn't worn in quite some time. Kelly had given it to Emma during one of the infamous purges of her overstuffed closet, but Emma had complained that the skirt was too short. It was the perfect reason to wear it tonight, though—Zack would probably love it. She paired the skirt with an off-the-shoulder white peasant top (also courtesy of Kelly) and a chunky silver necklace with a heart charm dangling from it. She gave her lashes a fresh coat of mascara, swiped some glossy lip balm on her lips, and voila—she was ready.

Emma used the remaining ten minutes to set the table, and when she had finished, the doorbell rang. *Perfect timing.*

She swung the door open to reveal Zack holding a colorful spray of fall flowers wrapped in cellophane.

"Thank you," she said, touched by the old-fashioned gesture. "Come on in."

Zack followed her into the kitchen, where she set the flowers down on the counter to look for a vase. She got up on her tiptoes to reach an upper cabinet when Zack came up behind her.

"Allow me," he said, his voice husky as he reached up and selected a crystal vase from the shelf. He set the vase on the counter next to them, and Emma slowly turned around. Zack had her penned in against the kitchen counter, and it didn't appear that he was moving anytime soon.

"I have chicken in the oven," Emma stammered, and she pointed behind him.

"Don't care."

"But aren't you hungry?"

Zack dipped his head down and nibbled on her bottom lip. "Yes, very."

His meaning was crystal clear, and Emma sighed as his hands began to caress her bare shoulders.

"This is pretty," he said, running his index finger along the top edge of her blouse.

Emma watched his finger travel back and forth a few times before he dipped his whole hand down the front of her top. "Zack."

His other hand had disappeared underneath her skirt, and he groaned when he touched her bare bottom. No days-of-the-week underwear tonight. Emma had recovered a red silky thong from the far recesses of her underwear drawer hoping that Zack would approve. By the sounds of it, he definitely did.

Suddenly Zack went down on his knees in front of her and started to pull up on her skirt.

"Here? Now?" *Why am I even questioning this?*

"I don't want to wait," he replied, and then his head was covered in denim. Emma felt a cool whoosh of air as her panties hit the floor. Zack gently lifted her feet out of them and spread her legs a little further apart.

Oh my! There was no more talking, no more thinking, no more worrying about burnt chicken. There was only Zack bringing her such excruciating pleasure that she wanted to scream. She settled for loud moaning instead, which Zack took as encouragement, and he intensified his movements.

Emma had always found oral sex to be a bit of a mystery. She never really understood what the fuss was all about, but Zack was giving her a whole new lease on the topic. She shattered against him with a stream of "oohs" and "aahs" and a few shouts of his name. She leaned against the counter for support when he peeked his head out from under her skirt.

Zack's hair was adorably disheveled, and his polo shirt had come untucked from his pants, but he looked as happy as, well, as happy as a guy should look after what he had just done! He picked up her panties and dangled them from his index finger while he rose to his full height.

Emma tugged her skirt down and reached her hand out to retrieve her underwear, but he held them just above her reach.

"Give me those," she said and tried to jump up to reach them.

"You won't be needing them," he stated and scooped her up with one arm.

Emma couldn't contain her giggles when he carried her into the living room he-man style and laid her on the couch. Her laughter faded away as she watched him strip, his sleek muscles contracting with every movement. In place of his trademark Superman boxers, he wore snug-fitting boxer briefs that left nothing to the imagination. Emma swallowed hard when he revealed himself fully. He didn't move for what felt like a long time, allowing her to look her fill, completely comfortable under her appraising eye.

When Zack started to approach, Emma held up her index finger. He stopped in his tracks and watched her undress. Her fingers fumbled with the strings that tied her blouse together, but it finally fell open, revealing her lacy white push-up bra. She lifted the blouse over her head and tossed it aside before reaching around to unhook her bra. When she pulled it down to expose her breasts, she heard Zack's loud intake of breath. Emma locked eyes with him while she shimmied out of her skirt, and then she stilled while he raked his eyes over her naked body.

"Emma" was the last coherent word she heard before he entered her. Zack propped himself up on his forearms and kissed her everywhere he could reach, starting with her forehead, the tip of her nose, her cheeks, and even her ear lobes. *Who knew those would be so sensitive?* He assailed all of her senses at once until her nerves became a mass of firing explosions. Their hips ground together, and Zack's chest hairs tickled her breasts as their movements quickened.

When Emma felt herself getting very close, she panted, "Zack, condom?"

Susan Coventry

"Crap, no time…"

Emma experienced a moment of panic, but a second later, Zack pulled out and released himself on her stomach. She instantly relaxed, but Zack's face was pulled tight, with anger or embarrassment she couldn't tell which.

"Hold still," he said and hurried down the hall to the bathroom. He returned with some tissues and proceeded to clean her up with the utmost precision. Afterwards, they sat side by side on the couch, both of them still naked.

"Is something wrong?" Emma ventured, unsure of the reason for his pensive mood.

He swung his arm around her shoulder and pulled her close. "Everything was great, too good actually. I'm mad at myself for forgetting about protection. If you hadn't said something…"

For some reason, Emma wasn't as concerned about their near-miss as he was. Not that she wanted to get pregnant, but if it happened she wouldn't be upset. She was curious about the real reason behind Zack's reaction. "It's ok, Zack. Don't beat yourself up over it. I'm not worried, so you shouldn't be either."

Zack looked at her with a mix of surprise and relief. "But what if you got pregnant? We're not even…"

"Together?" Now she felt her own dander rising.

"No. I didn't say that. I just think it would be bad timing, don't you?"

Emma pulled away from him and snatched her clothes up off the floor. "Why are you so hung up on the timing of everything? When we first met, it

194

was bad timing because we were both engaged to other people. I get that. But now we're single, and it's *still* not the right timing. It's too soon for Gracie. It's too soon for us to be more than friends. But there's never a bad time to have sex, is that it? Tell me something, Zack. When will it *ever* be the right time for us?"

Zack buried his head in his hands while Emma hurriedly redressed. Her ire rose higher and higher while he sat there without uttering a single word. The only man that she knew who had no trouble expressing his feelings now sat in miserable silence, naked on her couch. Emma shoved his clothes into a pile and threw them at him.

"Get out," she hissed.

His head jerked up, and he gaped at her in disbelief.

"I mean it, Zack. Leave now before I say something I'll really regret."

Zack heaved himself off of the couch, clothes in hand, and disappeared into the bathroom.

Absolutely unbelievable, Emma seethed while she waited for him to dress. A few seconds later, she decided not to wait. "Show yourself out," she shouted and stomped past the bathroom door and up the stairs. When she reached her bedroom, she slammed the door shut, locked it, and slumped down onto the bed.

A few minutes later, Emma heard the front door close and Zack's Range Rover start up. She told herself not to, but she couldn't help it. She walked over to her bedroom window and watched in stunned silence as he drove away.

CHAPTER 31

Emma relayed the entire sordid story to Kelly the next day during a lull at the bookstore.

"You were right, Kell. I don't do casual sex." Emma sighed and slumped against the counter.

Kelly rubbed her back consolingly and withheld her "I told you sos," which Emma greatly appreciated.

"None of this would have happened if we had just stayed friends," Emma continued, but she stopped short when the door chimed and Mike walked in hefting two large boxes in front of him. The day couldn't possibly get any worse, so Emma decided she might as well confront the *Mike situation* too.

He set the boxes on the counter but purposely avoided eye contact with Emma. He appeared to be looking around for Kelly, but as usual, she had slinked off when he came in. *Thanks a lot, Kell.*

"I can sign for those," Emma said and came out from behind the counter to stand beside him. She scribbled her name on the electronic device and handed it back to him. He grunted a "Thanks" and turned away, but she placed a hand on his arm to stop him.

"I owe you an apology," she said. "I'm sorry if I sent you mixed messages, and I'm sorry for Zack's boorish behavior toward you." *Zack had used the same word to describe himself, so she figured she could too.*

"You don't have to apologize, Emma. It's pretty obvious how you two feel about each other. I was just in denial."

Emma raised her eyebrows and cocked her head. "It's obvious how we feel about each other? That's amazing, because we can't seem to figure it out." She laughed, but it sounded hollow.

"Well, from where I stand, the guy's crazy about you, and I can certainly understand why." Mike gave her a shy smile and then looked away.

Emma felt herself blush, and instead of trying to hide it, she decided to poke fun at it. "Some pair you and I would make, huh?" She gestured back and forth between their pink faces and was rewarded with Mike's deep laugh.

"Thanks for being such a good sport," she said and spontaneously gave him a hug. With her arms around Mike's neck, she looked up right into a pair of piercing gray eyes. Zack stood outside the door, poised to come inside, but he frowned at her instead.

Talk about bad timing. Emma mouthed the words "Come in," but Zack turned his back on her and practically jogged back to his car. "Shit," she muttered, shaking her head in disbelief.

"What did I do? You hugged me, remember?" Mike had stepped back and looked at her with a confused expression.

"No, it's not you." She pointed toward the door. "It was Zack. He was just about to come in when he saw us hugging."

"Sorry, Emma, but I'm outta here. I don't want to be standing around if he decides to come back." With that, Mike made a hasty retreat, and Emma just stood there shaking her head when the door closed behind him.

It turned out that Mike had nothing to worry about. Zack didn't come back to the bookstore, nor did he call or text her. Emma stubbornly decided to let him stew over it, at least until she saw him on Saturday. *He certainly wouldn't deprive Gracie of story time due to a stupid misunderstanding, would he?*

The answer was yes, he would. Emma conducted story time with a heavy heart, discovering that she missed Gracie almost as much as she missed Zack. She went through the rest of the day in a fog, replaying the events that had led to this impasse between them. Had she been too hard on him the other day? But why did everything have to go according to his time line? Shouldn't she have a say too? The questions swirled around and around until she felt dizzy and begged off work early.

Kelly had been sympathetic and had told her to go home and relax, but now Emma was home, and she didn't know what to do with herself. The house felt emptier than usual, and whenever she looked at the couch where she and Zack had made love, she was flooded with conflicted emotions all over again.

The one thing that Emma knew for sure was that she missed him terribly. She missed his voice, his laughter, his presence. She missed everything about the man, even though he was being a stubborn ass. Of course, one could argue that she was being stubborn too. She could easily have picked up the phone to call or text him, but she hadn't. So Emma sat in her silent house and tried to distract herself with mundane tasks until it was time to go to bed.

She had just slipped into her favorite sleepshirt, the one labelled "I woke up like this," when the doorbell rang.

"No, it couldn't be." Emma padded to her bedroom window and peered out through the blinds. It was pitch black, and she hadn't left a porch light on because she hadn't been expecting company.

"Maybe it's Kelly, coming over to check on me," Emma mumbled while she went down the stairs.

The doorbell rang again, followed by a loud pounding of a fist against the metal door. *Only a man's fist could make that kind of noise.*

"Emma, open up. I know you're in there," Zack demanded.

"Just a minute," she replied haughtily.

She managed to unlock the door even though her hands were trembling. She flung it open, and a lump immediately lodged in her throat. Zack stood on her porch barefoot in a pair of gray sweatpants and a University of Michigan t-shirt. His hair was rumpled, like he had just rolled out of bed, and he sported a light smattering of facial hair.

He looked sexy as hell when he held up a McDonald's chocolate shake and said, "Peace offering."

Emma waved him inside and accepted the shake cup from his outstretched hand. "You brought me a shake at ten o'clock at night?"

He shrugged. "When I screw up, I bring food."

Emma gave him a slight smile. "If you bring food every time you screw up, I might get fat!"

Zack's expression told her that he deserved that comment. "Can we sit down for a few minutes and talk?"

"Sure," she said and led him into the kitchen. She purposely avoided the living room since it was the scene of the alleged crime. Once they were seated at the kitchen table, she took a long slurp of the shake and then said, "So, talk."

Zack ran his hands through his messy hair and sighed. "I don't know why, but it feels like I'm constantly screwing things up, when what I really want is for things to be perfect for you. For us."

Emma set down the shake and replied, "That's just it, Zack. I don't need things to be perfect. Life is messy, but that's also what makes it interesting. Life doesn't follow an exact time table, even when we want it to, so why not just let go and enjoy the ride?"

"How'd you get to be so smart?" He reached out for her hand and held it across the kitchen table.

"Lots of books," she quipped.

Zack gave her hand a squeeze. "I missed you, Em—so, so much."

"I missed you too," she admitted.

"I came to the bookstore the other day to apologize, but…"

"You saw me with Mike. I know, and what you saw was a conciliatory hug. I felt bad for him, but he understands that you and I are…"

"Together," Zack stated firmly.

"Together," she confirmed right before he pulled her into his arms. There was no mistaking the type of hug that Zack gave her; it was a possessive "you're mine and don't you forget it" kind of hug, and Emma ate it up. It was also the kind of hug that made her lady parts stand up and take notice.

After a minute or so, Zack pulled back and looked her directly in the eyes. "Emma, I need you to know something. The other day, when you made a comment about me just wanting sex—you're wrong. I want you for so much more than that, and…"

Emma put her finger to his lips. "It's ok, Zack. I think that you've apologized enough for one night." She was just about to lean in and kiss him, but he held her back.

"Let me finish. I'd like to stay with you tonight, but I don't want to have sex. I just want to hold you—all night long if you'll let me."

Emma's mouth gaped open until Zack lifted up on her lower jaw to close it. "Seriously?" she asked, torn between feeling touched and disappointed.

"Yes. Is that a problem?" He arched an eyebrow at her.

"No. No problem. It's just that you don't need to prove anything to me. I spoke out of anger the other day, but I didn't really mean it. At least, not all of it."

Zack leaned over and placed a tender kiss on her cheek. "Just let me hold you tonight."

He spoke with such sincerity that Emma realized he truly meant it. "Ok," she conceded, "But you better not be wearing the Superman boxers."

"And you better not be wearing your days-of-the-week underwear," he teased.

"Ha-ha. You wish!"

They climbed into bed together, and Emma snuggled in close to him, laid her head on his chest, and flung a leg over his. Being this close to him made her want to get even closer, but she restrained herself. Instead, she concentrated on the rhythm of his breathing and the warmth of his body next to hers.

"Zack," she said a few minutes later.

"Um-hmm."

"Thank you for this."

"No, Emma. Thank you."

They stopped talking after that, and even though she didn't think she'd be able to, Emma fell into a deep, blissful sleep.

CHAPTER 32

Emma awoke the next morning to find Zack's handsome face peering down at her, and it took her a moment to get her bearings. "What time is it?" she muttered. She was definitely not a perky morning person.

"Unfortunately, it's time for me to go," Zack said.

Emma forced her eyes open a little wider and realized that he was poised above her on all fours, looking fully alert and well-rested. "Go? Why? What time is it?" she repeated.

"It's nine o'clock, and Gracie is due home at ten."

"Oh, ok." She didn't try to hide the disappointment in her voice.

"I wish I could stay longer, but Alicia has some event to go to, so she has to bring Gracie back early. I have an idea though. Why don't you come over and have brunch with us in a little while?"

Emma perked up a little at the invitation. "Really?"

"Yes," he said and chuckled.

"Why are you laughing at me?"

"Because you're adorable in the morning," he replied, and he started to go in for a kiss.

She quickly turned her head to the side so that he caught her cheek instead. "I probably have horrible morning breath," she explained.

"Let me be the judge of that." Zack forced her head back to center and covered her protests with his mouth.

His warm, wet, delicious mouth tasted minty fresh, and when they broke apart, Emma swatted him on the arm. "No fair. You already used mouthwash!"

Zack chuckled again and hauled himself out of bed. Apparently he had removed his shirt sometime during the night, and Emma was treated to a daytime view of his gorgeous body. Zack's sweats hung low on his hips, and she admired his backside as he bent down to retrieve his shirt. She continued to admire his form while he pulled the shirt over his head and then ran his hands through his hair as if to tame it. Emma wished that her hands were in his hair instead, or on his biceps or his abs or his...

"Em? You want to walk me to the door?"

"Yeah, sure," she replied, and she sighed when she crawled out from under the covers.

He trailed her down the stairs until they stood by the front door. "What time will you be over?" he asked while twirling a lock of her hair.

"What time do you want me?"

Zack's eyes lit up with desire. "All the time."

Emma took a step closer to him. "You could have had me last night, but you wanted to cuddle instead."

"Ugh. Did I use the word cuddle?"

Emma giggled. "Not specifically, but you get my point."

Zack pulled her against him and buried his head in her neck. "I won't make that mistake again," he murmured against her neck.

Emma pushed her hips against his to remind him of what he had missed out on. They kissed for a few more minutes before reluctantly parting.

"Come over soon, ok?" Zack said on his way out the door.

An hour and a half later, Emma was greeted at Zack's house by a very exuberant four-year-old.

"Daddy, Daddy, she's here," Gracie called while she led Emma into the kitchen.

"Well, good morning, Emma. Nice to see you up and about." He winked at her over their shared secret.

"Daddy's making waffles," Gracie exclaimed.

Sure enough, the heart-shaped waffle maker that he had bought in Chicago sat on the kitchen counter with steam pouring out of it.

"Smells good. I love waffles!"

Zack smirked at her and went back to his cooking duties.

"What can we help with?" Emma asked.

"You two can set the table and pour the juice," Zack said.

Gracie excitedly showed Emma where to find the plates, forks, and glasses, and the two of them arranged everything on the table.

"I can pour the juice," Gracie said.

"Uh, Gracie, why don't we let Miss Emma do that. The last time you poured the juice, we ended up with a sticky mess, remember?"

Gracie looked like she was about to argue, but then she glanced at Emma and thought better of it.

"How about if you hold the glass while I pour?" Emma suggested.

Gracie nodded and gave her a sweet smile.

When the three of them sat down to eat, Gracie offered to pray again. They held hands around the table and bent their heads.

"Dear God, thank you for telling Robby not to pinch me, and thank you for letting Miss Emma come over for waffles. Amen."

Emma's heart was as full as her stomach by the time brunch was over. Gracie had bounded up the stairs to play, and now she and Zack were cleaning the kitchen.

"You're really lucky, Zack. Gracie is a great kid," Emma said while they worked side by side.

"Thanks. She thinks pretty highly of you too."

"You think?"

"I know. In fact, she was mad at me yesterday when I suggested we go to a movie instead of story time."

Emma was hesitant to dredge up the events of the last few days, but she was curious. "Did you end up going to a movie?"

"No. Gracie went into her room and refused to speak to me for most of the morning."

Emma giggled at the little girl's feistiness. "So that makes two of us who thought you were being a stubborn ass."

"Guilty as charged," Zack said, and then he swiftly changed the subject. "You have the day off, right?"

"Yes, why?"

"Gracie asked me to take her shopping for a Halloween costume. Come with us."

"Are you sure she'd want me to go?"

"Go where? Go where?" Gracie skidded into the room and stopped in front of them.

"I asked Miss Emma if she'd like to go costume shopping with us."

"Would that be ok with you, Gracie?" Emma asked, feeling cautiously optimistic.

"Yay! You can help me pick out a girl costume instead of a boy costume like Daddy would pick."

"Then it's settled. Get your shoes on, and then we'll go," Zack said, smiling at both of them.

"Are you sure you're ready for this?" Zack asked after Gracie left the room.

"Absolutely. What could be so hard about picking out a costume?"

Almost three hours later, Emma had her answer. They had gone to four different stores until Gracie finally settled on a Rapunzel costume, complete with a long blonde wig. Gracie was so exhausted from the experience that she had fallen asleep in the back seat on the way home. Zack carefully lifted her out of the vehicle and carried her upstairs before he rejoined Emma in the living room.

Emma was tired too and had kicked back on Zack's leather couch with her feet up on the ottoman. Zack sat beside her, but he maintained a respectable distance in case Gracie were to suddenly wake up.

"Thanks for spending the day with us," Zack said.

"It was fun, although I feel like I could take a nap too."

"Welcome to my life," he said off-handedly.

Emma turned sideways to see him better, but his eyes were closed, and his breathing was getting deep. She resisted the urge to kiss him and quietly got up from the couch. Emma would have gladly stayed with them for the rest of the day and night, but she didn't want to push things. The day had been perfect as far as she was concerned, and she decided to leave it at that. She went into the kitchen, scribbled a note to Zack, and then let herself out.

Emma went through the rest of the day in quiet contentment. When she crawled into bed that night, she realized that she didn't feel lonely, like she had on a lot of nights since her divorce. She read a few chapters in her book and looked forward to Zack's phone call, which came around nine thirty, just as expected.

"Hey, Em."

"Hey," she replied, smiling like a fool.

"Are you in bed?"

"Um-hmm."

"Wish I was with you."

"Me too."

Zack was quiet for a few seconds. "It was a great day, wasn't it?"

"Yes," she affirmed.

"I want more of those."

"Ditto."

"You're sure you want to be a part of our crazy life."

Emma hadn't been so sure of anything in a very long time. "Yes," she answered simply.

Zack was quiet again. "God, I really wish you were here right now."

Emma picked at a loose thread on her bedspread. "What would you do with me?"

Zack cleared his throat. "Well, first I would kiss that place on your neck that really makes you squirm."

"And then?"

"Then I would work my way down to your magnificent breasts."

Emma's eyebrows raised, and she felt herself getting warm. "And then?"

"Then I would check to see if you're wearing your days-of-the-week underwear."

Emma choked on her laughter. "That just ruined it!" she complained.

"Daaaad…"

"No, that just ruined it." Zack sighed.

Emma laughed again. "And so it begins…"

CHAPTER 33

After that day, Emma and Zack's relationship slowly expanded to include Gracie. They still exercised caution in how they interacted around her, adopting a mostly "hands-off" policy, and saved their affection for when they were alone. Emma and Zack had agreed to give Gracie more time to get used to Emma's presence before they revealed that side of their relationship. For now, Gracie accepted Emma as a "friend," and that was good enough for Emma.

The weeks rolled by, and soon, the holiday season was upon them. Emma held a special Halloween version of story time where the kids got to come in costume. Gracie had been thrilled to show off her Rapunzel costume that they had chosen together. Emma had even joined Zack and Gracie for trick or treating, and then she'd sat on Zack's living-room floor to help Gracie sort through her pile of candy.

Once November hit, business picked up at the bookstore, and Emma started working longer hours. Kelly also worked overtime, devising various promotions and events to boost sales for Christmas. Emma saw Zack as often as she could, but he complained that it wasn't nearly enough. Secretly, Emma was pleased that he missed her so much, and thought that it made the time that they spent together that much sweeter.

"Once the holidays are over, we'll have more time again," she said one weeknight after they had just eaten dinner. Emma had made dinner for him at her house, her first attempt since the burnt chicken fiasco weeks ago.

"Speaking of the holidays, what are you doing for Thanksgiving?" Zack asked nonchalantly.

They sat on her couch, holding hands and relishing the few hours that they would get to spend together that evening. "I don't know. I hadn't really thought about it." The truth was Emma had thought about little else. Up until this year, her holidays had been booked, first with her parents and then with Mark. Emma's mother had called a couple of weeks ago and said that they wouldn't be coming until Christmas, so Emma was on her own. Or so she thought.

"You're welcome to come to my folks' house with Gracie and me," Zack offered, his expression hopeful.

"That's really sweet of you, but I couldn't impose on your family like that." Emma hadn't even met Zack's parents yet, so she couldn't imagine just showing up to their Thanksgiving dinner.

"Impose? You obviously don't know my mother. She *lives* to feed people, Em. Believe me, she would be thrilled to have you there."

"But what about Gracie?"

Zack pulled her onto his lap. "Em, my daughter loves you. Of course she would want you to come."

Wait a minute—loves? Emma's throat closed up.

"Unless you don't want to…"

"No, no, I'll come," she said. "Will there be a lot of people there?"

"Yes, if my mom has her way. You'll even get to meet Damian. He's flying in from California, and he'll be here through the holidays. I offered to let him stay with me, but he hasn't given me an answer yet."

All of a sudden, Emma sat up straight and covered her mouth with her hand.

"What is it?" Zack asked, alarmed at her expression.

"I don't think I can come after all."

"Why not?"

"Because I just remembered a conversation I had with Kelly last week. Her parents usually fly up from Florida, but her father's been ill, and they might not make it this year. I'd feel terrible if she were alone on Thanksgiving."

Zack gave her a reassuring squeeze. "That's no problem. We'll invite her too."

Emma smacked her lips on his in rapid succession. "Really? Thank you, thank you, thank you!"

"How about if you continue thanking me upstairs?" He stood up with Emma securely in his arms and headed toward the stairs.

"How much time do we have left?"

He glanced at his wristwatch. "One hour."

"That'll work," she said and nuzzled against him.

Zack set her down once they reached her bedroom, and they both hurried to undress. They stood in the middle of the room, facing each other with their clothes pooled at their feet, and simply admired each other for a few beats.

"I will never get tired of looking at you," Zack said, his voice reverberating through her.

Emma closed the distance between them and wrapped her arms around his waist. She breathed in his all-male scent of spice and musk and gazed into his smoky gray eyes. "You're not so bad yourself," she whispered.

Zack hoisted her up so that her legs wrapped around his waist and backed them up to the bed. Instead of lying back, he perched on the edge, holding her firmly in his grip. Emma tingled with anticipation. Their lovemaking had become more intense as of late, and she basked in it. She wasn't sure if it was because their time was limited, or if it was because they were becoming more comfortable with each other. Whatever the reason, she embraced it and matched his passion with equal fervor.

Zack put his hands on her breasts and plucked at her nipples while they both watched. Emma sucked in a breath when he leaned down and pulled on first one and then the other with his mouth.

"So beautiful," he murmured.

Emma slid her hands into his thick mass of hair and massaged his scalp while he continued to use his hands and mouth on her. Her hips started moving of their own accord, and his hardness pressed against her belly.

Zack slid one hand between her legs and strummed her until Emma felt her whole body pulse with need. Her breathing became shallow, and she felt light-headed, but Zack had a good grip on her, and she trusted that he wouldn't let her fall.

"Hands on my shoulders and lean up a little," Zack demanded, his voice husky with desire.

Emma did as he asked and came up on her knees. Zack positioned himself at her entrance and slowly slid into place, filling her to the hilt.

"Ok?" he asked.

"Yes," she panted.

Emma squeezed her fingers into Zack's broad shoulders and held on tight. She was aware of his large hands on her hips, guiding her up and slowly back down again, over and over, bringing her to the brink and then easing off. Her head tilted back, and his lips were against her throat, warm and moist, kissing and nibbling.

She opened her eyes for a brief second and spotted the condom packet on the nightstand, just out of reach. But now Zack's hand was back between her legs, and the combination was too much. She couldn't stop—didn't want to stop.

Zack pulled his head away from her chest and gazed up at her, longingly, lovingly. "Em?"

She knew what he was asking, but at that moment, she was fearless. "Safe time of the month. Please... don't... stop," she groaned.

Stars, sparks, flames... it was the most intense experience she had ever had. She lost herself completely in that moment, and Zack followed right behind. They tumbled back on the bed together and waited for the tremors to subside. They clung to each other as if they could fuse together, and Emma felt the words bubble up in her throat and threaten to spill out.

I love this man. I truly, madly, deeply love this man. But I can't say it. Not yet. It's too soon, isn't it? Emma swallowed her words and nuzzled into his neck, pressing her lips against his warm skin to prevent her mouth from opening.

Zack rubbed his hand gently up and down her back and breathed deeply.

Whenever Zack was silent for long, it unnerved her. *Is he holding back too?* She decided to wait it out a little longer, and then…

"Emma, I want to tell you something."

She pulled her head out of his neck to look into his eyes, which, if she weren't mistaken, looked a little watery.

"Tell me," she managed.

"I…"

Brrring, brrring, brrring. Zack's phone buzzed insistently in his pants pocket.

"Shit," he muttered and scrambled off the bed.

Emma sat up against the headboard and waited.

"What? Wait. Slow down and tell me what happened."

Oh my God, Gracie. Emma jumped off the bed and started pulling on her clothes.

Zack tucked the phone in his neck and yanked his pants on.

"I'll be right there," he said and hung up.

"Is it Gracie?" Emma couldn't hide the panic in her voice.

"That was Alicia. Gracie fell off the monkey bars at Depot Park. She's at the emergency clinic in town. I have to go."

Emma followed him out of the room while he pulled his shirt on. "Is she ok? Zack? I want to go with you."

They were at the front door now, and Zack shoved his feet into his shoes. "No, Em. Just stay here. I'll call you," he said and raced out the door.

Emma crossed her arms over her chest from the chill that she felt in the open doorway. She watched Zack tear out of her driveway and hugged herself even tighter. "Please be ok, please be ok," she chanted.

She closed the door and leaned heavily against it. "I love her too," she said before she slumped to the floor, put her head in her hands, and cried.

Ten minutes later, Emma was in her car speeding toward the clinic. She didn't care if Zack was going to be mad; she had to find out about Gracie. Emma parked next to his Range Rover and raced into the clinic. Zack and Alicia sat side by side on the hard plastic chairs with their heads bent together, talking quietly. They both glanced up and noticed Emma at the same time.

"I had to come," she said unapologetically.

Zack motioned to the chair next to him, and when Emma sat down, he leaned over and gave her a brief kiss on the cheek. Emma caught Alicia's watchful stare over Zack's shoulder before quickly looking away.

"How is she?" Emma asked.

"They're taking x-rays of her right arm to see if it's broken," Zack replied.

"Won't they let you back there?"

Alicia bent her head down and wrung her hands. "It's my fault. The x-ray technician asked us to wait out here because I was crying like an idiot. She didn't want me to scare Gracie."

Zack laid his hand gently on Alicia's back, but then he quickly pulled it away. "Don't beat yourself up about it, Alicia. I'm sure a lot of parents react that way."

Instead of feeling jealous, Emma felt proud of the way Zack spoke to his ex-wife. He obviously put a lot of effort into keeping their relationship congenial for Gracie. It was just one more thing that she loved about him.

Just then, a female doctor poked her head into the waiting room and said, "Gracie's parents can come back now."

Zack and Alicia immediately stood up, while Emma remained seated. They took two steps away before Zack turned back and held out his hand to her.

"But?"

"I'm certain that Gracie would like to see you too," Zack said firmly.

Alicia raised her eyebrows, but Zack purposely ignored her and pulled Emma along behind them. They followed the doctor into the exam room, where Gracie was contentedly licking a purple sucker. Her right arm was in a sling, but other than that, she looked perfectly fine.

"Miss Emma! You're here too!" Gracie said enthusiastically.

Emma walked over and gave Gracie a careful hug. "I was worried about you," she said with a catch in her voice.

"I'm fine! I get to wear this sling, and the doctor said I can't do any work at school."

Her pronouncement caused a round of laughter among the adults.

"Gracie should avoid using her right hand for a few days, but she can still go to school," the doctor clarified.

The doctor went on to explain the results of the x-ray and gave instructions for Gracie's follow-up care while Emma let her thoughts wander. She was so grateful that Gracie was ok that she found herself tearing up again. *So this is what it feels like to love a child. How amazing! If I feel this strongly about Gracie, I can only imagine what it will feel like to have my own child someday.*

Zack's voice broke her train of thought. "Thank you, doctor. We appreciate you taking such good care of her."

The four of them walked out of the clinic together, but Emma stood back while Alicia said goodbye to Gracie.

"Mommy loves you, baby girl." She hugged Gracie on her left side and then turned to Zack.

"Call me tomorrow so we can make arrangements for her follow-up appointment."

"I will," Zack said, and they all waved as Alicia drove away.

"Can Miss Emma come over and watch a movie with us tonight?" Gracie asked, her eyes wide with hopefulness.

"I think you've had enough excitement for one night," Zack said and ruffled Gracie's hair.

"But Daaaad…"

Emma crouched down and laid her hands on Gracie's shoulders. "Your dad's right, Gracie. You need to go home and rest, but how about if I come over and visit you tomorrow?"

"Ok," she said and then popped the sucker back into her mouth.

After Zack tucked Gracie into the car, he walked Emma around to the opposite side of the Range Rover, where she had parked. Emma couldn't help it. She flung her arms around his neck and hugged him tight. Zack's arms went around her waist willingly.

"I'm so glad she's ok," Emma whispered against his chest.

"Me too," he said softly. "Thanks for being here."

"Thank you for not being mad that I came."

Zack chuckled. "Why would I be mad? I love being with you, Em."

She lifted her head, and they exchanged a look that acknowledged just how close those words were to "I love you."

"I love being with you too," she said. *Baby steps.*

"I should get Gracie home." He gave her a brief kiss on the cheek and broke their hold.

Emma waved while they drove away, and she couldn't help but wish that she were going home with them.

CHAPTER 34

"I can't believe you talked me into this," Kelly grumbled.

"I didn't think you'd want to be alone on Thanksgiving," Emma replied.

"It doesn't sound so bad now. There must be thirty cars here."

Emma and Kelly had followed Zack and Gracie to his parents' house on Whipple Lake. When they exited the car, Emma looked around with appreciation. The house was a sprawling ranch surrounded by a copse of trees, with the lake glimmering in the background.

"Thirty is an exaggeration, Kell. Just come in and eat with us, and then you can sneak out whenever you want."

"You ready to meet my family?" Zack asked when they joined him and Gracie on the porch.

"Sure," Emma said enthusiastically before shooting Kelly a look that warned, "Not a word."

When Zack pushed open the door, all of Emma's senses were assaulted at once. First, the smells: sage, pepper, nutmeg, and cinnamon. Then the sounds: loud, raucous laughter and high-pitched chatter. The foyer bled into the large, open living area, and twenty-five heads turned toward them at once. The sounds faded as if someone had lowered the volume on a radio.

A pleasantly plump woman with pitch-black hair and a ready smile approached them first. She gathered Gracie into a tight hug and said, "How's Nana's little girl?" Before Gracie could respond, she cupped Gracie's face and kissed first one cheek and then the other. When she finished, she repeated the process with Zack.

"Ma, I'd like you to meet Emma and her friend Kelly."

Emma immediately stuck out her hand, but Zack's mom used it to pull her in for a hearty hug.

"It's nice to meet you, dear. My name is Alexandra, but everyone calls me Alex. Welcome to our home."

The woman exuded such warmth that Emma couldn't help but smile. Kelly stood a couple of steps behind Emma to shield herself from the onslaught, but it was to no avail.

Alex pulled her in for a hug as well, and then she motioned them into the living room, where they were greeted by twenty-some inquisitive pairs of eyes.

To save Emma from individual introductions, Zack swept his arm around the room and announced, "Everyone, this is Emma and her friend Kelly."

Hellos and nods greeted them from around the room before the guests returned to their conversations.

Gracie ran off to join a board game in progress, and Zack scanned the area. "There they are," he said and grabbed Emma's hand. "I want you to meet my dad and brother."

Kelly tagged along behind them while they crossed the room. There, leaning against an oversized picture window with an extensive view of the lake, stood the men Zack wanted them to meet.

"Son," Zack's dad said by way of greeting. "Good to see you."

"Dad, I wanted to personally introduce you to Emma," Zack said proudly.

Mr. Kostas was almost as tall as Zack, and he sported a full head of salt-and-pepper hair. When he shook Emma's hand, she looked directly into a pair of light gray eyes that were identical to Zack's.

"Welcome to the nut house," he teased, clasping her hand in both of his. "I'm Joe." Kelly was hiding behind Emma again, but Joe leaned around Emma and gave her a little wave. "Brave girl," he added, pointing at Kelly. His jokey, easygoing manner immediately put them at ease, and Kelly cracked her first real smile since entering the house.

Kelly's smile turned into something else entirely when the man who had been standing with his back to them a moment ago, turned around.

Oh boy. Emma knew that look, and she tried to send Kelly a silent warning but failed to get her attention.

"And this is my brother, Damian," Zack said.

Damian tackled his brother, going so far as to lift him right off the floor, which couldn't have been an easy feat. They hugged each other hard before Damian unceremoniously set him back down.

Holy Greek God number two! Damian was a couple of inches shorter than Zack, but what he lacked in height, he more than made up for in muscle. He wore a short-sleeve t-shirt printed with the slogan "Pete's Custom Motors" above the image of a classic car. Emma noticed the edge of a tattoo peeking out from his right sleeve, and judging from the look on Kelly's face, she had noticed it too. Damian was basically an edgier version of Zack, with longer, messier inky black hair, a smattering of facial hair, and an "I'm sexy and I know it" attitude.

"Emma and Kelly, right?" he said, pointing to each of them in turn.

They both nodded, and he smiled even wider, showing off each and every one of his pearly whites. "Nice to meet you, ladies."

Zack thumped him on the chest with his fist. "You never answered my email, jerk. Are you staying with me and Gracie or not?"

Damian's eyes honed right in on Kelly, and he drawled, "Yeah, I think I'll stick around for a while."

Emma glanced back and forth between Damian and Kelly, and then she exchanged a knowing look with Zack.

"Hey, Em. Why don't I show you around the house? Damian, you mind keeping Kelly company for a few minutes?"

"It would be my *pleasure*," Damian replied without taking his eyes off of Kelly.

Zack took Emma's hand and pulled her down a hall that led to the bedrooms.

"Holy shit," she said when they were out of earshot. "Your brother is…"

"Hot? Yeah, I know. He's always been popular with the ladies."

Emma peeked into the doorway of one of the bedrooms, and finding it empty, she pulled Zack inside. She closed the door and leaned against it, motioning for him to step closer. "I wasn't going to say hot, although he is very good looking."

Zack's eyebrows raised while he waited for her to continue.

"Of course, he's nowhere *near* as handsome as you."

"That's better," Zack teased, and he pressed her against the door.

"What I was going to say is that your brother is Kelly's fantasy guy come to life. Did you see the way they looked at each other? Now that was hot!"

Zack put his index finger underneath her chin and tilted her face upward. "Kind of like the way I look at you, huh?" He trailed his finger down her neck and along the collar of her sweater dress. Kelly had insisted that they both dress up for the occasion, and Emma had chosen a cozy, ivory-colored sweater dress with a saddle-brown pair of knee-high boots. The dress skimmed over her petite body without being overtly sexy, and apparently, it had been a good choice, because Zack eyed her like a slice of pumpkin pie.

"We should probably get back out there," Emma said half-heartedly with her eyes trained on Zack's lips.

He had one hand braced against the door above her head, and the other had trailed down her side and now rested on her hip.

"Yes, we probably should," he said before taking her mouth in a demanding kiss. His hand wandered to her backside, and he pushed her hips against his. Their tongues tangled for a few seconds before they both became aware of voices in the hallway. They froze until the sound drifted away, and then Emma broke out in giggles.

"Come on," he said resignedly. "Let's go see if dinner's ready."

Emma and Zack sat next to each other at one of the two rectangular tables that had been set up in the spacious kitchen. Kelly sat on the other side of Emma, and Damian sat directly across from her. Gracie sat at a small "kid's table" that was set up nearby.

Emma kept sneaking glances at Kelly and Damian while dish after dish of mouthwatering foods were passed around the table. The conversation was lively, just as Zack had described in Chicago. Emma listened in and nodded politely, but it was difficult to follow any one conversation for long. Zack squeezed her knee under the table a few times to offer reassurance, but Emma enjoyed all of the activity. Everyone appeared to be having a great time, and the food was absolutely delicious. Zack was right; his mom did love to feed people, as was evident on Alex's glowing face.

After dinner, most of the men retired to the living room to watch football. Emma encouraged Zack to join them while she offered to help his mom clean up. Zack winked at her and hurriedly left the kitchen like he had just been given a free hall pass.

"I raised him better than that," Alex said, shaking her head while repressing a smile.

Emma wasn't sure how to respond. She wanted to tell Alex that her son cooked for Emma quite often—and cleaned up too—but how much had Zack shared about their relationship? Emma just smiled instead and concentrated on clearing the dirty dishes from the table. One of Zack's aunts helped as well, but Kelly was nowhere to be seen.

"So, Emma, how did you and Zack meet?" Alex asked innocently while she rinsed the dishes.

"Well, we first met about five years ago at my cousin's wedding, but then we ran into each other again about four months ago."

"Ah, yes, at the bookstore, right?"

So she does know some of the details after all. "Yes," Emma replied and handed Alex another plate.

"Gracie just loves books," Alex said conversationally.

"That makes two of us," Emma replied.

"She likes you a lot, you know."

Something in Alex's voice made Emma stop what she was doing. *Why does it sound like Alex is issuing a warning? Is she afraid that I might hurt her granddaughter the way that her ex-daughter-in-law did?*

"I care about her too," Emma began, and then she blurted, "I care about both of them."

Suddenly she realized that it was just the two of them in the kitchen. Alex turned away from the sink to face her.

"I'm sure you do, dear. Please forgive me for being an overprotective grandma. I just don't want to see my little girl get hurt again."

Although it made her feel slightly uncomfortable, Emma appreciated Alex's honesty. "I understand completely, and I have no intention of hurting either one of them."

Alex's face instantly relaxed, and she broke out in a trademark Kostas smile. "I believe you," she said.

Emma accepted Alex's remark as a stamp of approval, and they finished cleaning the kitchen in companionable silence until Gracie wandered in.

She tugged on Emma's dress and said, "Daddy wants you to come and watch football with him."

"Tell him I'll be right there," Emma replied before Gracie raced back out of the room.

Emma wiped her hands on a towel and met Alex's eyes. "You have a wonderful family," she said, and then she hurried out of the room before Alex could see the tears that had welled up in her eyes.

CHAPTER 35

The day after Thanksgiving, also known as Black Friday, brought in a steady stream of customers to A New Chapter. Emma, Kelly, and Brett were kept busy all day long with only a short break for lunch, which Zack and Gracie had kindly brought in.

"Guess what, Miss Emma? We're going Christmas shopping with Uncle Damian, and he's going to let me pick out my own Christmas present!"

Emma looked to Zack for confirmation, and he nodded in response.

"Well, what are you going to look for?" Emma asked with genuine interest.

"A puppy!"

"Oh no," Zack said. "We've already talked about this, Gracie. I said no pets until you're a little older."

"But Daaaad…"

Emma restrained herself from chiming in, but she had an idea that she would share with Zack later. "Maybe you could look for another doll instead,"

Emma suggested, and Zack gave her an appreciative nod.

"I already have a lot of dolls," Gracie replied.

Emma gave her a squeeze and said, "I'm sure whatever Uncle Damian buys you will be great."

Emma walked them to the door and automatically leaned in to kiss Zack goodbye, but he shot her a warning look. Emma didn't hide her dismay, and she was certain that Zack was aware of it when he left the store. *When will it be ok to show affection in front of Gracie?* They had certainly been spending a lot of time together, the three of them, and they had hugged in front of Gracie plenty of times. *Why is Zack still holding back? Is there some other reason that I don't know about?*

"Em, we need you over here," Kelly called, breaking Emma's chain of worrisome thoughts.

I'll talk to him about it tonight, she decided and delved back into her work.

It wasn't until eight o'clock that night that business slowed down enough for Emma and Kelly to chat. Emma had let Brett leave an hour earlier because he had "a hot date," which left her and Kelly and a few last-minute customers.

"So whatever happened with Luke?" Emma asked when they had perched on the stools behind the counter.

"The history teacher?" Kelly acted like she couldn't remember.

"Yeah. Was he as *worldly* as you thought he'd be?"

"I decided that history is kind of boring. It was never my favorite subject in school."

Emma laughed out loud and shook her head. "Have you decided that a certain custom car builder is more to your liking?"

Kelly's eyes twinkled, and her face lit up. "Perhaps."

"Hmm… so let's see, being a car builder makes him…"

"Skilled with his hands! What else can I say, Em? He's yummy!"

"So, Zack's delicious, and Damian's yummy. Maybe what you really need is a pastry chef!"

"Joke all you want, but we're going out tomorrow night," Kelly said haughtily.

"Do you really think that's a good idea, Kell? You know that Damian is only going to be around for a few weeks, right?"

"Yeah, so?"

"So, what's the point of it? What if you fall for him, and then he leaves?"

Kelly looked down and picked at a loose thread on her skirt. "I'm not looking for forever, Em. I'm not like you. I don't need hearts and flowers and white picket fences. I'm a good-time girl. If Damian and I have fun for a few weeks, that's good enough for me."

Emma sighed. *When will Kelly stop trying to hide behind this false persona that she's created? I know she's a true romantic at heart. When will she stop bluffing and just admit it?*

"Just be careful, ok?"

"I'll be fine, Em. I promise."

Emma tried to call Zack on her way home from the bookstore, but he didn't answer. "I guess you're still out shopping," she said aloud when she set the phone down. A few minutes later, she pulled up to find his Range Rover parked in her driveway. The lights from her car illuminated his outline where he leaned casually against his vehicle, and her body tightened with anticipation.

"Hey," Emma said once she got out of her car. "I tried calling you."

"I know. I was sitting right here."

"Why didn't you answer?"

"Because I wanted to surprise you."

Emma couldn't read his expression in the dark, but the desire in his voice was impossible to miss.

"I'm glad you're here," she stated. *Stay strong, Emma. Resist, resist, resist.*

"I was hoping that you'd say that."

"So we can talk," she said firmly.

"Oh."

Emma couldn't help but giggle when he visibly deflated before her eyes. "Come on in," she said.

She grabbed a bottle of water for her and a beer for him and led them into the living room.

Zack didn't waste any time with small talk. "Did I screw up again? Because I didn't bring any food," he added, attempting to distract her with humor.

Emma refused to give in to his charm. "I wanted to talk about Gracie. Don't you think she's smart enough to understand that we like each other—a lot?"

"Well, yeah, probably…"

"And don't you think she's getting used to seeing us together and touching on occasion?"

"Yes…"

"So why did you pull away when I tried to kiss you earlier? It's not like I planned on making out with you. I just wanted to give you a simple goodbye kiss."

Zack shrugged. "I don't have a good answer, Em. I guess I was just being overprotective. I don't want to cause Gracie any unhappiness. Any *more* unhappiness that is."

"And you think that I do?"

"No, I didn't say that."

"I love that little girl, and I think that she can handle a lot more than you give her credit for. I don't think that seeing us kiss is going to send her into a tailspin."

"You're probably right, but I should have a talk with her first."

"That sounds like a great idea. What will you say?"

"I'll start by reassuring her about how much I love her. Correction, how much we *all* love her: me, you, and Alicia. Then I'll explain how I feel about you."

How do you feel about me? Tell me, Zack. Their eyes locked, and he held out a hand to her, which she immediately clasped.

"Am I forgiven?" Zack asked, adopting a hopeful expression.

Baby steps, Emma reminded herself, and she pulled him toward her. Zack's arms wrapped around her, and she breathed him in. "Where's Gracie tonight?" It was better to ask before they got too carried away.

"With Damian," Zack mumbled against her hair.

"For the whole night?" She moved onto his lap.

"For a couple hours," he said apologetically, shifting her so that her legs wrapped around his waist.

"Superman boxers?" She quirked her eyebrows at him.

"You'll have to find out," he replied, and he stood up with her still seated around his waist.

"Where to?" he asked gruffly.

"The bathtub," Emma replied without hesitation.

"Hmm... sounds wet."

"I feel dirty from working all day," Emma said, letting the fog of lust settle around her.

"Well, then, let's clean you up."

Emma turned on the water and poured in a capful of vanilla-scented bubble bath. She was acutely aware of Zack undressing behind her, and when she turned around, he was already naked. Gloriously, happily, fully-at-attention naked.

"Great, now I'm going to smell like a woman," Zack said, hands on his hips, peering around her at the bubbles that were multiplying in the tub.

"Oops, sorry. I'm not used to having a man in my tub."

"Well, get used to it, because I'm getting in!"

Zack left her standing there fully dressed while he quickly immersed himself in the water. He leaned his head back against the tub and smirked at her. "What are you waiting for?"

Emma had been so mesmerized by the sight of him that she stood there mute, but now she snapped out of it. She pulled her sweater over her head and laid it gently on the bathroom counter. Next, she removed her skirt and tights, completely aware of Zack's eyes upon her. She unhooked her bra and slid it off her shoulders, and his gasp made her look up. His eyes were glazed over, and he motioned for her to continue. Emma slowly slid her panties down her legs and stepped out of them to the sound of his long, low whistle. Feeling giddy from all the attention, she finished her striptease with a flair by turning around in a slow circle and ending with a bow.

Zack chuckled appreciatively while she lowered herself into the water and leaned her back against his soapy chest. "You enjoyed that, didn't you?" he teased.

"Maybe a little," she admitted. "But more importantly, did you?"

"Loved it," he whispered into her ear.

The little puff of air in her ear trailed throughout her body and caused an instant flare of heat. Zack ran his warm, soapy hands down her shoulders and arms until he reached her hands. Their fingers entwined, and he brought their clasped hands up to her breasts, where he began massaging them in a circular motion. The water rippled around them, and Emma's nipples peaked in their hands. Her breath came in short pants when Zack slid their combined hands over her stomach and further down.

Emma started to protest and tried to untangle her right hand from Zack's grip, but he kept it firmly in place. The combination of the warm, steamy bath and the feel of his large, masculine fingers fondling her under the water had her so taut with need that it wasn't long before she found release. Her body was still pulsating when she sagged back against Zack's chest and let out a long sigh.

Zack pulled her hair off to one side so he could nuzzle her neck and then asked, "Feeling cleaner now?"

Emma shook her head. "No, I still feel *dirty*."

Zack's head snapped back when she twisted in his arms to face him. She balanced on his muscular thighs and reached under the water. It didn't take long to find what she was looking for, and Zack moaned when she clasped him with both hands. The suds had dissipated some, and they both looked down to watch what Emma was doing to him. After a few minutes, Zack said amidst a groan, "Em, we need to get out of here or…"

She let go of him and patted the edge of the tub.

He raised his eyebrows at her, and she said, "Just sit."

Zack perched himself on the edge of the tub, and Emma scooted up between his legs. She took him in her hands again before bending her head over him.

The sounds of Zack's pleasure filled the steamy bathroom while Emma ministered to him with her mouth and hands. When it was over, she sat back on her haunches in the lukewarm water and grinned like a Cheshire cat.

Zack gave her his own brand of smile in return. "Ya know, I decided that I like baths. No more showers. Just baths from now on."

Emma stood, dripping wet, and pointed to the towel bar behind him. Zack pulled two towels down and handed her one before wrapping the other around his waist. "So *baths* are your new favorite?" she teased.

"Everything with you is my favorite," he replied, and he pulled her in for a hug.

Emma leaned her head against his chest and breathed the scent of vanilla and raw masculinity. *If Bath and Body Works could bottle this, they'd make a fortune,* she mused.

Shortly after, Emma wore her sleepshirt, and Zack had redressed in his jeans and sweatshirt. They leaned against her front door to say their goodbyes.

"Will you bring Gracie to story time tomorrow?"

"Of course."

"I have to work until five."

"We could go out to dinner after."

"Can Gracie come too?"

"Sure."

Emma tilted her head up, and Zack immediately covered her lips with his. They were still warm from the bath, and Emma threaded her fingers into Zack's still-damp hair.

When he pulled back, they were breathless. "I don't like goodbyes," she stated.

"I know," he said, his hands still locked around her waist.

"I wish you could stay."

"Me too."

There was so much more to say, but they had already used up the allotted time. As if to remind them, Zack's phone buzzed. He pulled it out of his pocket and read Damian's text message.

"Gracie's waiting for me to tuck her in," Zack said. "You ok?"

"Yes, of course. I'm used to being alone." Good thing it was too dark for him to see her forced smile.

"I'll see you in the morning." He bent down and gave her one last kiss before walking out the door.

"It won't be soon enough," Emma said to the quiet house, and then she trudged up the stairs alone.

CHAPTER 36

A few days later, Zack found a quiet time to talk to Gracie about Emma. Damian was out, presumably with Kelly, and Emma was working, so that left Zack and Gracie home alone.

Gracie sat on the couch, flipping through a new Little Critter book that Emma had recently given her. Zack sat down beside her, and she snuggled close.

"Will you read to me, Daddy?" she asked politely.

"I will in a minute. First, I want to talk to you about something."

"Ok," she said, and she shifted her little body to face him.

Zack reached out and ran his hand over her wavy dark hair. As often as he'd looked into his daughter's eyes, he couldn't get over the fact that she was his. Even though he was no longer with Alicia, he would always be grateful for the beautiful gift that she'd given him.

"Gracie," he began, feeling uncertain of how to proceed. "How do you feel about Miss Emma?"

"I love Miss Emma," she replied immediately. "She's pretty and funny, and she tells the best stories. Better than you, Dad."

Zack chuckled at her honesty. "Well, I like her a lot too, but you probably already know that, right?"

"Um-hmm," Gracie nodded.

"And you don't mind that she spends a lot of time with us?"

"I wish she could stay here all the time!"

Gracie's admission caught him off guard, and he swallowed around the large lump in his throat.

"Do you really mean that, Gracie?"

She nodded again.

"I want you to know something. Someday, *if* Miss Emma stays here all the time, that doesn't mean that she's trying to take Mommy's place." Zack cleared his throat, thinking that this was a lot harder than he imagined it to be. Not for Gracie, but for him. "You already have a Mommy, and she loves you very very much, but Miss Emma loves you too. Do you understand?"

"Kind of like Robby. He has two daddies, his real one and his other one that drives him to school."

When Gracie said that, Zack realized that a lot of other kids were in the same situation as her. He had been so caught up in trying to shield Gracie that he hadn't even considered that she'd be exposed to the topic of divorce with or without his protection.

"Yes, kind of like that."

"If I get to have another mom, I hope it will be Miss Emma," Gracie said solemnly.

Zack gathered her in his lap and held her close. "I hope so too," he said, and he realized in that moment, just how much he meant it.

"Can I go play now, Dad?" Gracie had already squirmed off of his lap and was halfway up the stairs.

"Yes," he replied. "Thanks for the talk," he added when he heard her bedroom door slam.

"Does Emma know that you love her?"

Zack jerked his head around at the sound of Damian's gruff voice. "Dude, you almost gave me a heart attack. Don't sneak up on me like that."

Damian sauntered into the room and plopped down on the reclining chair. "You didn't answer my question."

"Not yet," Zack replied, settling back on the couch.

"What are you waiting for?"

"Easy for you to say, Mr. Footloose-and-fancy-free."

Damian cocked an eyebrow at him. "Hey, man, if you're off the market, that's one less guy for me to have to compete with for the ladies."

"Yeah, right. You and I don't even travel in the same circles, bro."

"That could change," Damian said, rubbing a hand over his stubbly face.

"What do you mean?"

"I mean that I might move back here."

Zack sat up straight. "Here? As in Michigan? Or as in my house?"

Damian chuckled. "Are you kidding? We would kill each other if I moved in with you. I'm thinking about moving back to Michigan, maybe even to Clarkston."

His news came as a big surprise, and Zack wasn't quite sure how to respond. "Do Mom and Dad know about this?"

"Not yet."

"This doesn't have anything to do with Kelly, does it?"

"Hell no. She's hot, but I just met her. I've been tossing the idea around for a while now."

Zack loved his brother, but he realized just how little he really knew him these days. Damian had moved to California shortly after Zack and Alicia were married, and he had only seen him occasionally since then. He'd heard snippets of news from his parents, but Zack was too busy with his own life to pay much attention. If Damian moved back home, it would probably be a good thing, not just for Zack, but for Gracie too. She seemed to have a soft spot for her secretive uncle.

"What would you do for a living?" Zack asked with genuine curiosity.

"Same thing I've been doing. Work on cars. Maybe open my own shop."

"Really? Wow, that's ambitious of you."

"I have goals too, you know," Damian said snidely.

Zack quickly realized his mistake. He knew that Damian wasn't lazy, but he didn't know much about his work. "Maybe I could help you out."

"How?"

"Well, I'm a financial guy. I could help you get your finances in order or get a business loan—things like that."

Damian shot him a wide smile. "Yeah, maybe," he said. "But do me a favor. Don't mention this to Mom or Dad or your future wife. I'm not ready for anyone to know yet."

Zack's mind went blank because all he heard was "future wife, future wife, future wife."

It had a nice ring to it, he had to admit, but was he ready? And, more importantly, was she?

CHAPTER 37

It was Thursday evening, one week prior to Christmas, and Emma and Kelly were getting ready to meet Zack and Damian at Hilltop Brewery, a popular bar/restaurant that had recently opened in Clarkston. Emma had been working such long hours that she really looked forward to a night out. Apparently, Kelly felt the same. She had changed clothes in the office and strutted out in a corduroy mini-skirt, high-heeled ankle boots, tights, and a V-neck angora sweater that showed off her... assets.

Kelly's appearance made Emma feel ultra-conservative in her knee-length plaid shirtdress and low-heeled leather boots. When they walked into the restaurant, Zack's eyes lit up at the sight of her, so Emma decided that her outfit wasn't so bad after all. Damian's eyes also sparked as he scanned Kelly from head to toe and back again. They squeezed into the booth next to their dates and settled in for a relaxed evening.

A waitress delivered glasses of water and took their order for appetizers and a pitcher of beer. The four of them talked easily about work, the upcoming holidays, and, of course, Gracie.

"She's with Nana and Papa tonight, but tomorrow is a school day, so I have to pick her up by nine," Zack said.

Emma had been contemplating what to give Gracie for Christmas, and she decided that now was just as good a time as any to bring up her idea. "Zack, remember the other day when Gracie mentioned that she wanted a puppy?"

"Oh no," Zack replied, shaking his head emphatically. "I already told her no pets until she's old enough to take care of one."

Damian grunted. "Dude, you're so uptight," he said, and Kelly suppressed a giggle.

"Hey, it's hard enough taking care of a four-year-old; I don't want to add a puppy to the mix!"

Emma squeezed his arm to regain his attention. "Wait, I have another idea. There's this cat that's been hanging around behind the bookstore, and..."

"A cat?"

"Yes, and I think it's homeless. Some of the other store owners in the plaza have asked around, but nobody's claimed it. What if..."

"I can see where this is going," Zack said, fighting not to smile.

"It's an adorable cat," Kelly piped in. "I bet Gracie would love it."

"And cats don't require as much work as dogs," Emma added. "As long as it has some food and a litter box, it'll be fine."

"What about scratching things and coughing up hair balls?"

"Geez, bro, lighten up," Damian said, obviously enjoying Zack's discomfort.

Glancing around the table, Zack must have felt outnumbered. He looked in Emma's pleading eyes and said, "I'll think about it."

"Yay!"

"But you need to make some more inquiries first. I don't want to give Gracie a cat only to find out that it belongs to someone else."

"We can also take it to the vet and get it checked out," Kelly offered, just as enthused by the idea as Emma.

"Looks like you're about to get a cat!" Damian said, flashing his toothy grin.

Emma glanced over at Kelly, who had her eyes trained on Damian's mouth. *Oh boy, Kelly has it bad! Almost as bad as I do for Zack.*

When the appetizers arrived, Emma took a few bites and felt her stomach contract. She hadn't said anything, but she had felt queasy on and off all day. At first, she'd blamed it on the Mexican food that Kelly had brought in for lunch, but that was hours ago. Emma set the mozzarella stick back on her plate and sipped some water. The rest of them drank beer, but just the smell of it made her stomach clench.

Zack and Damian were too busy talking about football to notice, but Kelly glanced over at Emma's plate and then made eye contact with her. She mouthed, *Are you ok?*

Emma gave her a slight nod and went back to sipping her water. She decided to avoid greasy food and ordered a salad for her main entrée. She picked at it through the remainder of dinner but left most of it on her plate. Finally, Zack looked over and noticed the untouched food.

"Don't you like your salad, Em?"

"It's ok. I'm not that hungry tonight. Kelly and I had a big lunch."

Luckily, the waitress came over to clear the plates, and they moved on to another subject.

"So, Alex and Joe wanted me to officially invite you two over for Christmas dinner," Zack said, motioning to Emma and Kelly.

"Really? How sweet of them." Kelly enthused.

Damian shifted in his seat and shot an undecipherable look at Zack. "That's the first I've heard about this."

Zack returned his gaze and replied, "Mom just mentioned it when I dropped off Gracie."

Emma attempted to dispel the awkward exchange. "Well, tell her that I would love to come."

Zack draped his arm around her shoulders and gave her a squeeze. She leaned into him, her chest tight with emotion. Emma looked forward to spending Christmas with Zack, Gracie, and the rest of his family. It warmed her heart that Alex had thought to invite her.

Kelly, on the other hand, looked distinctly uncomfortable. "If you don't want me to come, just say so," she snapped at Damian.

Damian appeared to be taken aback by her straightforwardness. "Hey, if you can handle the chaos, then by all means, come."

When Kelly didn't look pacified, he added more softly, "I want you to come."

His words did the trick, and the rest of the evening progressed smoothly. Shortly before nine o'clock, Zack announced that he had to leave, and Emma stood up with him. Damian and Kelly decided to stay for one more beer, so Zack and Emma walked out together. Zack followed her to her car and leaned against it.

"It would be nice if we didn't always have to come and go in separate cars," he said while she fished out her keys.

"I agree," she said softly.

Zack pulled her against him and put his lips on hers. Emma opened her mouth to him, vaguely aware of the people that came and went from the busy parking lot. A minute later, they reluctantly parted.

"Hey, did I mention that Gracie is with her mom this weekend?" Zack wiggled his eyebrows suggestively.

Emma giggled. "Yes, you might have mentioned that once or twice. You know that I have to work this weekend, right?"

"I know, but we'll still get some alone time."

"Sounds wonderful," she said and reached up on her tiptoes for another kiss.

Emma's warm feelings morphed into trepidation when she turned into the drugstore parking lot. She sat in her car for a few minutes and breathed deeply. Here she was, a grown woman, afraid to go inside the store. What must a teenager feel like in this situation?

Emma finally went inside and selected two pregnancy test kits. She added a few other items to her cart as if to disguise the real purpose of her visit. A young girl rang up her purchases and didn't even flinch when she handed Emma the bag.

"How ridiculous am I?" Emma said when she drove away. Not since her divorce had she felt this jumble of emotions. She drove home in a fog, collected her mail, and let herself in. Setting her package down on the counter, she checked her phone and discovered that she had two new voicemails.

The first one was from her cousin. *"Hey, Emma, it's Phil. Debbie and I were just wondering what you're doing for Christmas this year. You know you're always welcome to come down and visit us. We'd love to have you. Give me a call."*

The second message was from her mom. *"Hi, Emma, it's Mom. Dad and I plan to arrive two days before Christmas. After we get settled in at the campground, I'll give you a call."*

Oh my God. In all the hustle and bustle, Emma had forgotten about her parents, and now she had already accepted the Kostas's Christmas dinner invitation. Not only was her stomach queasy, but now her head hurt. Afraid to take anything for her headache in case she might be pregnant, Emma decided to head up to bed. According to the instructions on the pregnancy test, it was best to take it in the morning, so there was nothing more to be done tonight.

She had just snuggled under the covers when her phone rang. Despite all of the turmoil going on inside her, she smiled when she answered Zack's call.

"I miss you," he said first thing.

"You just saw me twenty minutes ago."

"Really? It feels like longer than that!"

Emma giggled and warmed at the rich tone of his voice. "I miss you too," she said.

"So what's happened in the twenty minutes since I've seen you?"

If you only knew... "Well, I listened to two voicemails. One from Phil and one from my mom."

"Funny, Phil called me a couple of days ago, but I haven't had a chance to call him back yet. What did he have to say?"

"He invited me to come down to North Carolina for Christmas."

"Hmm. You're going to tell him no, right? Because we're spending Christmas together."

Emma chuckled at the slight panic in Zack's voice. "I'll call him tomorrow and tell him. But about my parents..."

"I know what you're going to say, and it's no problem. You know that Alex will be thrilled to set two more places at the table."

"I don't know, Zack. I understand why they invited me and Kelly, but my parents too? Are you sure?"

"Emma, you were there at Thanksgiving, remember? You saw the joy on my mom's face when you said, 'Pass the stuffing.'"

Emma broke out in a full belly laugh that made her stomach hurt even more. "Ok, ok, I get it. I'll ask my parents when they get here."

"Whew, I'm glad that's settled."

"Speaking of getting settled, I need to get some sleep. I have to work all day tomorrow, and then I have a date with this hot Greek guy that I know."

"Hmm. What does this guy look like?"

"Let's see. He's tall and muscular, and he's got these really gorgeous light gray eyes."

"Sounds dreamy. What else do you like about him?"

"Well, he's caring and generous, and he has a great sense of humor. Not to mention…"

"That he's great in the sack?"

Emma giggled again. "I was going to say that he's a wonderful father."

"So, he's not great in the sack?"

"Goodnight, Zack."

"Seriously? You're going to leave me hanging like that?"

"Alright, fine. He's great in the sack. Correction, he's phenomenal in the sack. How's that?"

"Aah… now I can sleep good."

"Glad to help out."

"Em?"

"Umm-hmm?"

"You're phenomenal too, and I don't just mean in the sack."

"Thanks, Zack."

"I'm not going to say goodbye. I'm just going to say, I'll see you tomorrow."

Tears welled up in Emma's eyes, and she tried to blink them away. "I'll see you tomorrow," she said right before the first tear fell.

CHAPTER 38

Emma's eyes popped open at six o'clock the next morning, and she immediately remembered what she had to do. She shuffled into the bathroom, opened the test kit, and reread the instructions. Five minutes later, she sat on the edge of the tub, clutching the test stick in her trembling hand. Her heart pounded rapidly, and she broke out in a cold sweat. She considered taking the second test just to be sure, but she knew deep down that the first test was accurate. Plus, she could no longer deny the symptoms she'd been having for the past several days.

Emma wished that she felt elated about the news, but at that moment, she felt overwhelmed, scared, and alone. *What will Zack think? He already has Gracie. It's bad timing. How could I have let this happen?*

Emma ran through her list of options. She wasn't ready to tell Zack, Kelly, or her parents, but she desperately needed to talk to someone. She glanced down at her phone, and it struck her: Phil. He was close enough to her to understand, but far enough removed from the situation to be objective. In fact, he had no idea that she and Zack were dating, unless...

"Yes, Em. Zack mentioned that you two were dating," Phil said an hour later, when Emma had awakened him with her phone call.

"What? When?"

"Right before Thanksgiving. I had sent him an email just to check in, and he mentioned that you two were seeing each other."

"Funny, he didn't mention that to me," Emma said, clearly exasperated.

"What are you going to do, Em?"

"I honestly don't know. I'm supposed to see Zack tonight, but I can't. I need some time to process this."

"You're going to have to tell him sometime."

"And I will, but I just need a few days. I need to get my thoughts in order."

"I have an idea."

"I was hoping you'd say that."

"Come down here for the weekend. I'm sure you'd be able to find some last-minute flight deal, and we'd love to see you."

"And I already told Zack that you and Debbie had invited me down... it's perfect!"

"Why don't you check on flights and then let me know once you've figured it out," Phil said, suppressing a yawn.

"Thanks, Phil. Sorry I woke you."

Now that Emma had a plan, she was anxious to execute it. She made her flight reservations and then dialed Kelly. It was eight o'clock, and she was fairly certain that her friend would be up.

Wrongo!

"What happened? Who died?" Kelly answered groggily.

"Nobody died. Why are you still sleeping?"

"Well, I'm *not* sleeping anymore!"

"Sorry. I thought you'd be getting ready for work."

"We don't open until ten. I still have two hours."

Suddenly it struck Emma why Kelly might still be in bed. "Did you stay out late with Damian last night?"

"Maybe," Kelly answered, lowering her voice.

"Oh... my... God. He's there right now, isn't he?"

"Maybe," Kelly repeated, whispering this time.

"Ok, listen Kell. I need you to do me a huge favor, and you can't tell anyone, ok?"

"Of course. What is it?"

"I'm going out of town this weekend, and I need you and Brett to handle the store. I know it's last minute, and I'm sorry to put you out, but I really need your help."

"Hold on," Kelly said.

Emma heard her shuffle around, and a minute later, Kelly was back on the line. "Ok. What's going on, Em?"

"Phil invited me to come down for the weekend, and I decided to take him up on it. I found a last-minute flight deal, and I need to leave for the airport soon, so..."

"Emma Murphy, in all the time we've know each other, you've never once taken a spontaneous trip. Come to think of it, you never do *anything* spontaneously, so why don't you tell me what's really going on?"

Emma let out a long sigh. "I can't talk about it right now, Kell. Please. Will you just do this for me?"

"Ok, fine. But you owe me. Big time!"

"I know, and I promise to make it up to you when I get back."

"What about Zack? What if he comes into the store demanding to know where you are?"

"Don't worry about him. I'll call him from the airport." Emma glanced at the kitchen clock. "Gotta run."

"Call me when you land," Kelly said.

"Will do."

It was just before noon and fifteen minutes prior to boarding time when Emma called Zack. She had rehearsed her words at least a dozen times, but when his voice came over the line she wasn't sure she could go through with it.

"Hey, sexy lady. I didn't expect to hear from you until later. What's all that noise in the background?"

"I'm at the airport."

"The airport? Why? What's going on?"

"Zack, I know this is going to sound crazy, but I decided this morning that I wanted to go to North Carolina and visit Phil. I found a last-minute flight deal, so here I am. But I'll be back on Sunday."

She hoped her last sentence would pacify him, but she should have known better.

"Emma, are you all right? You sound kind of... frazzled."

"Yes, I'm fine, but I probably am a little frazzled. I had to rush like crazy to get here this morning."

"I don't get it, Em. I thought we were going to spend the weekend together. Why the rush to see Phil?"

"I guess I'm just feeling sentimental with the holidays coming and all. You have a big family that you get to see all the time, but I hardly have anyone, Zack. I rarely see my parents, and ever since Phil moved to North Carolina, it's the same with him. Please, try and understand."

Zack was silent for a few beats. "Ok. But I wish you would have talked to me about this sooner. Maybe I would have been able to come with you."

Emma breathed a sigh of relief. It sounded like Zack was going to accept her explanation after all. "I know, and I'm sorry that I won't be with you this weekend, but I really need to do this."

"I miss you already," he said gruffly.

"I miss you too," she said just as an airport employee made the initial boarding call.

"It sounds like you have to go. Call me tonight after you get settled, ok?"

"I will," she said, fighting the urge to cry.

"This isn't goodbye, Em. This is I'll see you soon."

Did he sense her distress? "Ok," she replied, and she hung up before she would be tempted to give her secret away.

Emma's mind whirled during the two-hour flight from Detroit to Charlotte. First, she questioned her decision to run away rather than to face Zack. She had jumped to the conclusion that he would be unhappy with the news, but maybe she was wrong. He was such a loving father to Gracie, so why wouldn't he feel the same about their child? Their child. Wow. It was hard to believe that she was actually pregnant. She had packed the second test kit just in case, but she had already felt nauseous that morning, a telltale sign if ever there was one.

When she thought of the possible reactions that Zack might have, she hoped that he wouldn't feel obligated. He was such a responsible man, which was an admirable quality, but in this case, she didn't want him to feel "responsible" for her and their baby. If they were going to have a future together, she wanted him to be in it all the way.

Emma now understood why Zack was so protective of Gracie, because she felt the same way about their unborn child. She placed a hand over her belly and looked down with tears brimming in her eyes. There was nothing visible—her tummy was still as flat as could be—but she knew that there was a life inside her, and it was the most beautiful feeling in the world. If only Zack were there to share it with her.

CHAPTER 39

Emma found Debbie in the pick-up area at the airport, just as planned. She stepped out of her sporty Audi two-seater and greeted Emma with a warm hug.

"It's so good to see you," Debbie said, and then she popped open the small trunk to stow Emma's bag.

"You too. It's been too long," Emma said, instantly relaxing in Debbie's presence.

Debbie and Phil had met in college and were part of a group of friends that had included Zack. Emma had always thought that Debbie and Phil made the perfect couple. He was energetic and spontaneous, while Debbie was calm and practical. They complimented each other beautifully.

"Thanks for leaving work early to pick me up," Emma said.

"No problem at all. Phil would have come too, but he had a meeting this afternoon. He'll be home for dinner though."

Emma looked out the window for a time as the city of Charlotte gave way to the sprawling suburbs. Even though she was far away from Michigan, she couldn't escape her thoughts of Zack. *I wonder what he's doing right now. Will he go out with Damian tonight or just stay in? Is he thinking about me too?*

"Do you want to talk about it?" Debbie's voice broke through, and Emma turned to face her.

"How much did Phil tell you?"

"He told me that you were pregnant with Zack's child and needed to get away for a few days. I'd guess by the look on your face that there's a lot more to the story though."

Emma put her head in her hands. "I can't believe I let this happen. I'm a grown woman for God's sake. I should have known better."

"Well, if it's any consolation, I can understand why. A man like Zack Kostas could make any woman lose her head—any single woman, I should say." Debbie gave her a broad smile, and Emma emitted a soft laugh.

"So Zack doesn't know yet?"

"No. We had agreed at the beginning that it was too soon for us to have a serious relationship. You know, after our divorces. Plus, there's Gracie to consider. She's been through so much already, and neither of us want to hurt her. We've been taking things slow, and now this happened."

Debbie sat silently for a moment as if she were weighing her words carefully. "Do you love him?"

Emma didn't hesitate. "Yes," she replied, and her heart flooded with emotion. This was the first time that she had acknowledged her feelings out loud, and it felt amazingly good! "I love Zack Kostas," she affirmed.

"Well, then, I think you owe it to him to share your feelings. The only way you're going to find out where he stands is by opening up to him like you just did with me."

"You make it sound so easy," Emma said, nerves fluttering in her stomach.

"Relationships are never easy," Debbie replied as they pulled into her driveway. "But anything worth having is worth fighting for."

Emma's eyes welled up, and a tear escaped. Debbie pretended not to notice when Emma swiped it away.

"Come on in. Let's get you something to eat and drink. You have to take extra good care of yourself now."

Debbie extracted Emma's bag from the trunk and led her directly into the kitchen of the cozy red-bricked bungalow. While Debbie bustled around preparing snacks, Emma checked her phone and found two text messages: one from Kelly and one from Zack.

Kelly: *I know you had to have landed by now, yet you didn't call me as instructed. Please call or text to let me know that you're ok!!!*

Zack: *I know I asked you to call me this evening, but I'd rather not wait that long. Will you please call me as soon as you get to Phil's house? I miss you.*

Emma texted Kelly first. *Sorry I didn't call right away. I'm safely at Phil's. Talk soon. Love you.*

Debbie set out a tray of cheese and crackers and poured a glass of iced tea for each of them. "Zack?"

"He wants me to call him."

Debbie smiled knowingly. "First, eat. Then call the man. Once he finds out that you're pregnant, he'll understand."

Emma made a cheese and cracker sandwich and realized just how hungry she actually was. "I don't think I should break the news over the phone. I'll be back in two days, so I'll tell him then."

"Do you think you can keep it a secret for that long?"

"I'm going to try. I want to be face to face when I give him the news."

Emma took a long swallow of iced tea and sat back. She felt much more relaxed now that she had made up her mind. She and Debbie moved onto other subjects while they nibbled on cheese and crackers.

"Let me show you to the guest room," Debbie suggested once they were finished. "I set you up in the spare bedroom that connects to a bathroom. Just in case you have to get up in the middle of the night!"

How strange. Emma would have to get used to the references about her pregnancy. It still didn't feel real and probably wouldn't for a while yet. Debbie left her to freshen up and closed the door behind her. After using the restroom, Emma sat down on the comfy daybed, took a deep breath, and dialed Zack. He would probably still be at work, but she didn't want to wait any longer.

He answered on the first ring. "Finally. I was about to contact the Charlotte Police Department to hunt you down."

Emma couldn't help but laugh at his overprotectiveness. "Hello to you too."

"Are you at Phil's? Are you ok?"

"Yes, I'm fine. What about you? Still at work?"

"No. I just picked up Gracie, and we're on our way to meet Alicia."

Wait, what?

Zack immediately cleared up her confusion. "Alicia has to work late tonight, so I offered to drive Gracie down to her office instead of waiting for her to get off work."

"Oh. Are you and Damian going out tonight?"

"No. He's hanging out with Kelly, so I'll be on my own."

Emma picked up on the disappointment in his voice. "Sorry, Zack. I didn't intend on..."

"Don't apologize, Em. It's ok. You'll be home in a couple days."

She might have been suspicious about his sudden change of heart, but she knew there was no way that he would drive down to North Carolina to see her. The drive from Detroit to Chicago was one thing, but Detroit to Charlotte... well, that would just be ridiculous!

Just then, she heard Gracie's voice pipe up from the back seat. "I want to talk to Miss Emma. Let me talk, Dad."

Emma smiled at the sound of Gracie's cheerful voice. "Go ahead and put her on, Zack." She heard the sound of the phone changing hands, followed by...

"Guess what, Miss Emma? There's only six more days until Christmas!"

"I know. I bet you're so excited."

"I hope I get a puppy!"

Emma heard Zack's deep voice in the background say, "No puppy until you're at least ten!"

How Emma wished that she were sitting in the front seat of Zack's Range Rover at that very moment. Instead, she was hundreds of miles away, all because she had been too afraid to face him.

"Are you coming to Nana and Papa's house for Christmas?" Gracie asked.

"Yes, of course. I'm looking forward to it."

Satisfied, Gracie said, "Here's Dad."

At the same time, Emma heard Phil's voice drift down the hall. She said, "Zack, I should go. Phil just got home, and I haven't seen him yet."

"Ok, sure. Call me later."

"I will." After Emma hung up, she realized that he purposely hadn't said goodbye.

That evening, after a delicious homemade dinner of pork roast and vegetables, Debbie suggested that Phil and Emma talk while she cleaned up.

Once they were comfortably seated in the living room, Phil said, "So, you and Zack, huh?"

"Quite a surprise, right?"

"No, not really."

Emma's eyes widened. "You're not surprised?"

"No. One, I never expected him and Alicia to last and, two, I saw how enamored he was with you at my wedding."

"Wow, Phil. You never said anything before."

"That's because I couldn't. You were both promised to other people, so what was I supposed to say?"

"Why do I get the feeling that everybody saw the mistakes that he and I were making except for us?"

"Probably not everyone, but maybe the people who were closest to you. I was in a unique position to see things from both sides, but it wasn't my place to do anything about it. Who am I to interfere in someone else's life?"

"So what do you think about me and Zack now?"

Phil leaned forward in his chair and clasped his hands together. He looked Emma directly in the eye and said, "I think that you're perfect for each other."

Tears immediately sprang to her eyes. Emma blamed it on her pregnancy hormones. "Seriously? You're not just saying that to make me feel better?"

"No, Em. I mean it. I love Zack like a brother, and I love you like a... well, like a cousin! I couldn't be happier that you two are together."

Emma let the tears flow freely now, and she flung her arms around Phil's neck. He held her tight and waited for her sobs to subside. A minute or two later, she sat back and accepted the tissue he handed her.

"It was wrong of me to run away from Zack. Not that I don't love being here with you and Debbie, but I should be at home with him and with Gracie."

Phil reached out and took her hand in his. "Don't beat yourself up about it. You're here now, so let's enjoy each other's company. I only get you for two days, but I have a feeling that Zack will have you for the rest of his life."

Emma willed herself not to tear up again. *Is this normal? Are all pregnant women this emotional?* "Thanks, Phil," she managed.

They stayed up talking for a while longer, but Emma was exhausted from her long, emotional day, so she excused herself somewhat early. Truth be told, she was also anxious to call Zack.

He answered in his usual style, by plunging right in with whatever was at the top of mind. "You know what I miss? Besides you, that is."

"What do you miss?" Emma snuggled further under the covers.

"I miss the good old-fashioned TV shows like *Friends* and *Seinfeld*. What's up with all these reality shows?"

"You're just now realizing this? You must not have turned on a television in a while."

"Actually, I haven't, unless it's to watch sports. Other than that, I'd rather read a book."

Emma smiled at their common interest. "So what were you doing when I called— watching TV or reading?"

"I tried both, but I can't seem to concentrate tonight."

"Hmm... and why is that?"

"Because you're too far away from me."

Emma's hand automatically went to her belly, and she choked up.

"It wouldn't be so bad if you were just a mile down the road at work or at home, but you're *hundreds* of miles away, Em."

When she remained silent, he gave a heavy sigh and continued. "Ugh. I promised myself I wouldn't do this. I don't mean to make you feel bad for leaving. I would just rather have you here—with me."

His heartfelt admission made her tongue-tied.

"Damn. You're not talking. Did I screw up again? I screwed up again, didn't I?"

Emma laughed through her tears. "No, you didn't screw up." *I'm the one who screwed up this time.*

"Well, then, say something, Em, anything. Tell me what's on your mind."

Now it was her turn to sigh. "I want to, Zack, I really do, but now is not the right time. I want to wait until we're face to face, and then I'll talk. I promise."

"Ok, fine. I guess I can wait two more days."

"It'll go by fast."

"I hope so, because I can only take so much bad television."

Emma giggled again. "Goodnight, Zack."

"I guess I could try to read again."

"Goodnight, Zack," Emma repeated, unable to suppress her huge grin.

"Maybe I should try reading a different genre. I heard about this series. You might know it. Something about a rich guy who wears a gray tie..."

"You don't need to read that series."

"Why not?"

"Because you have plenty of moves without it."

"Ooh. Tell me more."

"Goodnight, Zack."

"Talk to you tomorrow."

Emma barely heard Zack say, "I wonder what he does with that gray tie anyway?" before he hung up the phone.

CHAPTER 40

The next morning, Emma, Phil, and Debbie sat around the breakfast table enjoying the eggs, bacon, and toast that Debbie had prepared. Emma chewed slowly, hoping she would keep the food down despite the twinges of nausea she had felt since she'd woken up.

"I have an idea for what we can do today," Debbie said. "The Biltmore Estate is all decorated for Christmas, and it's only a short drive from here. What do you think?"

"Sounds great! I've always wanted to go there," Emma replied.

Phil looked back and forth between them. "As wonderful as that sounds, there's an important football game on today. Would you ladies mind if I bowed out?"

"I thought you wanted to spend time with your cousin," Debbie scolded.

He turned his attention to Emma. "Do you mind, Em? We could meet up for dinner later."

Emma couldn't blame him for wanting to watch a game rather than walk around an old mansion. *Zack would probably feel the same if he were here...*

"That's fine, Phil. I don't expect you to change your plans on my account, but I will hold you to dinner later."

Debbie sighed, but she smiled at her husband. "I guess you're off the hook. However, you're on kitchen clean-up duty. Emma and I need to get ready to go."

Phil started to protest but thought better of it. He leaned over and gave Debbie a quick kiss instead. "Thanks, babe."

An hour and a half later, they drove through the charming town of Asheville and then down the long tree-lined lane leading to the Biltmore Estate. When the magnificent mansion first came into view, Emma gasped.

"Wow, this is unbelievable," she said. The estate was set amongst rolling hills and was surrounded by elaborate gardens. Because of the state's temperate climate, there were still patches of green rather than the browns and grays that had taken over Michigan's landscape. The large pine and fir trees that framed the grand estate were exquisitely decorated with Christmas trimmings, and Emma felt the first real stirring of Christmas spirit. She had been so caught up with work and, more recently, her pregnancy that she hadn't fully embraced the joy of the season. Today, Emma decided that she would set her worries aside and simply enjoy the beautiful surroundings.

And that's exactly what they did. Emma and Debbie toured the house and the grounds, oohing and aahing as they went along. They took time out for a light lunch in one of the estate's restaurants that overlooked the vast property and chatted about everything but Emma's pregnancy.

This was exactly the kind of escape I needed, Emma thought when they drove back toward Charlotte a few hours later.

"Let's go home and freshen up before dinner," Debbie suggested as they neared her neighborhood.

"Sounds good to me," Emma agreed. *That will give me some time to call Zack.* She hadn't heard from him all day, but she'd decided that he was probably trying to give her some space. She had glanced at her phone several times during the drive home, but it remained silent.

A small black sedan was parked in front of the house when they pulled up. "I bet Phil called one of his buddies to come over and watch football," Debbie surmised when they got out of the car.

"What is it about men and football?" Emma said.

"They probably think the same thing about us and shopping," Debbie said, holding up her bag of souvenirs from the estate gift shop.

Emma tucked her own bag of goodies under her arm, followed Debbie into the house, and then stopped dead in her tracks.

Her hands flew to her mouth, and thankfully, Debbie caught her bag before it crashed to the floor.

Time stopped. Everyone froze, and then Zack stood up and started toward her.

"Deb and I will leave for a while so you two can talk," Phil said, breaking the silence. He hurried toward the door, turned Debbie around, and away they went.

Emma's hands still covered her mouth, and she hadn't budged. She felt the first tear prick the corner of her eye, but she was afraid to move, afraid to breathe, afraid of...

"You're probably wondering why I'm here," Zack said, his voice wavering a little.

He seemed nervous, which was only fair considering that her heart was pounding out of her chest.

"And no, I didn't fly to North Carolina to take you out to dinner," he added, his expression still serious.

He shoved his hands in his jeans pockets, cleared his throat, and took a step closer.

"I came here because I have a very important question to ask you, and I didn't want to do it over the phone."

Emma felt a tear trickle down the left side of her face, but she let it fall. Zack was two steps away, but he hadn't touched her yet. He just stared at her with his intense gray eyes, pinning her in place with his gaze.

Emma had dropped her hands to her sides, but she still felt incapable of speech. She gave him a slight nod to encourage him to continue.

"You see, I was wondering, when would it be the right time for me to tell my best friend that I love her?"

Emma gasped.

"Because I do. I love you, Emma."

Her name came out on a grunt because she had flung herself into Zack's arms, almost knocking them both over. She clung to him, and amidst the sounds of her half-laugh/half-cry, she managed to say, "I love you too, Zack. I love you so much."

After a moment, he pulled back, but he kept his hands locked on her forearms. "You're still crying." He searched her eyes for understanding.

"I know. I'm sorry. This is all so... overwhelming."

"But those are happy tears, right? You're glad I'm here?"

"Are you kidding? I'm thrilled that you're here. It's just that I have more to say. Let's sit down."

Emma led him across the room to the couch. They sat sideways to face each other, and Zack immediately clasped her hands in his warm, comforting grip.

"Talk," he urged.

Emma was bursting, and she made a split-second decision to use a direct approach. She took a deep breath, looked him right in the eyes, and said, "Zack, I'm pregnant."

Emma had done it again. The only other time she had rendered him speechless had been when they'd had their first argument. She watched several expressions flicker across his face and began to get nervous, until...

Zack jumped off the couch and yelled, "WOW!" with a big smile on his handsome face.

Emma watched him pace the room before she was hit with a barrage of questions.

"But when, how? Never mind the how. I know the how. But when? How long have you known?"

He came back to sit beside her and took her hands once again. She felt the tension drain from her body in the face of his reaction.

"I took the test yesterday morning, but I've had my suspicions for a couple of weeks."

Zack's mouth gaped open, but then his expression grew serious again. "Why didn't you tell me right away? Why did you run off instead of telling me?"

Uh-oh. Emma saw a blaze of anger flash in his eyes, and she shifted uncomfortably, realizing that she might have poked the bull. "I was scared, Zack."

"Scared of what? Of me?"

"Of your reaction. We hadn't even told each other that we loved each other yet, and I didn't know how you would feel about this... new development."

Zack stood up again and resumed pacing while shoving his hands through his hair. "My God, Emma. How could you not know that I would love this child just as much as I love Gracie, just as much as I love you?"

"Well, I wasn't sure. I didn't want you to think that I had trapped you in some way. I didn't want you to feel obligated to me."

The tears welled up in her eyes again, and Emma looked down at the floor. Zack softened immediately and came to kneel before her.

"Emma, look at me," he demanded, tipping her chin up.

"I don't feel *obligated* to you. I love you. I love you with every fiber of my being, and I'll love our child the same way. Please tell me that you know that and that you'll never doubt me again."

Emma responded by pulling him toward her. She wrapped her arms around his neck and pressed her forehead to his. "I love you too, Zack, and I'm so sorry for doubting you."

Their lips touched tentatively at first and then with renewed fervor. Just as Zack was about to scoop her into his arms, his phone buzzed.

"I better…"

"Go ahead," Emma said. She had become used to the interruptions because of Gracie, and with another child coming, there would be no letup.

Zack pulled his phone out of his pocket and grinned as he read the text message. "Phil says we can make out later. He sent me the address to a steak place and wants us to join them for a celebratory dinner."

"We better go," Emma said, even though she'd rather stay in Zack's arms for a little longer. "We can talk on the way."

After they were seated in Zack's rental car, Emma began with, "So, when did you decide to come down here?"

"Yesterday afternoon. I couldn't shake the feeling that something was wrong. It didn't seem like you to take off to North Carolina so suddenly."

Emma huffed. "Why doesn't anyone believe that I could be spontaneous once in a while?"

Zack shot her a *duh* glance. "Because you aren't. Anyway, after I dropped Gracie off with Alicia, I stayed at a hotel near the airport so I could catch an early morning flight. And here I am."

"Was Phil in on this?"

"I sent him a text last night, and he was all for it."

Emma giggled. "So that explains why he wanted to stay home and watch football today. He knew you would be joining him!"

Zack shrugged. "Us guys have to stick together. So now it's your turn. How are you feeling? About the pregnancy, I mean?"

Emma leaned her head back and sighed. "Gosh, so many things I don't know where to start."

"I'm all ears," he said encouragingly.

"Well, first of all, now I understand why you're so protective of Gracie. Our baby is no bigger than a pea, and I'm already fiercely protective of her."

"Her? Don't be so sure of that. There could be a Zack junior floating around in there."

"Lord help us," she said with a laugh.

"You're right. A baby Emma would be better. How are you feeling physically?"

"I've had some nausea, but so far, I've been able to keep food down. My breasts are tender, and I've felt overly emotional, but other than that, hey, I'm good!"

Zack chuckled. "That all sounds completely normal, although you should probably make a doctor appointment when we get back."

"I will."

They were silent for a few minutes, each lost in their own thoughts. Zack pulled into the parking lot of the steakhouse and shut the car off, but he made no move to get out. He rested his forehead on the steering wheel and let out a loud sigh.

Emma laid her hand on his back. "Zack? Are you ok?"

She gently rubbed his back and waited for him to get his thoughts in order. She'd already had time to get used to the idea of having a baby, but he had known for less than an hour. When he finally looked up, there were tears swimming in his eyes. "Yeah, I'm good. It just hit me. I'm going to be a dad again."

Emma smiled softly and nodded. "Yes," she said, "And lucky me, I already know that you're going to be a damn good one."

CHAPTER 41

Emma could hardly wait to be alone with Zack. Sitting next to him at the restaurant for two hours turned out to be a form of sweet torture. He constantly touched her in some way or another throughout the appetizers, dinner, and dessert. They were simple gestures: his hand resting on her knee, his arm draped possessively over her shoulder, his fingers entwined with hers under the table, his side pressed up against her in the tight booth. By the time they left the restaurant, Emma was on fire for him, and based on the smoldering looks he kept giving her in the car, Zack felt the same way.

A silent look of understanding passed between Phil and Zack once they reached the house, and now, finally, Emma and Zack were alone in the guest bedroom. Emma swore that the room was charged with their sexual energy. Whether it was because they had professed their love to one another or the surge of pregnancy hormones, or just because it was them, Emma couldn't be sure, but she welcomed the tension like a warm blanket soon to be wrapped around her.

They stood in the middle of the room, illuminated by the dim light of the bedside lamp, not speaking, hearts thumping. Zack raised Emma's arms above her head and gently pulled her sweater up and over. She instantly felt an involuntary shiver.

"Cold?"

"No."

Next, he unhooked her black bra and slipped it off her shoulders. Her nipples automatically stood up to greet him before he cupped her breasts in his large hands. He began to massage them, slowly, carefully, almost as if he were afraid to hurt her, and then understanding struck.

"Zack," she whispered.

"Hmm?" He answered distractedly, his index fingers tracing circles around her nipples.

"I'm not going to break, you know. I'm pregnant, not injured."

"Umm-hmm." He dipped his head down and drew a nipple into his mouth, sucking gently.

Ok, he really is trying to torture me. Emma thrust her breast forward, urging him to take more of her. If words wouldn't do the trick, then maybe actions would!

Her strategy worked, because Zack picked up the pace, drawing on her nipples with more intensity. As additional encouragement, Emma reached her hand between their bodies and stroked him over his jeans.

Zack jerked his head up, and Emma quickened her movements while he lifted his t-shirt up and over his head.

Finally! She left her post below his belt to travel her hands up and over the hard ridges of his chest, flicking his nipples on her way north. Zack's heavy breathing was the only sound in the room while she continued her own brand of torture. Her fingers blazed a path up to his shoulders, and then she trailed her fingernails down his muscular arms, leaving goosebumps in their wake. When she reached his hands, she entwined her fingers with his and squeezed.

"Finish undressing me, Zack," she pleaded and guided his right hand to the button of her jeans.

Zack nimbly unbuttoned and unzipped her jeans, hooked his fingers into her panties, and peeled her jeans and panties down her legs. He trailed his masculine hands up the inside of her thighs on his return trip and stopped right at the apex. Emma wanted him so bad she could already feel him inside of her, but she needed him naked first.

"Lose the jeans," she demanded and took a step back.

Zack's grin competed with the lamp for illuminating the room. In a flash, his pants and boxers hit the floor, and before she could get a good look, he scooped her up and placed her on the bed. Next came a jumble of hands and lips and tongues and limbs. Sweet caresses and hot kisses, whispers, sighs, moans and groans. Wrestling to get closer, the merging of bodies and the melding of souls. It reminded Emma of their first time, filled with urgency, passion, and desire, but there was something else now, and as she cried out his name, she realized what it was. It was love.

Afterwards, Emma nestled her head against Zack's chest and traced random patterns on his skin while he played with her curly locks.

"When do you think we should tell Gracie?" Emma ventured, asking the question that had surely been on his mind too.

"I think we should wait until after Christmas. I'm not sure what her reaction will be, but I don't want anything to spoil her fun."

"I agree, although I hope she'll be happy to have a little brother or sister."

Zack gave her a reassuring squeeze. "I hope so too."

"We should probably hold off on telling the rest of the family just in case someone slips."

"With the exception of Damian. The dude is like a vault. Plus, he's a man of few words, if you haven't noticed."

"Oh, I've noticed. Quite the opposite of his big brother," Emma teased.

"Hey, I can be quiet when I need to be."

"Seriously? You talk more than Kelly, and that's quite a feat! Speaking of Kelly, if you get to tell Damian, then I get to tell her. She already knows that something's up, so I won't be able to hold her off for long."

"Fine, Damian and Kelly, but no one else until after Christmas."

"So, what do you think is going on with them anyway?"

"Isn't it obvious?"

"I suppose, but you said that Damian isn't a one-woman type of guy, so I hope Kelly's not falling for him."

"Well, that would be kind of fast, wouldn't it?"

Emma cleared her throat noisily. "Um, excuse me, what about us?"

"That's different. I fell in love with you five years ago."

Emma smiled and nuzzled into his neck. "I probably fell a little too, but it took me longer to realize it."

"I'm glad you finally did," he said playfully.

"Back to Damian and Kelly."

"They're mature adults, Em. They'll figure it out without any interference from us."

His comment reminded her of what Phil had said the day before about not wanting to interfere when she and Zack got married. *Zack and I and married in the same sentence. Interesting...*

"Whatcha thinking?" Zack asked, pulling her in tighter.

"Oh, I don't know. Just wondering how everyone's going to react to our news."

"If I know Alex and Joe, they'll be thrilled. Especially Alex when she realizes there will be another mouth to feed!"

Emma giggled. "Do you think they'll be upset that we did things out of order?"

"What order?"

"You know the old saying, first comes love, then comes..."

"Aah, yes, that saying."

They had turned the light out a little bit ago, so now it was difficult to read his expression, but Emma could have kicked herself for even bringing up the topic. *Haven't I sprung enough on him for one day? Besides, I'm not sure I'm ready to get married again anyway.*

Zack twisted around to face her and laid his hand tenderly on her cheek. "Look what happened when we did things in the correct order the first time around. Maybe there's no such thing as the proper order. Maybe it's about whatever works for you and me and for our child. We'll figure this out, Em... together."

Emma leaned her head into the palm of his hand. She wasn't sure of everything, but she was certain about one thing. "I love you," she said softly.

"And I love you."

Three simple words, yet they held such meaning, such promise. Three simple words that wrapped around her heart until she drifted off into a deep, peaceful sleep.

CHAPTER 42

"It's not going to work," Emma insisted.

"Have a little faith," Zack argued.

Zack had been able to book the same flight home as her, but his seat assignment was in the last row right next to the restroom. He insisted that he would be able to persuade whomever had the seat next to Emma to trade with him, all in the name of love. *Foolish man.*

"It'll probably be some little old lady who reads romance novels. She'll be more than happy to give up her seat for us 'lovebirds.'"

Emma scanned the passengers as they filed onto the aircraft, looking for said "little old lady." A few minutes later, she appeared in the form of a burly, bearded man who wore a leather motorcycle vest— his bare arms covered in tattoos.

"I think you're in my seat," burly man stated with a voice to match his gruff exterior.

Emma had to suppress a laugh when Zack stood up, presumably to give up the seat.

"Excuse me, sir, but I wondered if you'd be willing to trade seats with me? You see, my lady is pregnant, and she's been suffering from morning sickness. I'm sure you would rather have her vomit on me instead of all over your good-looking vest."

Emma's eyes widened as she waited for burly man's response. He looked around Zack to Emma, seeking confirmation. She nodded her head and laid her hand over her belly for added effect.

"Yeah, sure, no problem. What seat is yours?"

After burly man left, Zack threw his hand up in the air for a high five, which Emma reluctantly gave him.

"I can't believe you did that," she said.

"Why not? It was the truth."

"No, I can't believe you called me 'my lady.' That's so... outdated."

Zack chuckled. "Well, it worked, didn't it? Let's just be happy."

She leaned over and gave him a brief kiss. "I am happy," she said.

Two hours later, after an uneventful flight (no vomiting!), Zack and Emma were forced to part ways. They said their goodbyes and got in their separate cars at the car park, with a promise to talk later that evening. Zack was off to pick up Gracie from Alicia, and Emma was off to the bookstore to check in with Kelly.

When she arrived at the store, she was pleased to find the place hopping. Christmas was only a few days away, and the shoppers were out in force. Kelly and Brett looked a little frazzled behind the counter, and there were several customers in line waiting to pay. Emma hurriedly set her purse in the office and jumped in to help.

Once the line abated, Kelly turned to Emma with her hands on her hips. "It's about time. It's been crazy in here all weekend!"

Brett must have felt an argument brewing, because he looked between the two women and hurriedly slipped out from behind the counter.

"I'm sorry, Kell. I shouldn't have left you like that."

"You're damned right! What was so urgent that you had to see Phil *this* weekend?"

Emma glanced around the store to see if anyone was within earshot. "Why don't we go out for dinner tonight, and I'll tell you then?"

"No can do. I'm meeting Damian tonight."

"Again?"

"Yes, again. He's only here through the holidays, and I want to make the most of it."

Emma was flooded with concern for her best friend, even though Zack had advised her not to be. "Kell…"

"Don't Kell me. Tell me why you flew off to North Carolina in such a hurry."

"Ok, let's step into the office." Brett was nearby, straightening the new release shelf, so Emma called out, "Brett, can you watch the counter for a few minutes?"

"No problem," he replied.

Emma and Kelly sat next to each other in the cramped office while Kelly waited expectantly.

"I'm pregnant," Emma blurted out.

Kelly's expressive eyes bulged, and her mouth gaped open. "Get out!"

"I'm serious. I took the test on Friday morning, and it was positive. I was afraid of Zack's reaction, so I took off to see Phil. But then Zack showed up and..."

"Damian said that Zack went after you. What was his reaction?"

Emma choked up at the memory of it. "He told me that he loves me and he's happy about the baby."

Kelly's expression morphed into one of pure joy. "Yay! I can't wait to be an aunt!"

Emma almost exploded out of her chair.

"Relax. I don't mean literally. I meant like an honorary aunt. Someone she can call aunt, even though I'm technically not one."

"You just called the baby 'she.' Funny, I did the same thing."

"I've got about a ninety percent success rate with predicting the sex. I'm pretty certain there's a girl in there."

"Speaking of girls, we're not going to tell Gracie until after Christmas. Besides Phil, you and Damian are the only two who know."

Kelly made the motion of zipping her lips. "Your secret is safe with me."

"We better get back to work," Emma said and stood up.

Kelly put a hand on her arm and then pulled Emma into a bone-crushing hug. "If you need anything, anything at all, and I don't care if it's the middle of the night or early in the morning and you're puking your guts out, you can call me. I mean it."

When Kelly let her go, Emma raised her eyebrows with skepticism. "Early in the morning?

The other day, I called you at eight o'clock, and you were still asleep."

"That was different. I had a warm man in my bed."

Emma watched Kelly's face light up at the reference to Damian, and even though her first impulse was to warn her friend, Emma decided to keep her mouth shut. Zack was right; it was none of their business.

"Thanks for the offer, but I think I'll get plenty of TLC from Zack. He's already texted me twice this afternoon to remind me to eat. Like I need a reminder!"

"He's a good man, Em. You're lucky to have him." Kelly looked almost wistful, but then she quickly snapped back into fun-loving Kelly mode. "This is going to be awesome. I can't wait to spoil my niece!"

That night, Emma relayed the entire conversation to Zack over the phone. "How did it go with Damian?"

"He grunted a few times and patted me on the back, so we're good."

Emma laughed at his description. "Did he actually *say* anything?"

"Yes. He said he can't wait to teach his nephew how to work on cars."

"Well, now we have one vote for a girl and one for a boy. I have to admit it felt good to tell Kelly. It's going to be really hard for me to keep my mouth shut until after Christmas."

"I know, but you haven't even been to the doctor yet, which reminds me..."

"I'll call and make an appointment tomorrow."

"Oh, and I plan on going with you."

"You don't have to do that. They probably won't be able to tell me much anyway."

"I don't care. I'm going with you," he repeated emphatically.

Even though Emma was secretly glad for his support, she couldn't resist teasing him. "Are you going to be an overbearing, overprotective dad-to-be?"

"No. Why would you think that?"

"Well, let's see. You texted me four times today to remind me to eat, and you left two voicemails asking if I drank enough water. If that's not overprotective, I don't know what is."

Zack had to chuckle. "Ok, fine. But I just want to take good care of you and our baby. I want you to feel like you're in good hands."

"Those hands are what got me into trouble in the first place!"

"Would you say these are *magic* hands?"

"Zack…"

"Sorry, couldn't help myself. I love you, and I wish you were here right now."

"I wish that too," she said softly.

"Which reminds me, we need to talk about our living arrangements. I don't like the idea of us living apart while you're pregnant."

Emma sat up straighter in bed. "I only live a mile down the road."

"I know, but what if something happens and I'm not there."

"You're being overprotective again."

"Maybe, but I also want you with me. With me and Gracie."

Emma's heart squeezed, and she suddenly felt light-headed. She was afraid to bring up the m-word, but was marriage what Zack was alluding to? "Shouldn't we take this one step at a time? I'm still reeling over the fact that I'm pregnant. I don't know that I can handle any big decisions right now." *There, at least that was the partial truth.*

There was a brief pause before Zack replied, "Oh. I guess I thought you'd want to be with us too."

"I do. I just don't want to rush things. I don't want us to have any regrets."

"Funny, it used to be me who was afraid to move forward, but now it sounds like you might be the one who's scared."

He said it matter-of-factly and without malice, but his words still managed to put her on the defensive. "Zack, I just found out that I'm going to have a baby. Forgive me if I'm feeling a little overwhelmed."

Something in her voice must have caused him to back off. "You're right. Again. In fact, from here on out, you're always right, ok?"

He was back to teasing, but knowing him, he wouldn't give up that easy. "Why don't we table this discussion until after my first doctor appointment?"

"Agreed. Now, you should probably get some sleep. You've had a long day, and you and Zeus need your rest."

"Zeus? You're kidding right?"

"No. My little boy should know his heritage, and what better way than to name him after one of the Greek Gods."

"We are not naming our child Zeus, unless you want him to be bullied for the rest of his life."

"Do you even know who Zeus was? No one will mess with a guy named Zeus. Believe me."

"I'm a little rusty on Greek mythology, but I'm still nixing the name."

"We'll see."

Emma sighed. "Goodnight, Zack."

"Aren't you forgetting something? It starts with an I and ends with a U."

"I love you."

"Aah. I like the sound of that. I love you too. You and Zeus sleep well!"

Emma hung up and snuggled under the covers, the sound of Zack's laughter still ringing in her ears.

CHAPTER 43

"It's going to be fine Em," Zack assured her.

Emma's parents had arrived in Clarkston two days prior to Christmas, and Emma had invited them, along with Zack and Gracie, to dinner at her house. She had decided that her parents should meet the father of her child prior to meeting his entire family on Christmas day.

Zack and Gracie had arrived early so that Zack could help her prepare the food, but honestly, she needed him more for moral support. It had been almost one year since she had last seen her parents, and their meetings were always slightly awkward. She supposed that was normal for families who didn't interact frequently, but it still put her on edge. Hopefully, Zack's and Gracie's presence would help lighten the mood.

Zack tossed a salad while Emma ladled homemade meat sauce over spaghetti noodles. Gracie had been given the task of setting the table, which she assured them that she could do without help.

"They should be here any minute," Emma said nervously while she carried a steaming bowl of pasta to the table. "I hope I didn't forget anything."

Zack looked up from the salad. "Gracie, I think Emma needs a hug. What do you think?"

Gracie's response was immediate. She wrapped her arms around Emma's legs and squeezed. "Now you'll feel better," Gracie proclaimed.

"Thank you, pretty girl. I do feel better now." And she did. The comfortable comradery between the three of them warmed her heart. She could easily envision such scenes every night, although their dynamic would change once the baby arrived. Emma squashed the feeling of panic that rose within her whenever she thought about telling Gracie the news. Gracie's reaction was more important to Emma than that of all of their other family members combined.

The doorbell rang before she could think any more about it.

"We'll wait in here," Zack said and gave her a reassuring nod.

Emma answered the door. "Mom, Dad, good to see you," she said and greeted each of them with a brief hug. "How was your trip?"

"Fine. Uneventful," her father replied. *And Zack thought Damian was a man of few words!*

"We're anxious to meet the new people in your life. Where are they?" Emma's mother asked, peering around her.

"They're in the kitchen. Follow me."

When they entered the kitchen, Emma's throat swelled with pride. Zack and Gracie stood side by side, the epitome of a loving father and daughter, spit-shined and polished, while they anxiously awaited their introductions.

"Mary and Hank, I'd like you to meet Zack and Gracie."

Zack immediately stepped forward to shake her father's hand, and then he gave her mother a quick hug.

"Oh," Mary said, obviously surprised by the gesture.

Gracie stepped forward next, her smile as bright and joyful as only a child's can be. "My name is Gracie Marie Kostas. I'm four years old," she added proudly.

If Mary and Hank had seemed a bit stiff before, Emma swore she saw them both soften.

"Well, it's nice to meet you, Gracie. Do you go to school?" Mary asked, bending down to the little girl's level.

"I go to preschool, and I go to story time at Emma's bookstore."

Emma smiled widely at that pronouncement. She was also happy that Gracie no longer referred to her as "Miss Emma." She and Zack had agreed that it was time to drop the formal title.

"It's wonderful that you like books," Mary said.

Her mother seemed enthralled with Gracie already, and Emma breathed a sigh of relief while she ushered everyone to the table.

They were quiet while the plates were passed around until Gracie blurted, "I get to say grace!"

Zack shot Emma an apologetic look, but she just nodded. Everyone bowed their heads as Gracie began. "Dear God, thank you for letting Emma's mommy and daddy come over for dinner. And I'm glad that we're having noodles, because they're my favorite! Amen."

Their heads popped up simultaneously, and Emma looked over at her parents, who were trying to suppress their laughter.

"So, Zack, what do you do?" Hank asked a few minutes later.

"I'm a financial consultant. I work with people mostly on retirement plans."

"You do ok, then?"

"Dad!" Emma scolded.

"Yes, sir. I do very well," Zack replied, and he squeezed Emma's knee under the table.

Satisfied with Zack's answer, Hank returned to eating.

"I'm done. Can I go play now?" Gracie asked.

"Sure, honey," Emma said, and they all watched Gracie scurry away from the table.

Silence descended again, and then Mary asked, "When did you two meet?"

"Well, now, that's a funny story," Zack began, ignoring Emma's warning glare.

"Tell us," Mary encouraged.

"We first met five years ago at your nephew Phil's wedding…"

"I thought you looked familiar," her father piped in.

"I was enamored with your daughter back then, but as you know, she was engaged to someone else."

Emma swallowed nervously and avoided eye contact with her parents. *Why is he doing this?*

"So, I didn't see Emma again until this past summer when Gracie and I moved here from Ann Arbor. Our love of reading led us to Emma's bookstore, and the rest, as they say, is history! I like to think that we were destined to be together."

Emma wiped at a miniscule speck of spaghetti sauce on the tablecloth and willed Zack to stop speaking. But apparently, he wasn't finished yet.

"The bottom line is that I love your daughter, and Gracie does too."

"Does anyone want dessert?" Emma blurted, rising from the table abruptly.

"Not yet, dear, but would you like help with the dishes?" Mary asked, seemingly looking for a distraction.

"No. Zack will help me. Why don't you and Dad go into the living room and check on Gracie?"

As soon as her parents left the room, she turned on Zack and hissed, "Why did you do that?"

"Do what?" he asked innocently.

"Tell them all that stuff about us? You shared more information with my parents in five minutes than I've shared in the past year!"

Zack took the dish out of her hands and set it on the counter before pulling her into his arms. Against her will, Emma melted against him.

"I wanted your parents to know how much I love you. I didn't want them to think that I was just some stranger who swooped in on their daughter."

Emma peered up at him through damp lashes. "You're too good to me. Do you know that?"

Zack kissed the tip of her nose. "I love you, Emma, and I will always be here for you and for our baby."

He laid his hands on her belly just as Mary and Gracie re-entered the kitchen. Mary's hands flew to her mouth, and Gracie's eyes widened with confusion.

Emma felt the blood rush from her head, and she suddenly went limp in Zack's arms. In a swift movement, he scooped her up and rushed out of the room, barking orders as he went. "Get her a cool washcloth and a glass of water. Quick!"

Zack gently laid Emma down on the couch and instructed her to breathe. Seconds later, Mary and Gracie came in bearing the requested items. Hank stood in the center of the room, looking bewildered by all of the commotion.

"What's going on? What's wrong with my daughter?"

Emma was still fuzzy-headed, but the cool washcloth on her forehead helped, and she sat up to accept the glass of water from Gracie's little hands.

Zack rubbed his hands up and down her arms in a soothing motion. "Are you ok, babe?" he asked, his eyes full of concern.

"Yes, I'm fine," Emma managed, feeling herself slowly return to normal.

"Is someone going to tell me what's going on?" Hank demanded.

Zack gathered Gracie in close and gave her a reassuring squeeze. Emma looked between her mom, dad, and Gracie. Then she took a deep breath and said, "I'm going to have a baby. *Zack* and I are going to have a baby."

"We were waiting to tell everyone until after Emma's first doctor appointment," Zack added, concern still etched on his face.

Mary opened her mouth to speak, but Gracie surprised them all by shouting, "Am I going to have a baby too?"

"You're going to have a baby brother or sister, but not for a little while yet," Zack answered calmly.

Gracie appeared to mull the idea over and then said, "It better not be a brother because I don't like boys!"

A rumble of laughter filled the room, Mary's and Hank's included.

"Well, this is some news!" Hank said.

"It is indeed," Mary added, her eyes welling up with tears.

The rest of the evening smoothed out after that. Emma's parents seemed genuinely thrilled with the news. Mary refused to let Emma serve them dessert, and she and Gracie served it instead in the living room, where Zack kept a close eye on Emma. Zack and Gracie flanked Emma on either side while they indulged in chocolate cake and talked about the baby.

Naturally, Gracie had the most questions, starting with, "Where will the baby sleep?"

"In a crib," Zack answered, hoping to bypass the next question.

"At whose house?"

"Umm... we're not sure yet."

Mary and Hank exchanged a curious glance but didn't say a word.

"Will I get to play with the baby?"

"Of course, but when babies are first born, they don't really play," Emma answered.

"Well, can I hold it?"

"Yes," Zack said.

"And feed it?"

"Absolutely," Emma said, already accustomed to the barrage of questions. Gracie was her father's daughter after all!

"What will we call it?"

Zack's face lit up with the Kostas trademark grin. "If it's a boy, we were thinking Zeus."

Mary bobbled her spoonful of cake, and Hank broke out in a coughing fit.

"He's kidding," Emma said, rolling her eyes at Zack.

"What if it's a girl? I want it to be a girl," Gracie said emphatically.

"We haven't decided on any names yet, but we still have plenty of time," Emma replied, rumpling Gracie's dark curls.

"Gracie, why don't you help me take these dishes to the kitchen?" Mary suggested.

Grateful for the reprieve, Emma leaned her head against Zack's shoulder.

"Are you feeling better now?" he asked, cupping her face in his hands.

"I feel wonderful," she replied and gave him a brief kiss, aware of her father's eyes upon them.

"So, Dad, what do you think of our news?"

Hank cleared his throat noisily and answered, "I think that I'm going to be a grandpa."

CHAPTER 44

It was Christmas Eve, and Emma geared up for a whirlwind of activity, starting with work. A New Chapter would be open until five o'clock, and she and Kelly expected to be busy right up until closing time. After her fainting spell the night before, Zack had tried to convince Emma to take the day off, but she didn't want to abandon Kelly. Besides, it would help keep her mind occupied before she met up with him later. Now that her parents knew about the baby, she and Zack had decided to tell his parents too. They figured that if they waited, Gracie would surely spill the beans on Christmas Day, so this was the better alternative.

If Emma had been nervous about her parents' reaction, she felt doubly nervous about telling Zack's parents. She recalled the conversation she had had with Alex on Thanksgiving, when Alex had expressed her concerns over her granddaughter. Even though Gracie had reacted positively to the baby news (as long as it was a girl!), would Alex feel the same?

Emma worried that Alex and Joe might have difficulty accepting the idea of Zack and Emma having a child out of wedlock. Emma would find out soon enough, but in the meantime, she would immerse herself in the comfort of the bookstore.

The store bustled with activity until the noon hour, when shoppers took their lunch break. Emma was forced to do the same when Zack showed up bearing sandwiches.

"How's my girl doing today?" he asked, setting the bag of food on the counter.

"Which one?" Kelly flirted and gave him a wink.

"Save it for your own man," Emma reprimanded while she dug through the bag.

On cue, Damian walked into the store clutching a tray with four drink cups.

Kelly instantly lit up at the sight of him. "Oh, I didn't know you were coming too," she purred.

Damian's lips curled up in a seductive smile, and he handed her a drink.

"So, since we're all here, what's the latest on Gracie's Christmas surprise?" Zack asked before biting into his ham and cheese sandwich.

"I took the cat to the vet yesterday, and she checked out fine," Kelly replied. "According to the vet, he sees cases like this quite often. Someone probably decided that they didn't want a pet anymore and just let her go. Since no one has claimed her, she's all yours!"

"Oh, goody!" Zack said.

Emma swatted him on the arm. "Just think about how excited Gracie will be on Christmas morning."

"Something about this reminds me of the heart-shaped waffle maker," Zack said, raising his eyebrows accusingly.

Kelly and Damian looked confused, so Zack, completely enjoying himself, continued the story. "Emma convinced me that I *had* to buy a heart-shaped waffle maker for Gracie when, in fact, Emma got a bigger kick out of it than her. I'm sensing a pattern here."

"You're probably on to something. Emma always wanted a pet, but her parents wouldn't allow it, and then Mark was allergic," Kelly offered.

"Hey, whose side are you on?" Emma asked, glaring at her friend.

"Sorry," Kelly said with an amused smirk.

"So, what's the plan? Are you and Damian bringing the cat over on Christmas morning?" Zack asked before taking another hefty bite of his sub.

"Yup," Damian said with his mouth full.

"Eight o'clock sharp. Don't be late," Zack ordered, looking pointedly at his brother.

"Don't worry. I'll make sure he's *up*," Kelly said.

Emma felt herself flush as she looked between Kelly and Damian, and then she quickly turned her attention to Zack, who had a similar glint in his eye.

Oh boy! I have a feeling that this is going to be an eventful night—in more ways than one! Gracie is staying with Alicia, and Damian is staying with Kelly, so that means...

A few minutes later, some customers drifted into the store. Emma and Kelly quickly finished their sandwiches and shooed Zack and Damian out.

"See you tonight," Zack whispered in Emma's ear.

She still had goosebumps when the door closed behind him. She knew her hunch was right when, a short time later, she received a text from Zack that read: *Bring your overnight bag when you come over later. Xoxo*

Emma arrived at Zack's house only a few minutes before Alex and Joe pulled up. That gave her just enough time to stash her overnight bag in Zack's bedroom and check herself in the mirror. Of all times to look like Medusa! Emma had recently purchased the bestseller *What to Expect When You're Expecting*, and she had read that hormonal changes could have an effect on her hair. *Just great!*

"Hello, darling," Alex said, and she immediately gave Emma a kiss on each cheek, European style.

Emma couldn't help but reflect on how different Alex was from her own mom. She had such a strong and vibrant personality, fluttering in with her colorful clothes and dangly earrings and smelling as if she had taken a bath in her perfume. Emma couldn't help but be drawn to Alex, just as she had been to Alex's son.

Joe followed in her wake, wielding a bottle of wine and his million-dollar smile. Compared to his wife, he exuded a casual elegance, dressed in pleated khakis and a black crew-neck sweater, still handsome and virile in his mid-sixties.

Zack led them all into the living room, where he had set out some appetizers. His parents had just come from dinner with friends, so they weren't going to have a formal sit-down meal. That suited Emma just fine, since her stomach was already clenched with nerves.

"I'll grab some wineglasses and be right back," Zack said, and he left Emma alone with his parents.

"How's business at the bookstore?" Joe asked once they were seated.

Ah, thank God, one of my favorite topics! "Great. We've been really busy due to the holidays, and I hope we'll have a lot of repeat customers after the season's over."

"I've heard a lot of good things about your store, but I have to admit that I don't read much these days," Alex said.

"Zack mentioned that you belong to a lot of clubs, so I'm sure that keeps you busy."

"It does, but I love to be busy! Bring it on, I always say!"

Does that apply to grandkids too?

Zack came in bearing a tray with three wineglasses and a bottle of water for Emma. Alex gave her a curious glance but became distracted when Joe poured the wine. Emma looked longingly at the cheese tray but opted for a sip of water instead. The last thing she needed was to vomit while Zack's parents were over.

"So, what is the reason for this little tete-a-tete?" Joe asked after taking a sip of wine.

Alex's hand reached out and swatted his arm so fast that Emma barely saw it. "Joe, don't be rude. Maybe they just called us over for a cup of Christmas cheer."

"Dad's right. We have some exciting news to share…"

"I think I already know," Alex said, smiling directly at Emma.

Hot flashes—another symptom of pregnancy. "You do?" Emma asked with a quiver in her voice.

"Mom, can I please continue?"

"Yes, of course, dear. Go ahead."

"Emma and I are going to have a baby."

"I knew it! I was right!" Alex exclaimed, clapping her hands like a seal.

"Wow," Joe said and smiled broadly.

Emma felt her whole body relax when she witnessed their enthusiasm, and Zack reached over and squeezed her hand.

"When are you due? Does Gracie know? Who else have you told?"

Alex launched her questions in true Kostas style, which caused Emma's head to spin. She grabbed on to her seat cushion for added support while Zack took over.

"Mom. One question at a time, please." His voice was firm, but he gave his mother a warm smile.

Joe slung his arm over Alex's shoulder as if to anchor her to the couch. "Let them tell us," he said softly.

"We don't know the due date, because Emma hasn't been to the doctor yet. We had planned on telling everyone after the appointment, but I slipped the other night at dinner. So now, all of our immediate family members know, and Kelly."

Alex appeared to have calmed down some, and she asked, "How did Gracie take the news?"

Emma chimed in before Zack could answer. "She took it very well, although she was pretty emphatic that she doesn't want a baby brother."

Everyone chuckled.

"That's our Gracie," Alex said.

"So, Mom, if you don't mind, we'd rather not make a big announcement at dinner tomorrow. You can tell our extended family after Emma's appointment next week, ok?"

Emma watched various emotions flicker across Alex's face, the primary one being disappointment.

"You heard him, Alex. No spilling the beans tomorrow!" Joe added for good measure.

Realizing that she was outnumbered, Alex caved. "Ok, fine. I'll keep my mouth shut, but as soon as you find out that Emma and the baby are ok, call me!"

"You'll be at the top of our list," Emma said reassuringly. Now that her stress had abated, Emma decided it would be ok to indulge in some cheese and crackers. She hadn't had anything to eat since lunch, and she was famished. She had just taken the first bite when...

"I have one more question. When are you two getting married?" Alex asked.

The cheese and cracker morsel flew out of Emma's mouth with such velocity and accuracy that it landed with a splat on the front of Alex's colorful blouse! Zack immediately jumped up to get a napkin, and horrified, Emma quickly swallowed what remained in her mouth.

"I'm so sorry, Alex. Oh my God. I hope I didn't ruin your blouse."

Alex wiped feverishly at the stain while the rest of them hovered around her.

"Well, this has been an exciting evening," Joe said deadpan.

Zack looked back and forth between Emma and his mother, obviously needing a moment to formulate his response.

Embarrassed over what had just transpired, Emma decided to step in and save him. "We only just found out about the baby, Mrs. Kostas"—it seemed like the right time to use her formal title—"so we haven't made any definite plans yet."

"Hmm…"

Zack interrupted before his mother could say anything more. "We'll be sure to keep you apprised of any new developments."

After his parents left, Zack thumped himself on the forehead. "Apprised of any new developments? Did I really say that? Please tell me that I didn't say that?"

Emma giggled. "Well, how about me, with the cheese incident? I didn't know cheese could fly that far."

Zack rolled back on the bed, buckled up with laughter, which caused Emma to go into hysterics too.

"And then Joe says, 'This has been an exciting evening.'" Zack imitated his dad's voice to perfection, setting off another round of raucous laughter.

Once their laughter subsided, Emma propped herself up on her elbow and gazed down at him. "Do you really think they're ok with it?"

"Yes, I do. Just wait until Zeus is born, and then you'll see. Everyone is going to love him."

"Again with the name? What if it's a girl?"

"Already on it. There's Athena or Artemis or…"

"Zack?"

"Hmm?"

"Shut up and kiss me."

Zack pulled her over on top of him, took her face in his hands, and did as she had asked. His lips moved slowly, deliberately, kissing across her mouth from corner to corner in a tantalizing pattern. Emma threaded her fingers through his wavy hair and massaged his scalp until he sighed.

All of the stress of the past several days melted away, and it was just the two of them in the quiet of his darkened bedroom. Zack's hands had moved down to cup her bottom, and she began to grind against him, enveloped in the fabulous friction that they generated.

"Too hot," Zack muttered between kisses.

"We are, aren't we?" Emma replied, tracing his lips with her tongue.

"No, I mean me. I'm too hot. Need… to… get… naked."

The thing she was doing with her tongue had obviously revved him up, and Emma smiled against his lips. She sat up on his pelvis while Zack reached behind him and yanked off his thermal Henley.

"Better," he panted.

"I agree," Emma replied. Her hands were already on his bare chest, and her fingers skimmed over his collar bone, his pecs, and down the midline of his body.

"Aren't you hot too?" His husky voice reverberated through her.

Emma loved seeing him this way, all hot and bothered because of her. "I'm hot for you," she teased, and she lifted her arms as an invitation for him to remove her sweater.

Zack's warm hands skimmed up her sides, which made her squirm against him. He made quick work of removing her sweater and bra, but then he stalled.

"Are they still sore?"

"Not right now."

"Are you sure?"

"Zack! Please touch me." *Why must he talk at such crucial moments?*

He put his hands on her breasts and squeezed gently, using his thumbs to circle her nipples until they were taut peaks.

The truth was that her breasts were still sensitive, but he didn't need to know that. She wondered if he could tell that they were a little fuller in his hands. Her answer came seconds later.

"They feel... bigger," Zack said in an exhale of breath.

"One of the benefits of pregnancy," Emma managed, even though his tugs and flicks and *oh my...* licks made it hard to concentrate.

Some women experience increased sexual desire during pregnancy were the words that came to mind as Emma's head fell back and Zack's arms encircled her waist.

Zack buried his head in her neck, nibbling and sucking where her skin was so sensitive that she felt the sensations all the way down to her toes. She had a vise grip on his shoulders, and they rocked together, the momentum building with each stroke.

"Need to be... inside... you... now," Zack whispered in her ear, sending a delicious shiver down her spine.

Recognizing the urgency of the situation, there was no time for a seductive striptease. They broke apart just long enough to tear off their jeans and underwear and toss them off the side of the bed. They immediately resumed their previous position, an obvious favorite, but this time, it was bare skin on bare skin.

Emma was so ready for him that he glided in easily, and they breathed a collective, "Aah."

Amidst their groans and gasps and jockeying to achieve the best possible contact, Emma reflected on how wonderful their union was. Zack was the man she truly loved with her entire being, without doubts, without fear, without inhibitions. This was the man she wanted to be with forever, to raise a child with, or children if they were lucky. To give herself to completely, to... *oh God, hold that thought...*

Once they had collapsed flat on their backs, sweaty and satisfied, Emma was able to finish her thought.

To marry.

CHAPTER 45

On the day after Christmas, Gracie and Zack sat at the kitchen table eating heart-shaped waffles while their new house member purred underneath the table. Gracie hadn't wanted to part with the cat since she had received it bright and early on Christmas morning. The five of them, Zack, Emma, Damian, Kelly, and Gracie, had sat around the Christmas tree testing out different names for the gray and white fur ball until Kelly had suggested Duchess, the name of her favorite cat in the Disney film *Aristocats*.

The adults had given Kelly a good ribbing for having watched Disney films on her own, sans children, while Gracie had clapped delightedly.

"I saw that movie at Nana's house," she had exclaimed, and so, Duchess it was!

The rest of the day had gone wonderfully as well. Alex had honored her promise not to tell anyone about the pregnancy, although Zack had noticed his Aunt Helen eyeballing him and Emma intently throughout the day. In any case, both sets of parents seemed to get on fine, and Alex had been thrilled to set two extra places at the table.

The only negative in the day was when Zack and Emma had parted ways later that evening. When he had climbed into bed alone that night, he had never felt so empty. It was worse than after he and Alicia had first separated. They had been arguing so much prior to filing for divorce that Alicia's absence had been a welcome relief. No, this was completely different. This was an ache that he felt deep in his bones, and that was when he made up his mind. Once the decision was made, Zack had fallen into a deep sleep, but now he had two hurdles to get past before he could get to the fun part.

"Gracie, I need to talk to you about something important."

"Ok," she replied, but she dipped her head under the table to look for Duchess.

"I need you to pay attention to Daddy for a few minutes."

She popped her head back up and gave him her full attention, which would probably last all of two minutes.

"You know how Emma is going to have a baby?"

"Um-hmm."

"And you know how much Daddy loves her, right?"

"And me too," she added, not to be outdone.

Zack smiled. "Yes. So, what would you think if I asked her to live here all of the time? With us."

"And Duchess," Gracie corrected.

"Yes, Duchess too."

"Ok, Daddy," she said, and she jumped off the chair to chase after the cat, who had just darted out from under the table.

Yep, he was right. That had taken about two minutes, but the real challenge was yet to come.

"So, what did you want to talk to me about?" Alicia asked suspiciously. She had arrived that afternoon to pick up Gracie for the weekend, but Zack had asked to speak with her in private first.

They stood awkwardly in the den, behind the closed glass-paned door so that he could still keep an eye on Gracie.

"There've been some new developments lately, and they involve Gracie, so I wanted to tell you before she does."

"Developments?"

He should be used to Alicia's icy stare by now, but it still unnerved him. Still, he had to do this, so he plowed ahead. "Emma is pregnant."

Zack saw a flicker of surprise pass over her face before it was swiftly replaced with a mask of indifference. Alicia visibly composed herself before speaking. "Are you two getting married?"

He could always count on her to come straight to the point. "I hope so."

"I see. So how does Gracie feel about this?"

"She's good with it, although she's not too keen on the idea of having a brother." Zack's chuckle sounded hollow to his own ears, but Alicia's lips turned up in a brief smile.

"Life is crazy isn't it? Who would have thought six years ago that we'd be standing here today having this discussion?"

Zack was dumbfounded. It wasn't like Alicia to wax poetic, but her honesty tugged at him. What he did next surprised them both. He pulled Alicia toward him and hugged her. It only lasted for a few seconds, but it made a stronger statement than words could.

When she stepped back, she looked up at him with tears in her eyes. "I want you to be happy, Zack. I really do. And of course, it goes without saying that I want that for Gracie too."

"Thank you," he said with a lump in his throat.

"So, when's the baby due?"

"We find out on Monday, which is why I asked you to keep Gracie a little bit longer. Our doctor appointment is at ten in the morning, so we should be done by noon."

The term "we" hung in the air for a moment as they both stood there.

"Ok then. I should go." Alicia put her hand on the doorknob, but then she turned back around. "I hope everything goes well."

She left the room before he could respond, and they spent the next few minutes gathering Gracie's things, including Duchess. There was no way that Gracie was going anywhere without that cat!

After they left, Zack breathed a loud sigh of relief. His talk with Alicia had gone much better than he could have hoped for. Satisfied, he rubbed his hands together and began to formulate the next part of his plan.

CHAPTER 46

"Are you nervous?" Zack asked while they drove to the obstetrician's office.

"No, but I really have to pee." Emma had consumed more water than was probably necessary to make sure that she could produce a urine sample for the doctor.

Zack and Emma had just spent the entire weekend together, minus the hours when Emma had needed to work, and she was grateful that he had taken Monday off to accompany her to the appointment.

"I brought a list of questions," Zack said in an attempt to distract her.

"Of course you did."

"Well, I want to make sure that we cover everything."

"Zack, this baby is really, really tiny. How much do we need to cover?"

When they signed in at the front desk, Zack leaned way over the counter like he was about to tell the receptionist a secret.

"Can Emma give her urine sample right away? She's really uncomfortable."

Emma was torn between wanting to punch him and wanting to hug him. The receptionist was obviously enamored by Zack, and it was no wonder: a great-looking guy who also cared enough about his woman to want to relieve her discomfort! It didn't get much better than that!

"Of course," the receptionist replied. "She can go through the door to the first room on the right." The receptionist shot them an empathetic smile and then went back to work.

Zack started to walk through the door with Emma, but she stopped him with a mild scolding. "I can pee by myself," she whispered, well aware of the several pairs of eyes upon them.

"Oh, right," Zack replied, and he sat down to wait.

When Emma rejoined him, she felt like a whole new person. "Thank you," she said and leaned over to kiss Zack on the cheek.

A very pregnant woman who sat in the chair across from them watched with great interest. She looked to be similar in age to Emma, and she rested her hands proudly on her rotund belly. "Is this your first child?" she ventured.

"My first, but his second," Emma replied, and then she wanted to kick herself. This stranger didn't need to know about her and Zack's *situation*.

The woman didn't even flinch. "This is my second. I'm hoping for a boy this time."

"It looks like you're about to pop at any second," Zack said rather loudly. The other women who sat nearby snickered.

"I'm due in two weeks," she said, unfazed by his childlike terminology.

A nurse poked her head out the door and called Emma's name. "Good luck," the woman said.

Once Zack and Emma were seated in an exam room and Emma had changed into a paper gown, she said, "Why did that woman say 'good luck'? That just made me think of all the things that could go wrong."

"Em, it's just a saying. What should she have said instead?"

"I don't know. Maybe something like, 'Having a child is the best thing ever!'"

Zack chuckled and threw his arms around her. "I love you."

"I love you too," she replied and basked in the comfort of his arms.

A few minutes later, a petite female doctor walked in looking like the model of efficiency, holding a clipboard and with a stethoscope slung around her neck. Suddenly, Emma felt very nervous, and the room started to spin. She gripped the sides of the exam table and prayed for it to pass.

Zack stepped forward immediately and put his arm around her. "She's had a few dizzy spells recently. Is that normal?"

The doctor stepped closer and checked Emma's pulse. "It can be. There are a lot of hormonal changes that accompany pregnancy, so anything is possible."

"I'm ok now," Emma assured Zack, and then he reluctantly took the seat in the corner of the room.

The doctor did the routine checks, asking numerous questions along the way, and then she helped Emma back up to a seated position. "We'll need to draw some blood, but everything looks good. I'd estimate your due date to be around the middle of August, but we can narrow it down once you get closer. Do you have any questions for me?"

Emma raised her eyebrows at Zack and waited for him to whip out his list, but he just sat there, hands clasped tightly in his lap. "No, I don't think so," Emma answered, disconcerted by Zack's silence.

"The most important thing is for you to take good care of yourself. Eat regularly, drink lots of water, and take prenatal vitamins. I'll leave a prescription at the check-out desk. Other than that, I'll see you back here in four weeks." The doctor gave them both a reassuring smile and slipped out the door.

"Zack? What's wrong?" Emma asked as soon as they were alone.

"It's real, Emma. We're going to have a baby."

"Yes, silly. That's why we're here!" She hopped off the table and went over to him. She knelt down in front of him and placed her hands over his. "You're happy about this, right?"

"Yes, of course. I don't know what happened. Once the doctor started talking, the reality of it hit me, and I froze. Damn, now I didn't get my questions answered!"

Emma giggled. "I happen to have access to hundreds of books on this topic. I'm sure we can find the answers to all of your questions."

All except one, Zack thought.

After the appointment, Zack dropped her off at the bookstore.

"Don't forget to eat lunch, and I'll pick you up at five," he reminded her when she hopped out of the car.

"If I forget, I'm sure your ten text messages will remind me," she teased, and she blew him a kiss.

Emma felt buoyant when she entered the store, and Kelly bombarded her right away.

"How did it go? Tell me everything," Kelly demanded.

Emma relayed the details while Kelly listened intently.

"I'm glad everything went well, because now we can start to plan a kick-ass baby shower!"

"Kell, you know you're going to have to curb your language when this baby arrives, right?" Emma admonished her friend while trying to hide her smile.

"Pfft... piece of cake!" Kelly said.

"You'll have to go shopping with me for maternity clothes soon. Zack gave me a really generous gift card for Christmas to that swanky maternity store at Somerset Mall."

"I'm in! Maternity clothes can be sexy, you know, and your boobs will be bigger, so you can really show them off."

"Kell, we're talking about me, not you. I don't see myself buying provocative maternity wear."

"But I bet Zack would love it." Kelly wiggled her eyebrows.

Which reminded Emma of the other Christmas gift he had given her in private. Zack had bought her an extremely sheer white baby-doll lingerie set from a high-end lingerie catalog. She recalled his words: "Not that I don't love your 'I woke up like this' nightshirt, but I wanted to see you in something like this." Emma had worn it for him over the weekend and had been amply rewarded! He'd reciprocated by wearing the Superman pajama pants that she had bought for him and nothing else.

"Em, are you still with me?"

"Oh, yeah, sorry. I have a lot on my mind."

"I'm sure you do," Kelly said knowingly. "Probably the same things that are on my mind about Damian."

"So you two are still hot and heavy?"

"Emphasis on the *hot*!" Kelly replied.

Emma didn't want to burst her friend's bubble by reminding her that Damian was flying back to California on New Year's Day. She assumed that Kelly already knew but didn't want to acknowledge it. It was too bad, really, because Emma would have liked it if Damian stuck around, not just for Kelly, but for all of them. Gracie was especially fond of him, and it would be difficult when the time came to say goodbye.

Emma and Kelly's discussion was halted when Mrs. Simmons walked in, leaning on a cane for support.

"What can we help you with today?" Emma asked sweetly.

"I finished that *Fifty Shades* series, so now I need a new romance novel," she stated.

Emma had to suppress a giggle while Kelly quickly stepped in. "I'm your resource for romance, Mrs. Simmons. Follow me!"

As they walked away, Emma thought, *Good for her! I hope I'm still that spry at her age.*

Three rapid pings of Emma's phone interrupted her musings.

Did you eat yet?

I hope so, because Zeus needs his nourishment.

Plus, you need to keep your energy up for tonight. Hint. Hint.

Emma thought for a moment and then typed her response:

If I keep having to answer your texts, I won't have any energy left over for tonight. Hint. Hint.

There, that should hold him off for a while!

She'd underestimated him, because, a second later, her phone pinged again.

Nice try! Eat. xoxo

She rolled her eyes and went to her office in search of a carry-out menu.

Zack and Gracie pulled up in front of the bookstore at exactly five o'clock. Emma had just opened the car door to get in when Gracie shouted, "We have a surprise for you!"

"Gracie," Zack warned, and he shot her a scolding look.

"You do? But Christmas is over," Emma said.

Gracie could barely contain her excitement, but Zack shifted uncomfortably in his seat. "First, you need to eat dinner, and then we'll give you the surprise," he said without his usual humor.

Emma was curious, but she could tell that the topic was closed, so she let it go.

When they arrived at Zack's house, Gracie raced inside, presumably in search of Duchess.

"So, what can I feed you?" Zack asked, leading her into the kitchen.

"I'm not hungry yet. Kelly and I ate a big lunch."

Zack's mouth was still set in a rigid line, which was unusual for him, so she had to ask. "Zack, what's bothering you?"

Just then, Gracie came bounding down the stairs with a wrapped package in her hands, and Duchess pranced along behind her.

"See, Emma. This is your present, and I helped wrap it," Gracie said proudly.

"Gracie, I told you we were going to wait until after dinner," Zack snapped. He then turned his attention to Emma and said, "You want to know what's wrong? This is what's wrong. This is not how things were supposed to go."

"What things?" Emma was truly confused. She put a hand on Zack's arm. "What's going on?"

Zack took a deep breath and composed himself. "Ok, Gracie. We'll give Emma our present now. Let's go into the living room."

Once they were seated on the couch, with Zack on one side of her and Gracie on the other, Gracie handed Emma the package.

Truth be told, Emma loved presents. She felt just as excited to open it as Gracie was to give it to her. She flashed Zack a big, goofy smile, and he visibly softened.

"Go ahead and open it," he urged.

Gracie bounced up and down while Emma tore open the paper to reveal a musical jewelry box decorated with pink hearts. "It's for my baby sister,"

Gracie said, which caused tears to spring into Emma's eyes.

"Gracie picked it out herself," Zack explained.

"Daddy said if I get a brother instead, I get to keep the jewelry box!"

Emma giggled and swiped a tear away. She was just about to open the lid of the jewelry box when Zack placed his hand on her arm. "The second gift is from me," he said gruffly.

"What? What... second... gift?"

"Open the lid."

Gracie had suddenly gone quiet. She had picked Duchess up and was busy petting her when Emma opened the jewelry box. Inside was another smaller box, which looked like it had been professionally wrapped, with crisp corners and a neatly tied white bow.

Oh my God. It can't be. Could it be?

Zack took out the smaller box and handed the jewelry box to Gracie, which was just as well because Emma's hands were shaking and tears clouded her vision.

"Emma," Zack began.

Oh my God. I think it is.

"First of all, I want you to know how much I love you..."

"I do too, Daddy!"

"How much *we* love you," he corrected.

Oh my God. I'm going to pass out. No, don't!

"Second, we want you to know how much we're going to love this baby—whether it's a girl or a boy, right Gracie?" he asked pointedly, but his smile was warm and wide.

Just as Zack had found his stride, Emma fell apart. Her face was a crumpled-up, teary mess, and she was sure she sported lovely racoon eyes by now.

"So, I was wondering... well, *we* were wondering..."

"Will you marry us?" Gracie finished, springing off the couch to stand in front of Emma.

Emma's hands flew up to her tear-stained cheeks while Zack unwrapped the box and opened the lid.

She launched into full-fledged sobs then. Her vision was so blurry that she couldn't see the details on the sparkling diamond ring, but she knew it had to be extraordinary because it had come from them. Her family. Zack and Gracie.

Gracie had run out of the room, and now she returned with a tissue box.

"Thank you, sweetie," Emma somehow managed to say while she hurriedly wiped her eyes.

"Um, Em? We're still waiting for your answer," Zack said with a mixture of impatience and hopefulness.

Finally, her vision cleared, and she could actually see him, and the ring, and Gracie in vivid detail. Her heart was bursting with love and joy, and she prayed that she wouldn't pass out before she gave them her answer.

"Yes," Emma said, and she would have said more, but she was suddenly enveloped in a tight, three-person hug, and the wind had been knocked out of her.

This is love, she thought. *This is family.*

EPILOGUE – 8 MONTHS LATER

"Be careful with her head," Alex instructed, peering over Gracie's shoulder at her new granddaughter.

Gracie sat stiffly in the chair by Emma's bedside, with her baby sister propped carefully in her arms. Ava Kostas had come screaming into the world at close to midnight the night before, and everyone in the room was a little bleary-eyed. She was surrounded by her parents, both sets of grandparents, and her honorary Aunt Kelly, each waiting for their turn to hold the newborn bundle of joy.

Emma was especially exhausted, having labored for ten hours, but it was a good kind of tired, a happy kind of tired. She was surrounded by the people she loved, but she couldn't take her eyes off the masterpiece that she and Zack had created.

Zack hadn't left Emma's side during the labor and delivery unless he'd absolutely had to. He had been Emma's rock throughout it all, and the experience had only made her fall deeper in love with him.

There was only one person missing from the Kostas/Murphy group, and he was due to arrive at any minute. Damian had called from the airport about an hour ago to let them know that he was on his way. While they were all anxious to see him, one person in particular looked up every time someone passed in the hallway outside of Emma's room.

Kelly hadn't seen nor heard from Damian since New Year's Eve, eight months ago, when he had returned to California. What Kelly didn't know, because Emma had been sworn to secrecy, was that Damian was coming back to Michigan to stay. Zack had only recently told Emma the news, but he'd made her promise to let Damian tell Kelly himself. Emma could hardly wait to see the look on her best friend's face once she found out. Kelly had put up a good front during Damian's absence, but Emma knew that she still carried a torch for the devilish Kostas brother.

"Time's up, Gracie. I think it's *Aunt* Kelly's turn now," Zack said, smiling softly at his two daughters.

"But Daaaad... that was only one minute," Gracie complained as Kelly carefully lifted the baby out of Gracie's arms.

"That was actually five minutes, and you will have plenty of time with Ava once we take her home," Zack said.

Kelly took the chair that Gracie had vacated, and Mary stepped in to distract Gracie. "Why don't you show me that new doll that you brought with you?" Mary suggested.

Emma watched Gracie rush over to her soon-to-be step-grandma without hesitation, and her heart leapt to her throat. One of the unexpected benefits of her pregnancy had been the closer relationship she had formed with her parents. When they had left after the holidays, Mary had promised Emma that they would return in time for the birth and stay indefinitely to help out. Emma was afraid to be too hopeful, but based on her parents' reaction to the birth of their first grandchild, she could visualize them staying for good.

"Now that Ava is here, we can really start to focus on the wedding," Alex said enthusiastically.

"Mom, she was only born yesterday," Zack scolded.

"You know your mother. Any mention of a party, and she's all over it!" Joe teased from the corner of the room.

"Your Mom's right, Zack. The wedding is only a few months away, and we still have a lot to do," Emma piped in.

"Not to worry. I'm on it," Kelly said while she gently rocked the baby.

"What's this I hear about a wedding?" Damian asked, startling them all. The family had been so busy talking and admiring Ava that they hadn't noticed him sneak in.

"Uncle Damian!" Gracie shouted, and she rushed across the room to jump into his arms.

"How's my big girl?" he asked gruffly, spinning her around.

Gracie giggled with delight. "I got a sister, I got a sister!"

"That's what I heard," he replied as he stepped further into the room.

Kelly's head had snapped up at the sound of his voice, and now she sat frozen with a strange mix of emotions stamped on her face.

"Hey, everybody," Damian said as he sauntered toward Kelly. "Hey, Kell," he said more softly once he reached her.

"Hi," she said with a slight waver in her voice.

"Mind if I hold my niece?"

Kelly snapped out of her trance. "Oh, yeah. Of course." She transferred the warm, sleepy bundle into Damian's bulky arms, and he gazed down at her.

"Yep, she's a Kostas alright!" He ruffled the baby's tuft of pitch black hair with his beefy hand. "Hopefully, she has Emma's disposition though!" He shot Zack a teasing grin.

"It's nice to see you too, bro," Zack replied, returning the grin.

"This is so wonderful! The whole family together. As soon as Emma has a chance to recuperate, I'm inviting everyone over for dinner!" Alex stated.

"I've only been here for two minutes, and Mom's already talking about feeding people," Damian said.

"Welcome home!" Emma said and giggled.

Damian acknowledged Emma's comment with a brief nod of his head, and then he directed his attention toward Kelly. "It's good to be home."

THE END

Find out what happens next for Kelly and Damian in a new stand-alone novel, coming soon...

Also by Susan Coventry

"As Coventry describes the complex issues of age and love that Jason and Sam must navigate, she also touches on other weighty topics, such as grief, friendship, and emotional renewal. She tells the story at a fast clip, building the suspense in a way that will keep even the most experienced romance fans engaged. The story artfully explores the difficulties inherent in unconventional relationships without skimping on steamy sex scenes." - *Kirkus Reviews*

Website: www.susancoventry.org
Facebook: www.facebook.com/authorsusancoventry/

Nikki Branson swore off men a long time ago. She runs a successful real estate business and has a cuddly cocker spaniel to keep her company. What more could she possibly need? When a Hollywood agent contracts Nikki to find a rental home for his superstar client, she hadn't even heard of Nate Collins. Her first mistake, looking him up on Google... Nate Collins is Hollywood's latest sensation and most eligible bachelor. All he wants is a quiet place to stay while he's in Michigan filming a movie, and who better to find it for him, than the most sought after real estate agent in town. When Nate and Nikki meet, sparks fly, but their lifestyles are worlds apart. Logic tells Nikki it will never work, now if she could only convince her heart of that...

Made in the USA
Lexington, KY
06 April 2017